# Fit to Die

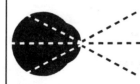

This Large Print Book carries the
Seal of Approval of N.A.V.H.

A SUPPER CLUB MYSTERY

# FIT TO DIE

## J. B. STANLEY

**WHEELER PUBLISHING**
*An imprint of Thomson Gale, a part of The Thomson Corporation*

Detroit • New York • San Francisco • New Haven, Conn. • Waterville, Maine • London

# THOMSON

## GALE

™

Copyright © 2007 by J. B. Stanley.
Wheeler, an imprint of The Gale Group.
Thomson and Star Logo and Wheeler are trademarks and Gale is a registered trademark used herein under license.

Wheeler Publishing Large Print Cozy Mystery.
The text of this Large Print edition is unabridged.
Other aspects of the book may vary from the original edition.
Set in 16 pt. Plantin.

**LIBRARY OF CONGRESS CATALOGING-IN-PUBLICATION DATA**

Stanley, J. B.
    Fit to die / by J.B. Stanley.
        p. cm. — (Supper Club mystery) (Wheeler Publishing large print cozy mystery)
    ISBN-13: 978-1-59722-595-3 (alk. paper)
    ISBN-10: 1-59722-595-9 (alk. paper)
    1. Overweight men — Fiction. 2. Dieters — Fiction. 3. Virginia — Fiction.
4. Large type books. I. Title.
PS3619.T3655F57 2007b
813'.6—dc22                                          2007021004

Published in 2007 by arrangement with Midnight Ink,
an imprint of Llewellyn Publications, Woodbury, MN 55125 USA.

Printed in the United States of America on permanent paper
10 9 8 7 6 5 4 3 2 1

*For Anne Cunningham Briggs,*
*A woman of many talents*

*"The only way to keep your health is to eat what you don't want, drink what you don't like, and do what you'd rather not."*

— MARK TWAIN

# ONE:
## ÉCLAIR

**Serving Size:**
1 éclair · 4 oz.

**Witness to Fitness Points**

8

"Would you care for an éclair, sir?"

James Henry stared at the attractive, chocolate-covered delight nestled in its crinkled paper cup. He knew he shouldn't even think of eating the tantalizing pastry.

He was *supposed* to be on a diet. For the last six months he was *supposed* to have been on a good-carbohydrate, good-fat diet. And at first he *was* good — almost a saint — but lately, more and more, his cravings for forbidden foods had overpowered him and he had cheated. Just a little bit at first, but as the months went by, he found himself eating something deliciously fattening every day. What began with a slice of pizza once a week had morphed into a jelly donut on the way to work, a small bag of cheese puffs at lunchtime, a tub of buttered popcorn at the movies, or a candy bar during evening television. It was when he began eating the cheese puffs again that James knew his diet had officially become a failure.

All his life, James Henry had had a love affair with cheese puffs. The crunchy, salty, cheesy ambrosia that seemed to be comprised of baked air and that addictive, electric-orange dust drove James to his knees. During the first two months of the diet, in which he was determined to lose weight alongside his new friends and supper club members, James had resolutely passed by the snack food aisle in the grocery store. If he didn't go anywhere near a bag of cheese puffs, he could resist buying them. He had been so strong and the pounds had come off. Slowly at first, just a few a week, as he had been told was healthy. In two months, he lost more than twelve of the extra fifty-plus pounds he carried on his tall frame and had felt confident and hopeful for the first time in years.

That was back in autumn, though. Then Thanksgiving had come, and Christmas. It was during the holiday season that he and the other members of the supper club, who had humorously dubbed themselves the Flab Five, could be seen sneaking little sugary treats on the sly. "What's a piece of sweet potato pie here or a little candy cane there?" they reasoned with one another. At their last supper club dinner, Gillian, the barrel-shaped pet groomer with the nest of wild orange hair and garish clothing sense, admitted that she had already gained back half of the weight she had lost over the fall. Now, in March, James Henry, head librarian of the Shenandoah County Library Branch, also ruefully confessed that he had steadily been gaining weight instead of losing it.

Shrugging his shoulders as if to brush off all thoughts of dieting, James finally accepted the éclair from the woman wearing a green apron and an artificial smile. He popped the soft pastry into his mouth and happily exhaled as warm custard oozed onto his tongue. He licked a centimeter-sized smudge of chocolate from his left knuckle and pushed his cart farther up the frozen food aisle. He really had no reason to be walking down this aisle. If he admitted the truth to himself, which he wouldn't, James would have to acknowledge that the only reason he came over to this side of the store was that it took him closer to the display of jumbo-sized bags of tortilla chips, potato chips, pretzel rods, and of course, cheese puffs.

As head librarian, James made quarterly runs to the discount warehouse in Harrisonburg, Virginia. His purpose was to restock necessary office supplies such as Scotch tape, staples, printer paper, ink cartridges, and the like. The small town of Quincy's Gap, where James worked, was nestled in a verdant valley beneath the Blue Ridge Mountains and didn't support a large enough population to have more than one grocery store, let alone a mammoth warehouse store. James had grown up in Quincy's Gap, so he was accustomed to driving to larger towns like Harrisonburg or Charlottesville for specialty items. And even though James worked a Monday–Friday schedule at the library, he deliberately came to the warehouse during his time off over the weekend in order to partake of the food samples.

Steering a cart the size of a compact car down the wide yet congested aisles of refrigerated food, James paused in front of a shelf containing tubs of chocolate-chip cookie dough before noticing that another green-aproned woman was serving samples of pizza bagels up ahead. James darted forward and immediately stuffed one into his mouth, ignoring the molten tomato sauce, bubbling mozzarella cheese, and the woman's sales pitch as he greedily pivoted toward the juice sampler station behind him. Tossing back the doll-sized Dixie cup filled with sugary berry juice as if he were doing a shot at a bar, James blotted his purple-stained lips with a napkin and hustled in the direction of what could only be a cart set up to offer samples of choco-late.

A clot of eager customers surrounded this particular sampling station, which was strategically located at the section of the store displaying a contradictory combination of health foods and candies. James pushed his cart into a side aisle and shoved his bulk in front of a small boy, fearing that all the free samples might be given away before he could get his share. Glancing at the stacks of cartons containing sugar-free gum, honey-roasted peanuts, and protein bars in disdain, James elbowed forward until he could see the surface of the white stand being manned by a hassled-looking elderly lady. The poor woman was cutting up squares of chocolate from a slab the size of a shoebox as fast as she could. Shoppers grabbed a square and rapidly returned to their carts, like snakes seeking some privacy in order to properly swallow their prey.

"Hey! You cut!" the boy behind James whined.

Ignoring him, James stretched a long arm through a narrow gap between the hips of two chatting women and snagged a piece of chocolate. As he attempted to retrieve both his limb and what he now saw was a caramel-filled confection, one of the women abruptly turned. Her purse, acting like a thirty-pound pendulum, smacked James roughly in the arm, which he was holding high in the air in order to avoid having his chocolate touched as he reeled it in toward his salivating mouth. He watched in horror as his caramel-chocolate square flew out of his battered hand and above a tower of granola bars. Taking advantage of James's dismay, the disgruntled boy lunged forward, seized the last square on the tray and melted away into the crowd.

"Damn!" James muttered. He cast a sidelong glance at the old woman with the green apron. "Are you going to cut another piece?" he asked, hating the pathetic tone of his plea, but unable to stop himself from making it.

The woman fixed a pair of angry, blue eyes on him. "Not only am I *not* going to open a new bar," she seethed, "but I am going *right* home to read the paper."

James was confused. What did reading have to do with sampling chocolates? "The paper?"

"Yes. The classifieds! I'm going to find another job!" the woman squawked. "I've never seen such rudeness or gluttony in my whole entire life. And mine hasn't been a short one, mind you. For Pete's sake! It's just a piece of candy. I'm not handing out hundred-dollar bills here!"

James flushed, wondering why he had been fortunate enough to have been the sole recipient of this woman's tirade. Seeing the combination of an empty tray and a lack of activity on the sampler's part, most of the other shoppers had dissipated like mist.

"I'm sorry." James offered a weak apology to the woman. Then, in a final attempt to coerce her into renewing her sampling, he decided to lie. "I don't know about the rest of these people but I forgot to have breakfast today. Suddenly, that piece of chocolate looked awfully darned good to me. I guess I forgot any sense of manners in the face of hunger."

The woman eyed him as she untied her apron. "Sonny," she said, leaning toward James. "That's a bunch of horse manure and you know it. You don't look like you've *ever* missed your breakfast, or any other meal for that matter." And with that, she stomped away.

Indignantly, James reversed his cart, stormed down the main aisle, and practically skidded to a halt in front of the cheese puff display. Just as he was reaching up to pull a bag down from the shelf, he heard a familiar voice.

"James!"

As James swung around, his elbow grazed the cheese doodles display, knocking four or five bags from the shelf. They dropped into his cart with a crinkly plunk. He tried to block the cart with his body as he gave his friend Lindy a guilty smile.

"Who are *those* for?" she asked in her familiar teasing manner, her large round eyes twinkling in mischief.

"Uh . . ." James fumbled for an excuse. "Well, I *was* going to buy one bag, but those others just fell in, I swear."

"*Tsk, tsk.*" Lindy waved a finger at him as she simultaneously tried to block his view of her cart.

Lindy was barely over five feet tall, but her round, curvaceous body was wide enough to prevent James from getting a clear look at what his fellow supper club member was trying to hide. As James noted the blush creeping into Lindy's nougat-colored cheeks, he suddenly stood on his tiptoes and spied that the high school art teacher was preparing to purchase three five-pound bags of mixed candy.

Pink roses bloomed on Lindy's full cheeks. "They're just bribes for my students." She gestured at the bags defensively, swinging a long lock of glossy, black hair over her shoulder in defiance.

James sighed as he took all the bags of cheese puffs out of his cart and replaced them on the shelf. "Well, you caught me out. Not only have I eaten every sample in this place, but I was going to gorge on cheese puffs all the way home." He looked at the snack display with longing.

"I've eaten everything in sight here, too." Lindy glumly pointed toward the checkout area. "Let's get out of this place before we get any fatter."

"Ha! We're going to lose five pounds before we ever get out of here," James said, indicating the long lines. Every shopper's cart seemed to be exploding with stacks of books, cartons holding three-dozen eggs, ten-gallon Tide bottles, steaks the size of footballs, and sixty-four rolls of toilet paper.

James and Lindy pulled into adjoining lines. The woman in front of Lindy had a similar body type to her own, being short and round with large hips and full, heavy breasts. James couldn't help but notice that the woman's cart was stuffed with cookie assortments, two cheesecakes, potato chips, ice cream bars, a giant-sized box of Frosted Flakes, rice pudding, and several varieties of candy bars. As James watched with interest, the woman opened the box of Twix bars, pulled out a single candy, and began to struggle with the foil wrapper. The gold packaging, which seemed to be illuminated with an ethereal glow beneath the fluorescent lights, was successfully preventing her from having a tasty treat while waiting in the endless line.

As James and Lindy stared, the woman tugged at the wrapper, grunting with exertion. She even put it down for a moment, then wiped her hands on her purple floral dress, and tried again. Just as her line moved forward, she was able to rip the stubborn wrapper apart, sending one of the chocolate and caramel-covered Twix bars soaring through the air and into the cart of a stick-thin brunette dressed in workout clothes standing in front of her.

Lindy's eyes grew large as she, and every-one waiting in line around the Twix Lady, ogled the brunette as she fished the candy bar out of her cart. The brunette's mouth compressed into a thin-lined smile as she turned around and looked appraisingly at the plump woman behind her.

"I'm so sorry!" Twix Lady gushed, holding out a pudgy hand in order to retrieve the offensive snack. If she was expecting to have her piece of candy returned however, she was to be disappointed.

"I'd rather stab myself in the heart than give you this" — the brunette eyed the candy as if it were a piece of dung — "disgustingly unhealthy, chemical-filled piece of trash! Darlin'," she cooed as if talking to a baby, "you don't really want this back."

Twix Lady put her hand over her heart in shock. James and Lindy looked at one another with wide eyes. As the cashier waved James forward and he scurried around the other side of his cart so that he could unload it, he now found himself standing parallel to the brunette.

"Look at your cart, dear!" the woman continued, her voice rising in concern as she rifled through Twix Lady's cart with frantic energy. "Nothing but sugar, nasty carbohydrates, and nicely disguised lard! Honey! How can you *do* this to your body?"

Twix Lady looked around for help, but the other shoppers only stared in embarrassed fascination. It was like watching a lioness circle calmly around a wounded wildebeest.

"Don't you know that you are too beautiful to ruin yourself with food like this?" the brunette asked in a deep drawl, her hand held over her heart as if to express her earnestness. "If I were your friend, and I'm sure you have tons of friends, I wouldn't let you out this door with this cart, sugar."

"I dunno." Twix Lady looked as though she would burst into tears at any moment. She then frantically opened a new Twix bar and desperately bit off an end as if the sweetness could ward off any further attacks from the brunette. "I like this stuff. It makes me feel good."

The brunette smiled at her victim in sad

disbelief. "Darlin', this doesn't *really* make you feel better. I mean, only for a few minutes. But later . . . ," she let the words drift away as she took a step closer to Twix Lady. "You are killing yourself," she said so softly that James almost couldn't hear. "And it's breaking my heart." Then, smoothing back a few wisps of hair that had escaped her ponytail, the brunette perked back up and spoke in a singsong voice. "See my cart? I've got fruit, vegetables, cheese, lean meats, and sugar-free candy for when I need a little reward. My cart is why I look the way I do and your cart is why I'm real worried about your future, sweetheart. Do you live around here?"

Twix Lady blinked, overwhelmed by the brunette's concern and startled by her question.

"Um . . . not really. I live north of here."

"Anywhere near Quincy's Gap?" James and Lindy quickly exchanged wary looks.

"I live in Hamburg. It's 'bout twenty minutes drive from Quincy's Gap."

"That'll be close enough." The brunette handed Twix Lady a business card. "My name's Veronica Levitt. I'm opening a new fitness and weight loss center called Witness to Fitness in Quincy's Gap. Matter of fact, the Grand Opening is next weekend. Why don't you come by and I'll help you change what you put in your cart *and* in your mouth. I will save your life, if you give me the chance." The brunette put a hand on Twix Lady's shoulder and squeezed it tenderly. Twix Lady began to cry, her shoulders and chest jiggling as she wept.

"You can help me?" she sobbed, a bit of chocolate drool running down her chin.

It seemed to James that Veronica hesitated for a fraction of a second before her lips curved upward into an enormous smile. "Oh, yes, my dear. Now, it's going to be tough. Real tough. But if you stick with me, you're going to be a newer, stronger, *sexier* you in just six weeks!"

"I'd like that." Twix Lady sniffed, holding the business card to her chest as if it were a treasure she might lose. "Thank you." She reached out and hugged Veronica.

"Excuse me!" Lindy called to Veronica from behind Twix Lady. "Did you say six weeks?" Lindy's tone was clearly dubious.

Veronica's bright green eyes fixed on Lindy's figure. "That's what I said. Are you interested as well, hon?"

Lindy hesitated. "I've been on a diet for over six months, actually."

Veronica began unloading her cart. "And is it working for you?" she called back, eyeing Lindy sweetly as Twix Lady turned around to get a good look at the person who might next be transformed by the magical fitness guru.

Lindy shrugged. "I've lost some weight." She pointed across the way at James. "There are five of us on the diet together. We've got a supper club going."

"Good for you!" Veronica cheered Lindy. "But now . . . is that candy a part of your supper club's menu?" she asked, using the type of chiding tone that a doting grandmother might use on a child who has eaten too many of her homemade cookies before dinner.

Lindy looked down at her cart guilty. "It's for my students! Look, I still have some curves," she added sulkily, "but we don't all have your kind of bone structure. I have always had a very full-figured build."

Veronica finished paying for her purchases. "Of course we're not all the same," she said soothingly, pushing her cart out of the way so that Twix Lady could check out. Veronica then approached Lindy as if she were a lost puppy in need of adoption, her face a perfect mixture of sympathy and friendly concern. "But you can still have the curves of Jennifer Lopez instead of the fat rolls of Jabba the Hutt. Why, with that gorgeous hair and those huge chocolate eyes, you could have men lined up for miles just to get your phone number!"

Lindy's jaw seemed to have come unhinged as her face burned red with embarrassment. Veronica seemed oblivious to the emotions she was provoking. "Here, just take my card. I'm giving discounts to all those who sign up for the six-week plan during my Grand Opening." She bent to retie the shoelace on one of her spotlessly white running shoes. "But I've got to warn you. You won't be eating any candy with me as your food advocate, so you may as well get out of this line and put it back on the shelf. That'll show you just how much you want to change your life. Go on, darlin', put it back. You don't need that candy to make you happy."

James waited for Lindy's Brazilian half to raise its hot-tempered head and verbally reduce Veronica Levitt into a smoldering pile of ash. Customarily, Lindy was an easygoing and fun-loving person, filled with a positive energy that seemed to infect all those who spent time with her, but on occasion, she could have a fit of rage not unlike a two-year-old throwing a tantrum in the toy store. Lindy always blamed these infrequent bouts of passionate wrath on her

Brazilian mother, a former supermodel. Lindy claimed that the traits she had inherited from her mother were limited to her skin tone and her ability to pitch a fit when backed into a corner. But amazingly, Lindy's temper remained completely checked. She simply nodded her head in silent agreement, scooped up the bags of candy, and left her place in line in order to return them to their proper shelf.

As a dumbfounded James began unloading his cart, Veronica appeared at his side and gave him the once over with her calculating green eyes. She placed a pair of tanned hands on her nonexistent hips and offered him a flirtatious nudge in the side.

"So you've been on a diet for six months, too?"

James slapped a heavy carton of copier paper onto the conveyer belt. "Yes."

Veronica smiled with encouragement. "You'd do *so* well on my program. Men always do." She reached out an arm to help James empty his cart. He stared at the appendage. It looked more like a jungle vine, sinewy and leathery in texture, than a part of the human anatomy.

"You know, you've got a good frame and a *real* handsome face hidden beneath all of that cushion," Veronica said, tossing a very weighty carton filled with printer paper onto the belt as if it were a box of Kleenex. "I bet you were a looker in high school and college, weren't you?"

James was amazed by her strength, considering her overall lack of body mass. He was more than a little intimidated as well. He felt more comfortable with women who had softer bodies. He liked curves and solid limbs and dimples in the cheeks. Suddenly, he had a vision of Lucy Hanover, another supper club member who worked for the Sheriff's Department. The only thing sharp about Lucy was her mind. The rest of her was all softness, like a warm and cozy chair that one longs to sink into at the end of the day. A flash of her sunlit, brown hair, eyes the shade of bachelor's buttons, and a pair of plump lips that he had dared to kiss just once a few months ago made James forget all about Veronica's presence.

Veronica was not the type of woman to be ignored, however. She shoved a business card into James's hand and then patted him on the protruding mound that formed his belly.

"Let me help you. We can change you from looking like Santa Claus to looking like one sexy . . ." she eyed his empty ring finger, "bachelor." She smiled again as

James shifted uncomfortably. Veronica traced the curve of his cheek with her finger and then moved off to collect her cart. "Hope to see you next week, handsome!" she called over her shoulder as she exited the store.

James flushed as he noticed the other shoppers gawking at him. He quickly balled up Veronica's pink business card and shoved it deep into his jeans pocket just as Lindy reclaimed a place in the checkout line. James waited for her by the exit, standing close enough to the outside doors to note that the cold March rain had ceased and the formerly congealed clouds were finally showing signs of thinning.

"I thought you needed that candy for your students," James said as Lindy pulled her cart next to his.

She shrugged. "I'll have to get them something else as a reward. Truth is, I *would* have eaten half of that stash if I had it at school."

James shook his head in disbelief. "How could you listen to a sanctimonious woman like that? She's part cheerleader, part used-car salesman, part Dr. Phil."

Lindy paused in the middle of the parking lot and turned to look James in the eye. "I don't know, James. But let's face it: we haven't done so well on our own. Maybe it's time we seek professional help."

"But she's . . . she's like Richard Simmons on speed!" James spluttered in protest.

Lindy unlocked her car, a red Chevy Cavalier with a sizeable dent in one of the rear door panels, and began loading her boxes into the trunk. "Exactly! That woman will get our energy levels up and get us to be more honest about ourselves. We haven't been accountable to one another. When was the last time we ever shared our weight loss progress?"

James fidgeted with his key chain. "At least two months," he admitted.

"That's 'cause there hasn't been any! It's time that *someone* coerced us to get back on a scale and made us exercise. If it means that Veronica's going to be the Head Diet Cheerleader, so be it. We need someone to champion us, someone who truly cares about our health and happiness. Tomorrow night, during our dinner, I'm going to suggest we all go to her Grand Opening. It's time to face the fact that we've slipped." Lindy opened her car door and squeezed inside. "The Flab Five is about to get back in the swing of things and Veronica Levitt is just the woman for the job."

James groaned. There was something

about the fitness instructor that he didn't like. His instincts were warning him not to trust her, but he couldn't explain his feelings to Lindy, let alone come up with a good argument as to why they shouldn't join Veronica's program.

On the way back to Quincy's Gap, he stopped at a Food Lion and bought himself a large bag of cheese puffs.

# Two:
## Chilly Willy's
## Praline Caramel Kiss

**Serving Size:**
1 sundae · 189 g

**Witness to Fitness Points**

13

"You got another one of your *social* dinners tonight?" Jackson Henry asked grumpily, dissecting the tuna casserole James had cooked for him earlier in the afternoon. The elder Henry probed beneath the layer of paprika-covered cheddar cheese in order to ascertain whether the pasta used in the dish was that of a shape he favored. "Is this some kind of new-fangled noodle?"

"No, Pop. That is elbow macaroni," James sighed with impatience. "It's the same kind you've had in your tuna casserole for the last twenty years. I followed Ma's recipe to the letter."

Jackson furrowed his bushy white eyebrows. "Except you didn't use that ole orange casserole pot. The cheese broils better when you use that pot. Gets all nice and crispy. You could snap it in two like a twig. I suppose you've gone and used it makin' some fancy meal for your friends."

James rolled his eyes. "The pot's in the freezer, Pop. I used it to make you shepherd's pie last week, remember? You said there were too many peas in the pie and that you'd eat it when you felt *in the mood* for peas." James couldn't help but add a sarcastic tone to his voice.

"Well, I *ain't* in the mood for peas. Matter of fact, I might never be." Jackson sulked childishly as he flipped through the worn pages of his *TV Guide.*

James refused to be provoked any further. "I'll see you later, Pop."

"Wait just a minute." Jackson grumbled

loudly. "You gotta stop at Goodbee's first to get me my pills."

James looked at his watch. He was already running late and he'd be even later if he had to pick something up at the pharmacy before heading over to Bennett Marshall's house.

"Pills for what, Pop?" James asked suspiciously. His father was notorious for trying to ruin any chance of his son acquiring a healthy social life. Jackson never took messages when people called and ripped open all of the mail, whether his name was on it or not. He dumped all the bills on the kitchen table, read his son's personal notes, and carelessly crinkled each and every page of any magazine, newspaper, or catalogue as he read them while watching hours of game shows.

Recently, he had accidentally smeared peanut butter all over James's treasured copy of *The New Yorker,* which Jackson considered unequivocally snobby and written in a manner impossible for "simply country folk" to read. He even complained about the cartoons, grumbling that not only were the artists untalented, but they were also missing any trace of a sense of humor. James would normally read such a magazine at the library, but the limited budget of his branch did not allow him to order magazines according to his own taste. Instead, he ordered subscriptions to *Better Homes and Gardens, Outdoor Life,* and *NASCAR Illustrated,* as those were the publications his patrons were interested in reading.

"Pop," James prodded. "I'm not going to be late going over to Bennett's unless it's over something important. What are the pills for?"

"That's my own business. Can't a man get some privacy?"

"You get plenty of privacy. Too much, if you ask me!" James retorted, crossing his arms over his chest. His father was practically a recluse. Ever since his business, Henry's Hardware, had been bought out by one of the country's larger home improvement chains, Jackson had begun to sink into a depression. When his wife died suddenly of heart failure a year ago, Jackson stopped going out altogether.

At the time of his mother's death, James had been a professor of English Literature at the College of William and Mary in Williamsburg. James was living the good life. He had a tenure-track position, a quaint brick townhouse, and a lovely wife named Jane. But one day, after James returned home from his afternoon lecture on William

Faulkner, Jane had announced that she wanted a divorce.

"I'm sorry, honey. You're just too dull for me," his wife of two years had said. A few months later, James's mother went to sleep at her usual ten o'clock bedtime, never to wake again. James resigned his position as a professor, the only thing that still brought a fraction of happiness to his life. He grimly moved back to his childhood home of Quincy's Gap in order to take care of his ill-tempered and reclusive father. At first, James considered that his new job as the head librarian of a small town library branch was a step down in his life, but he was pleasantly surprised to discover that his new career suited him well. He loved being surrounded by books and enjoyed his co-workers. Most of all, the friendship James had forged with the members of the Flab Five had made his relocation an unexpectedly positive change.

Every time James even thought about one particular member, Lucy Hanover, his heart began to race like a marathon runner spotting the finish line. If only he weren't so shy and insecure. Months after their first kiss, he had yet to ask her out on an official date. Plagued by fears that the dullness his wife had hated would destroy any possibility of

Lucy remaining interested in him, James had withdrawn inside his shell. Now, he treated her like all the other supper club members. Lucy had responded by following his lead. Even though they never discussed the kiss, they still threw each other significant looks from time to time. But it was as if their fall from the diet wagon had also stripped them of the courage to pursue a romantic attachment. So with the exception of his weekly supper club meetings, James had no social life. He came home every night to his dilapidated childhood home and his irascible father.

"I thought you were in some kind of hurry?" Jackson asked, raising one of his bushy eyebrows in amusement.

James snapped out of his stupor, stomped off to his truck, and tore down the gravel driveway, leaving an irritated cloud of dust in the wake of his old white Bronco. Goodbee's pharmacy was due to close in a matter of minutes, so James drove fifteen miles over the speed limit and barely paused at one of the town's four-way stops in order to get in the door before closing time.

Mr. Goodbee raised a kindly, freckled face from a pile of paperwork to greet James.

"Sorry to stick my foot in the door at the last minute, but my father said he had a prescription waiting here." James paused to catch his breath. "Though I don't see how. He hasn't been to a doctor in years."

The pharmacist laughed. "Oh, he called me with this very creative yarn about how his doctor told him he could call in his own prescriptions from now on. Luckily, when he described his symptoms — bloating, pain, and a feeling of pressure in the lower belly — I knew what was wrong."

James leaned over the counter. "Which was?" he asked anxiously.

"No need for concern," Mr. Goodbee rifled through a box containing prescription envelopes. "Your father has gas. Pure and simple. Now, I know a lot of old folks feel better about gettin' their medicine in old-fashioned and official-lookin' types of pill bottles instead of packages from the shelves, so I went ahead and dumped a batch of Gas-X in one of my vials and typed up the Latin name on the label." Mr. Goodbee chuckled as he wiped his glasses off using the corner of his white lab coat. "Works every time."

"You sure know your customers," James said with admiration as he paid for the pills. "Pop had me thinking this was some kind of emergency."

"Well, that man should see a doctor.

Someone his age should be checked out on a regular basis. See if you can talk him into visitin' Doc Spratt sometime soon." Mr. Goodbee wagged a finger at James. "Just tell him it's for his own good, Professor."

Everyone in Quincy's Gap called James "Professor" even though he no longer taught any students. James knew that vanity prevented him from correcting the townsfolk or suggesting that they simply call him Mr. Henry. He had worked hard to earn the title of Professor and he was reluctant to let it go.

James shook his head helplessly. "For a physical, I assume? I'll try, but there's a better chance of an iceberg forming in the Sahara than me getting my father to a doctor without him being knocked unconscious."

"No problem. I've got pills for that!" Mr. Goodbee teased as he walked James to the door.

"There are plenty of times when I could use 'knock-you-unconscious' pills for Pop," James mumbled as the door was locked behind him. He glanced at the orange pill bottle and then at his own reflection in the pharmacy door. His pouch hung out over his pants like a hot air balloon trying to squeeze out of a narrow cave opening. The double chin that had shrunk so nicely during the fall was filling itself back up. James shook his face from side to side and could see an unhappy resemblance between his fleshy neck and a pelican with a bill loaded with fish. He sighed as he headed back to his truck. "And there are times I could use them on myself."

"Oh, here's James!" Lindy exclaimed. "I was just telling everyone about our encounter with Veronica Levitt. I stopped by her fitness center and peeked through the window today. She had some brochures sitting in a display case outside so I grabbed a couple. Here, take one." Lindy slid a pink brochure across the table to James. "We can look them over while we eat."

The brochure, which looked as though it had been created by a printer with low toner, was covered with illustrations of smiling red hearts lifting free weights. The text on the front panel read:

**ARE YOU READY TO GROW ...**
- *FITTER?*
- *LEANER?*
- *STRONGER?*
- *MORE TONED?*
- *SEXIER?*

**ARE YOU READY FOR ...**
- *A NEW CLOSET OF CLOTHES?*
- *CONFIDENCE?*
- *A LONGER LIFE SPAN?*
- *A CHANCE TO TAKE CONTROL?*
- *HAPPINESS?*

**JOIN WITNESS TO FITNESS TODAY!**

"I'll take sexier." Gillian O'Malley giggled, patting her orange cloud of hair. Gillian was barrel-shaped and tried to draw attention to her shapely legs by wearing billowy shirts. A few months ago, she had begun wearing rather form-fitting tops that were more flattering to her figure, but recently she had resumed wearing the blouses James secretly called her "circus tent tops" due to their voluminous shape and brilliant hues.

U.S. Postal Service employee Bennett Marshall examined his brochure cautiously. "I'd like to be stronger, but offering happiness to another person by puttin' them on some diet seems like a bit of a stretch if you ask me." He stood and cleared the remainder of their meal, which had consisted of cheddar burgers (without buns), spinach salad, marinated mushrooms, and ricotta cheesecake. As he cleaned off a water ring from beneath a tumbler filled with diet soda, Bennett cast suspicious glances at the brochures scattered across the surface of his dining room table.

"I, for one, am pretty sick of eating the food we've been eating," Lucy said as she gestured at the pile of dirty plates stacked near Bennett's sink. "I love your company, you guys. You have become my closest friends, but . . . well, I haven't been honest with you lately. See, I haven't been eating this kind of stuff on my own any more. I think I got kind of burned out on it."

Lindy nodded in agreement. "It's been hard packing the right lunches to bring to school, too. I've had to eat the same things week after week. For the last two months I've started eating cafeteria food again. Stuff that we shouldn't have like macaroni and cheese, garlic bread, and even those crispy, seasoned fries every now and then."

"Stop!" Lucy shrieked. "Please! I'll run right out to McDonald's for fries this instant if I think about them too much."

James cleared this throat as he often did before he was going to speak. "Did Lindy tell you about Veronica's . . . uh . . . coaching style?"

"Lindy told us the woman was really persuasive. A little bit bossy, but in a good way. A take-charge kind of person." Lucy flashed her blue eyes at James. "I think we could use someone like that at this point."

James squirmed in his chair. He wondered if Lucy was referring to the group's failure to stick with their diet or his inability to develop a romantic relationship with her. The disappointment in her eyes reminded James all too much of the looks he had once seen, but not recognized, reflected in his ex-wife's dark brown eyes. It's better not to risk our friendship, James told himself. Still, he found that his desire to impress Lucy had not diminished over the long winter and that he wanted her approval as much as ever. "Do you really think Veronica can get us all back on track?" he asked her.

"On a whole new road. Look!" Gillian interjected emotionally as she pointed at one of the interior pages of the pink brochure. "She will even provide meals for us for the six-week period. And, praise Buddha, some of them are vegetarian. That would make *me* feel so much better about myself. My *chi's* been completely out of whack since I've been eating so much . . . meat." Gillian whispered the last word as if she had used an expletive.

"Woman." Bennett stared at Gillian as if she were an extra-terrestrial. He pulled on his toothbrush mustache and then clasped his espresso-colored hands together. "Where do you come up with this stuff? Here I thought I was an educated man, but in all of my forty-one years I have never heard of *chi.*"

Gillian inhaled a large breath, a sign that she was about to provide them all with one of her lectures about a myriad of subjects falling under the category of New Age. "Chi is an energy." She spread her arms out into the air theatrically, her polka-dotted top opening up like an umbrella. "It's all around us. It's *very spiritual.* One needs to keep one's chi balanced or —"

"Oh! So it's like the Force in *Star Wars,*" Bennett interrupted, looking pleased. "Cool. I'm down with that. Now, listen y'all. Are we gonna sign up to do this program or what?"

"Let's vote," Lindy suggested. "Raise your hands if you're ready to try Veronica's method of getting healthy. Who is in for joining Witness to Fitness?"

"Wait." James held off the vote by waving his hands over the brochure. "This system seems kind of complicated. Do you think we can figure out how to count all these food and exercise points and stuff?"

"It says here that we'll be 'provided with all the tools needed to achieve guaranteed success,' " Lucy read from the brochure.

James frowned dubiously. "And how much is this going to cost us? Meetings, meals, and exercises can't be cheap."

Lindy laughed. "Probably not, but if Witness to Fitness can offer us happiness after six weeks in the program, then who cares what it costs? All in favor?"

Everyone raised a hand, including a reluctant James.

"It's starting to feel like spring!" Lindy exclaimed as she opened the front door of Bennett's tidy ranch, preparing to leave. "Your neighbor's crocuses are coming out. I can see every blade of grass in their yard with the amount of outdoor lighting they have. They afraid of rabid deer or something worse, like their neighbor?" She asked, nudging Bennett with her elbow.

Bennett sniffed the evening breeze. "Dunno. One of their garden gnomes was stolen last year, right around Halloween, and next thing I know, I can see spotlights out my bedroom window. It's like sleeping next to a disco. Shoot, one day a small plane is gonna land here, thinking it's an airstrip. Maybe *I* should hire someone to do it as a joke. After all, April Fool's Day is this weekend and then I could get some sleep."

"April Fool's *and* the Annual Brunswick Stew Dinner at the fire department." Gillian pulled on a knit poncho in a pattern of violet and saffron stripes. "I *strongly* believe in supporting local causes."

"Shoot, I go just to look at the firemen." Lindy grinned sheepishly.

"What about your Principal Chavez? Aren't you still in love with him?" Lucy asked her friend.

"Of course, but I don't dare make a move until I've got a little less meatball and a lot more sauce to this body." Lindy patted her round hips. "Does anyone want to ride down to that Asian building they put up where the Dairy Drive-Thru used to be? I saw some lights on as I drove past earlier tonight."

Filled with energy due to a combination of the temperate evening air and their decision to begin a new weight-loss program, the Flab Five members all agreed to extend their supper club evening a little longer. Dividing themselves into two cars, they drove through the center of a quiet town and headed west to one of the town's two strip malls nestled beneath the comforting shadow of the Blue Ridge Mountains.

"So this is where Witness to Fitness is, too?" James asked Lindy.

"Yeah. Veronica moved into that place where Mrs. Posillico used to give dance lessons. Her oldest daughter is in my ceramics class this year and she told me her mama's arthritis just makes teaching dance too painful." Lindy uttered a sympathetic sigh. "Bless her heart."

"Hey!" Lucy shouted from the back seat. "There's a sign on that funky building. Chilly Willy's Polar Pagoda. Pagoda? Is that a Chinese type of architecture?"

"Japanese," Lindy promptly replied.

"Actually, it's both," James corrected his friend. "It's probably an Indian word in origin. It's a Buddhist building resembling a temple. If I remember correctly, the dome shape was supposed to create balance. I'm sure Gillian could tell you more about the whole religious part of the history."

"No thanks!" Lindy answered firmly. "There's someone washing the glass front door. I wonder if he's the new owner."

"Howdy folks!" A light-skinned African American man with a neat goatee dropped his squeegee into a bucket with a splash and waved to James and his two female passengers. A few seconds later, Bennett and Gillian joined the group and introduced themselves.

"Welcome to Quincy's Gap!" Lindy added

with a flourish.

"Mighty kind of y'all. I'm Willy Kendrick, but you can call me Chilly Willy. Everyone always does in the end." He laughed. The sound was rich and throaty and filled the night air like a song.

James smiled at the man's infectious laugh. "So, if you don't mind me asking, why the pagoda theme?"

"Well, it's pretty darn eye-catching, wouldn't you say?" Willy chuckled and he jerked his thumb at his new building.

"Are you a Buddhist?" Gillian asked hopefully.

"No ma'am. Southern Baptist born and raised, but I could use all the heavenly help I can get. I lost everything I had durin' the Fall of '05. I used to have my own restaurant in Biloxi, Mississippi. It was totally wiped away by that wicked woman known as Hurricane Katrina. No offense, ladies."

"You poor thing!" Gillian's eyes instantly grew misty.

"Now don't you go gettin' yourself all upset on my account." Willy's middle-aged face grew somber. "Lots of folks got a lot worse hurts than I did. All my family came out okay and that's what really matters. I worked a few jobs in Florida and lived through a few more storms until I decided that I was damned tired of hurricanes. Figured the mountains of Virginia get their share of snow, but no tornadoes, typhoons, tsunamis, or hurricanes. Am I right?" Willy laughed again, his warm brown eyes dancing with vivacity.

"You might not need to worry about those kinds of storms," James began as he watched a BMW pull into the parking lot. "But there are other kinds of natural disasters in this town and here comes one of them."

The BMW screeched to a stop within a few feet of the small group and a petite, silver-haired woman wearing a fur-trimmed suede jacket scrambled out of the car and fixed a pair of angry, narrow eyes upon Willy.

"I suppose this is *your* doing?" she demanded, gesturing wildly at the black and red painted pagoda.

Willy issued a welcoming smile. "Yes, ma'am. Do you like it?"

"Like it?" The woman panted. "It's an abomination! This town has a two-hundred-year-old history of Southern architecture and then you come along and build this . . . this . . ." She sucked in a great breath. "Atrocity!"

Willy remained nonplussed. "Yes, ma'am. It *is* different. But you can't get upset with me until you've tried one of my special praline caramel kiss sundaes. Come on in and you might feel a little friendlier toward the world at large once you've had a taste. I'm Willy, by the way." He stuck out his hand.

"*I* am Savannah Lowndes, President of the Shenandoah County Historical Society," the woman snapped while ignoring Willy's outstretched hand. "And I'd rather see this place burn to a cinder than *consume* anything that came from inside such a despicable eyesore!"

"Suit yourself, ma'am." Willy shrugged. "Not everybody's got a sweet tooth. How about the rest of you? I've got some coupons for next weekend's Grand Opening, too."

"We'd love to!" Lucy exclaimed and they turned to follow Willy inside. Savannah Lowndes snorted and climbed back into her car. She raced out of the parking lot, her face clouded with anger.

Suddenly a peppy voice that sounded all too familiar to James hailed the group. "Hi there! I hope you all enjoy your ice cream!" Veronica Levitt called from outside her storefront, which was four stores down from the Polar Pagoda. "I expect to see you all here next Saturday. And then you," she wiggled a skinny finger flirtatiously at Willy, "can kiss *this* precious little group of customers goodbye! If I have *my* way, they are all going to be lean, lovely, fruit-and-vegetable-eating gods and goddesses by June!"

"Hmm," Willy sighed as he held open the front door. A bell tinkled merrily as they entered the ice cream parlor, but Willy's face had turned grim. "I do believe that woman's gonna be bad for business."

# Three:
# Fat-Free Popcorn
# (Butter Flavored)

Serving Size:
5 cups

Witness to Fitness
Points

1

Chilly Willy was serving up frozen delights as fast as his two arms would allow. Due to the unusually mild spring night, a long line of townsfolk snaked out the front door of the Polar Pagoda and along the entire length of the strip mall. These animated patrons, having just finished their dinners at home or watching one of the two movies showing at the local theater, studied the colorful cones, cups, and sundaes mounded with candy toppings as their cheerful owners carried them outside. People exchanged waves, offered tastes of their frozen desserts, and chatted with friends as if they were guests at a cocktail party. In fact, the very evening air seemed brimming with a sense of vivacity and friendliness that infected the majority of the population of Quincy's Gap.

A band of teenage boys, satiated by extra-large cones of chocolate-chip cookie dough ice cream and bottles of cold root beer, sat on the curb outside the Polar Pagoda and flirted noisily with any pretty girl who passed by. Preteens propped bicycles against the red wooden walls of the ice cream shop and spoke in high-pitched squeals or giggled in unsuppressed excitement as they attempted to read the board containing the day's flavor specials.

After waiting twenty minutes, James Henry finally made it inside the front door. He peered over the heads of the adults standing clustered in front of the counter and was hailed by Willy as if he were a long-lost friend.

"Hello there, Mr. Henry!" Willy's voice boomed. "So glad to see you! Are you here for something sweet to eat?"

"Absolutely." James returned Willy's warm smile. "It sure looks like you're having a successful Grand Opening," he observed pleasantly, fascinated by the manner in which Willy was folding a glob of gummy bears into a slab of white ice cream using two tools resembling spackling knives.

"Sure am, my man. It's 'cause of this fine March evening and my even finer home-made frozen custard. This here is Sweet Cream mixed with Gummy Bears, red hots, and pieces of licorice. I call it the Kid in the Candy Store mix."

James watched in wonder as Willy scooped up the concoction and folded it neatly into a Styrofoam cup. "Who's next?" the grinning proprietor called out merrily.

"Me!" A woman's voice declared. James recognized the trim form and shimmering brown hair belonging to Murphy Alistair, reporter and managing editor of *The Shenandoah Star Ledger,* the county's small daily paper. "I'd like chocolate custard with peanut butter cups, please. Oh, and topped off with chocolate sprinkles. Do you mind if I take some photos for *The Star* while you work?"

"I'd be much obliged to you if you would, pretty lady. And don't you even think about tryin' to pay me, ya hear? Anyone who might get Chilly Willy some free business gets her pretty little self a free frozen custard."

Murphy smiled. "Are you attempting to bribe me with ice cream?"

"Absolutely, miss, absolutely."

After shooting a few pictures of Willy with her digital camera Murphy retreated to the back of the small store. "Hello, Professor." Murphy turned to James. "You here to buy what will soon become the most famous T-shirt in all of the Shenandoah Valley?"

James craned his neck in order to view the cobalt T-shirts hanging next to the menu board. The white text on the front of each shirt read, *HAVE YOU GOT A CHILLY WILLY?*

"That's an attention getter if I ever saw one." James laughed. "Every teenager in Quincy's Gap is going to be advertising for you, Willy."

"Lord willing!" Willy handed another customer an ice cream float. The next customer ordered pumpkin custard covered in hot fudge sauce as James desperately tried to decide which of the flavor varieties he was most in the mood for.

"Aren't you cheating on your diet?" Murphy asked, nudging James playfully in the ribs. Her hazel eyes sparkled and James wondered if she was flirting or simply being friendly.

"I'm joining Witness to Fitness tomorrow," James confessed softly. "I've been kind of sliding on my own, so I'm hoping to get back on track. You know, I'll just do their program until I can figure out how to do it by myself."

Murphy was listening intently. "Hey! That would make a great article. I could track your progress, kind of like one of those TV reality shows. The readers would love it and you're such a likeable personality. I bet a lot of people would be inspired by you."

James cleared his throat nervously. "Uh . . . I don't think I'd care to share my weight with the entire town."

"Now would I do that to you?" Murphy frowned playfully, but James believed she would print anything to sell more papers. "It would be more about your experience at Witness to Fitness. I think our readers need to hear a genuine story about this new business before they all race in and spend their hard-earned money there, don't you?"

"What'll it be, my friend?" Willy asked, holding his trowel-type tool above the mounded containers of custard.

"Peppermint with hot fudge and marshmallow, please," James stammered.

"Come on, what do you say, Professor?" Murphy pleaded, slowly licking chocolate custard off her plastic spoon.

James watched her tongue in a semi-hypnotic state as his brain struggled to form a reply. "I . . ."

"Thanks, Professor. I knew I could count on you." And with that, Murphy patted him on the arm and sauntered outside to interview some of the Polar Pagoda's satisfied customers.

Just as James had received his bowlful of heaven, a troupe of middle-aged women pushed aside the patrons in line and began shouting at Willy in unison. From what James could make out, they were furious about the T-shirts and wanted them immediately taken down from the display area and destroyed.

"They should be burned!" shrieked a mousy woman wearing a heavy wool jacket despite the balminess of the evening. "I am Mrs. Gloria Emerson and I am a minister's wife." She gestured to the group of heaving bosoms behind her. "And these are leaders of our church's youth group. We will *not* have our impressionable youth sporting such . . . such *indecent* apparel."

Willy remained nonplussed. "Indecent? It covers up everything, now don't it?"

Several onlookers chuckled. Mrs. Emerson ground her teeth until James thought they might crack.

"Don't you mock me, sir! I have influence in these parts and I will make it my duty to make sure that no *decent* folk come here until you agree to remove those offensive shirts from our sight. And!" she proclaimed as if she, and not the Reverend Emerson, were accustomed to giving the sermons, "I want you to give the money back to those innocent boys who have already purchased those filthy rags from you."

"They're not dirty, ma'am. They're fresh out of the box," Willy teased and the crowd cheered him. The customers were clearly on his side.

Mrs. Emerson reddened. "This is not the last you'll see of us. We're going to get those shirts gone and this I swear to you!"

"Well, at least have some ice cream before you go!" Willy called after the huffy women, and even though he continued to serve out cups and cones in a jolly manner, his eyes betrayed a hint of worry.

Outside, Murphy was busy interviewing Mrs. Emerson and her crowd. She then took a photograph of a teenage boy proudly wearing one of the controversial T-shirts.

"I'll be damned if I'm gonna get rid of it!" the boy shouted, eyeing Mrs. Emerson and her posse. "It's not like it's got swear words on it or Satanic symbols or anything. Those biddies need to lighten up."

"See the disrespect that kind of garment produces?" Mrs. Emerson shrieked and several members of the crowd nodded their heads in agreement. Murphy scribbled wildly on her notepad as the teenager strutted proudly up and down the parking area. Within minutes, two of his friends were in line in order to purchase T-shirts for themselves.

James strolled over to where Murphy was standing. "Poor Willy. This makes three threats on his new business and all from women," he muttered and then scooped custard into his mouth.

Murphy's eyes widened. "Who else threatened him?"

James instantly regretted mentioning anything to the reporter so he quickly regaled her with the barest of details regarding how Savannah Lowndes had tried to pick a fight with Willy and how Veronica Levitt wanted to sweet talk his clients away from him.

"It's hard to be a newcomer in this town," Murphy said, surprising James with what sounded like heartfelt sympathy. "A lot of folks here aren't comfortable with change."

"Can't say I blame them," James answered, thinking back to how he hadn't wanted to move back home. "Unless it's the kind of change that brings people like Willy to our town. We could all use more of his kind of jauntiness and optimism."

"Isn't *that* the truth? You're all right, James Henry." Murphy suddenly stood on her tiptoes and kissed James on the cheek. "I'll give you a call tomorrow to see how Witness to Fitness went."

As a stunned James pivoted to watch the reporter walk away, his hand touching the spot on his cheek where Murphy had brushed his skin with her sticky, custard-covered lips, he found himself facing an angry glare from Lucy Hanover. He offered a feeble wave, but she pretended not to have seen him and disappeared inside the Polar Pagoda.

James finished his dessert while debating whether or not to explain to Lucy that he and Murphy weren't an item, but he didn't see much point in doing so. On the other hand, the anger and hurt in Lucy's eyes made it clear to James that she still had feelings for him. Warmed by this thought and the giant bowl of custard filling his stomach, James was just about to pursue Lucy inside. He would ask her out for coffee and finally come clean as to why he had succumbed to his fears and insecurities and pray that he still had a chance to become more than her friend.

Before he could take a step forward, however, Veronica Levitt appeared on the sidewalk and began turning a series of cartwheels to the amusement of the waiting crowd.

"Hey everyone!" she shouted brightly. "I'm Veronica Levitt, the owner and manager of the brand-new Witness to Fitness. We're just a few stores down. Now, I know that you all are here tonight to enjoy a delicious dessert, but by the morning, you're going to be sorry. That fat is going to stick on your thighs," she pointed to a woman in tight jeans, "your waistline," she pointed to a man with an impressive spare tire, "and your rear," she pointed at a woman who had bent over to retrieve a set of dropped keys. All three of the crowd members unsuccessfully tried to fade into the background. "But you are all too, too beautiful to do this to yourselves!"

Veronica put her hands out as if embracing the crowd and continued her sales pitch. "Wouldn't you rather have the energy to do a cartwheel, or dance with your husband or wife, or live ten years longer than spend any more time in this line?" She brandished some pink brochures in her hands. "Come to *my* Grand Opening tomorrow and I'll give you a whole new life — one that will be *so* sweet that you won't even need desserts anymore."

"Ha! *That* can't be possible," someone mumbled and several people snickered.

"Yes it can!" Veronica seized the opportunity the dissenter had provided her. "You can be slimmer, stronger, younger looking, more energetic. No surgery, no pain. Just a different way of eating and some easy exercise and you can have a whole new body and a whole new outlook by beach season!"

Several people murmured and nodded their heads. Hands reached out to take brochures from Veronica.

"This looks expensive," a man pointed out sourly.

Veronica glided like a cat on ice to the man's side. She offered him a dazzling smile, grasped his shoulder, and whispered intimately, "Darlin', I think your life is worth the expense, don't you?"

The man said nothing. He blinked a few times as she moved away and then began seriously studying the pink brochure. By the time Veronica had reached the front of the line, Willy must have heard about the sideshow being produced for the benefit of his first customers. He propped open one of the front doors and spoke loudly, but politely.

"Do you mind letting my customers be *my* customers tonight? You've got your day comin' up tomorrow."

Veronica thrust her angular chin in the air and swept her arms around in order to indicate her rapt audience. "I'm trying to *save* the bodies of these lovely people while you're trying to send them to an early grave. Look at all of this potential standing right here in front of me! I won't lose a single opportunity to help someone live a longer, healthier life."

"Sometimes, folks have gotta have something that's just plain fun, too. Now scoot and do your business in your own time, at your *own* place."

"I'll just finish handing out these brochures." Veronica turned her back on Willy and bounced farther up the line, her ponytail bobbing along enthusiastically.

In a flash, Willy ran up and jerked the

brochures from Veronica's hand and stuffed them in the nearest trash can, which was predominately filled with sticky ice cream containers and dripping soda cups.

Veronica's fists clenched with anger. She took a step toward Willy and James scuttled sideways in order to get out of her way, but not far enough to avoid hearing her whisper, "That was *not very nice,* ice cream man. You'll learn to be nicer to me in the future."

On Saturday, as James stood outside the Witness to Fitness storefront gathering the courage needed to face a new diet and a disgruntled Lucy, Bennett appeared and hastened him inside.

"Man, let's just get this over with," his friend muttered.

Inside, the space was divided into the office section in the front, where four cubicles had been constructed out of sleek gray materials, and the exercise room in the back. Here Veronica had arranged a group of folding chairs in the middle of the floor with an aisle going up the center. Gillian waved James and Bennett over to the two seats she had saved for them. Lucy and Lindy also smiled and greeted their friends, and although James could sense no animosity coming from Lucy, he felt agitated all the same. In addition to the members of the Flab Five, at least twenty other people with an evident love of food had gathered in the room. Avoiding their own reflections in the wall-length mirror opposite them, the men and women fidgeted nervously or attempted to strike up conversations with those seated next to them.

Abruptly, the lights in the room were dimmed and then turned back to their full brightness. Upbeat dance music began to play from a boom box set up in one of the rear corners of the exercise room. The crowd immediately fell silent.

Once again, Veronica displayed her gymnastic talents by doing two cartwheels and a roundhouse on the empty space of hardwood floor in front of her future clients. Several of these people clapped hesitatingly as she completed her routine and gave a short, stiff bow.

"Welcome to Witness to Fitness!" she beamed. "I'm Veronica Levitt, but since you and I" — she pointed at people randomly as she spoke — "are going to be *very close* in the next few months, you should call me what my friends do, and that's Ronnie."

"I wonder how many friends she's got. I mean, who could tolerate all of that perkiness?" James muttered under his breath and

Gillian shot him an admonishing look.

Ronnie ran a hand over her hair, which was pulled back so tightly into a high, bouncing ponytail that it seemed like the woman had just had a brow lift. "All of you sitting before me are brave and intelligent people. You have made the choice to live a better, healthier life and I plan to reward you for the decision. You see, right now you are all like a bunch of caterpillars. You are overweight and you spend too much of your time eating. But *inside!*" She reached out to an overweight teenage girl in the front row. "Inside of each and every one of you is a butterfly. Something beautiful and new and *filled* with energy is just dying to be let loose from its shell. *You* are holding yourself back!" Ronnie pointed to Lindy next.

James turned and was surprised to see Lindy nod in silent agreement. Gillian was dabbing tears from her eyes with a pink and purple tie-dyed scarf. Lucy's face was blank and Bennett simply appeared amused.

"Quite a show," he whispered to James as Ronnie skipped around the room.

"Quite," James agreed.

"Now, in the next six weeks, I am going to get a little bit tough with you, because that's the kind of help you need." Ronnie grabbed the shoulder of a fleshy man sitting near the aisle. "But you'll have lots of loving support, too. How many of you out there have tried other diet plans?"

A dozen hands rose into the air. Ronnie stared down at the man whose shoulder she had clamped onto until he raised a trembling hand.

"And here you are, back in bad shape. After six weeks on my plan, I will have taught you how to eat and exercise so that you can continue changing your life on your own. I will help you break out of your shell!" she exclaimed gaily. "My friends, you will fly like a butterfly and begin living the life that has always been confined to your dreams!"

Several women to the right of James broke out in sporadic clapping. One of them was Twix Lady from the discount warehouse. She sat with a look of rapt fascination as she watched Ronnie's every movement. Her hands were clutched together as if in prayer.

"That's the spirit, ladies. Now, you can't do Witness to Fitness as a piecemeal plan. You must eat my food, keep a food journal, come in every week for counseling and weigh-in sessions, and attend at least three exercise classes a week." Ronnie paused and clasped her hands over her flat breasts. In a dramatic stage whisper, she pronounced, "If you cheat on any of these items you will be removed from the program with NO MONEY RETURNED!" Several people began twittering amongst themselves.

"Oh dear, no refunds?" someone behind James whimpered.

"This is for your own good, my friends. You must place your *complete* trust in us. Paying us up front will motivate you to return for your required sessions." Ronnie ran her hands over her gaunt cheeks as she surveyed her future clients. "I have two assistants I would like to introduce to you. First is Phoebe Liu. Phoebe is in charge of counseling and finances."

Phoebe stood up from where she sat in the front row. She was a petite Asian American with attractive, exotic looks and a demure smile. She raised a small hand and waved shyly at the crowd saying softly, "Please don't hesitate to call me if you need any extra support during your time with Witness to Fitness. I am here to help you."

The sincerity of her simple statement made more of an impact on James than any of Ronnie's cartwheels or butterfly analogies.

"Next," Ronnie called out, "we have Dylan Shane. Dylan is our primary fitness instructor."

A door in the rear of the exercise room opened and the women in the room issued a collective gasp. A man of average height with white-blonde hair, sparkling brown eyes, and limbs that looked like they were sculpted from tree trunks, offered the crowd a dazzling smile. His aquamarine workout shirt strained against his chiseled pectoral muscles and a whiff of his musky cologne drifted out into the first two rows of seats. "Hello y'all. I'm Dylan," he boomed in a deep, manly voice. "I live over in Harrisonburg but will be commuting here every day except on Saturdays. Today is an exception, as I usually volunteer for the elderly on Saturdays." The women turned to one another and prattled in approval.

"How many twenty-something hunks would do that with their free time?" A woman behind James asked the man seated next to her.

"Honey," the man stated matter-of-factly, "I'm sure he's gay. No one who looks that good is straight."

"Dylan has made you all a special snack to celebrate your decision to join our team." Ronnie issued a wink of flirtatious collusion at her co-worker. "Dylan?"

Dylan bounded back into the room from whence he made his original entrance bearing a tray laden with paper bowls. James smelled popcorn and immediately perked up.

"Here's a sample of the kind of snack you'll be enjoying as a Witness to Fitness member," Ronnie said as she and Phoebe helped Dylan distribute the popcorn. "It's 98% fat free and has a butter substitute spray to give you that movie theater taste."

James grabbed his bowl and hurriedly stuffed a handful of popcorn in his mouth. His taste buds were disappointed by the cardboard nature of the popcorn and even though he could smell the butter-flavored spray, he couldn't taste it at all.

"Movie theater popcorn?" Bennett scoffed beside him. "The only way this stuff tastes like that is if she's been eating the paper tub instead of the popcorn."

James laughed as Lucy chimed in defensively. "I think it's just fine. Though it could use a bit more butter," she added wistfully.

"I don't care what we have to eat as long as I get to come in here and feast my Brazilian eyes on Dylan three times a week!" Lindy announced cheerfully.

"Amen to that, sister," breathed Gillian who was eyeing the male fitness instructor appreciatively.

"Now we're going to divide up into three

groups in order to discuss how many food points you'll each be allowed." Ronnie pointed at Phoebe. "Phoebe will take all the lovely ladies weighing between 150 and 185 pounds in this corner. Dylan will take all of the ladies who weigh above 185 in this corner. I will meet with all of our *fine* gentlemen in the front of the store."

As James stood up to join the other men, he noticed that several of the heavier women seemed torn between pretending they weighed less than 185 pounds and the chance to bask in the glow of Dylan's beauty. As if reading their minds, Ronnie added, "And don't worry if you're unsure of your weight, we've got *very* accurate scales that can tell us an exact number."

As the men huddled around Ronnie's spartan cubicle, James detected a pungent and rather sour odor coming from one of the men to his right. Unable to focus on Ronnie's lecture about choosing the next week's meals and snacks based on their current weight, James sniffed and grimaced as Bennett began to do the same.

"Some of you might be feeling a bit depressed over your current weight, but on my program, those of you weighing over 200 pounds get more food points. More food points means more food. Now, let's share what the scale said about your weight. That will bring you closer together as a group." Ronnie looked each of them hard in the eye, a patient smile fixed upon her face.

One by one, the six men began to quietly and humbly admit how much they weighed. The only person who refused to answer turned out to be the source of the ripe smell filling the cubicle area. James was pretty certain that it was a mixture of whiskey and the fetid sort of body odor a person carries when they haven't visited a shower in several days.

"Come now, Mr. . . . ?" Ronnie prodded. "We're all friends here."

"Name's Vandercamp, Pete Vandercamp." The man coughed repeatedly and then spit something solid into a foul-looking handkerchief. James suddenly recognized him. Pete was the former night janitor from Blue Ridge High. He had been a young man when James was in high school and all the students had dubbed him Mr. Vandercough due to the constant wet hacking noises he made as he cleaned the floors at the end of the school day.

"Why don't we get to know each other a bit?" Ronnie suggested, deciding to ignore Pete. "Tell us what you do for a living, for example."

James and Bennett already knew that one of the men named Leo worked for Shenandoah Savings & Loan. Another man, named Dane, was a plumber, and Pete Vandercamp triumphantly announced that he had come out of an early retirement in order to work nights at the Polar Pagoda.

"That's sure some good ice cream," he rasped as Ronnie clucked her tongue in disapproval.

"Did Willy send you here to spy on me?" she teased, but James thought he detected an undercurrent of tension in her voice.

Pete cleared his throat nonchalantly. "Hey. It's a free country, lady. Folks can eat ice cream if they wanna."

Ronnie took Pete by the arm and pulled him toward the front door. "Honey, if you're not here to join Witness to Fitness then let's not waste the time of those who have come to change their lives." Under her breath, James thought he heard her mutter nastily. "And you might want to take a bath before your shift starts tonight."

Pete, who seemed to be in no hurry to exit, stared at her. "I know you from somewhere, lady. Weren't you on TV a few years ago?"

Trying to mask her impatience, Ronnie turned to see the group of men watching her exchange with Pete. It was evident that her clients were enjoying themselves, so she quickly tried to guide Pete to the door but he refused to budge.

"Well," Ronnie quickly uttered a high-pitched squeal. "I *have* been told I look a little like Hilary Swank, the actress."

Pete's eyes narrowed as he struggled to remember. "Nah. It wasn't like that."

Ronnie opened the front door and practically shoved Pete outside with an exaggerated giggle and a powerful bump of the hip. She then followed him out and said something else that no one could hear as the door had shut after her. The rest of the men began to talk among themselves about their concerns about joining a diet group, but James kept his eyes riveted on Pete Vandercamp, who reached into his pocket, removed a tin of Skoal chewing tobacco, and put a wad inside his left cheek.

Staring at Pete, it was obvious that the older man had suddenly remembered something, because he pointed accusingly at Ronnie and then began to laugh. His whole body seemed to shake as he mocked the fitness instructor. James could see from Ronnie's profile that the color had drained from her flushed face, but she seemed to recover quickly. She raised her fist and took a step toward Pete in what was unmistakably a threatening manner. Guffawing, Pete spit a thin stream of brown tobacco juice on the ground, turned his back, and then casually strode away as Ronnie stood motionless, calling angrily after him. James watched as Ronnie took several deep breaths in order to compose herself before she reentered the store.

When she returned, a wide smile was once again plastered on her face, but James noticed that both of her hands were still clenched into tight fists, as if the rest of her body hadn't received the message that rage must be completely controlled in front of the customers.

# FOUR:
## BRUNSWICK STEW

**Serving Size:
2 cups**

**Witness to Fitness
Points**

**12**

Brady Gerhardt was the newest member of the Quincy's Gap Volunteer Fire & Rescue Station. Even though he knew about as much as everybody else did about putting out fires, the veterans of the department called him "rookie" and forced him to do all of the menial tasks around the station, such as stocking the pantry and cleaning out the restrooms. Brady didn't mind. He was an affable young man in his early twenties and felt proud to have joined the grizzled and seasoned men of Fire & Rescue. He also knew that as soon as someone else signed up to volunteer he, Brady, would be able to call that person "rookie," regardless of the newcomer's age or station in life.

At the moment, Brady couldn't dwell on thoughts of rising in status within the department. It was the annual charity dinner and he was far too busy ladling steaming spoonfuls of homemade Brunswick stew into deep ceramic bowls neatly lined up on a tray in the station's kitchen to do any thinking at all.

"Come on, rookie!" Dirk Maguire shouted gruffly. "We got payin' customers out there and they're starvin'!"

Brady wiped a line of perspiration off his brow with the back of a potholder and carefully pushed the tray, filled with delicious-smelling stew, in Dirk's direction.

"Keep 'em comin'. We're gonna be able to keep the lights on after tonight's dinner for sure." Dirk hoisted the tray high on his shoulder, as expertly as a waiter in a four-star eatery. Brady was impressed. Dirk worked at the landfill and was noted for his strength and direct mannerisms, but he was clearly graceful as well. "We might even be able to buy that second-hand pool table we've been wanting for so long."

Other members of the department came noisily into the kitchen, clapping Brady merrily on the back and taking deep swallows of beer from red plastic cups.

"This dinner's a record breaker!" bellowed a jovial Chief Lawrence. "Get on out there and enjoy yourself, boy. I'll spot you for a bit. There's a lot of pretty women who'd just love to meet a handsome firefighter like yourself." The chief winked and took the ladle from Brady's hand.

"Thanks, Chief!" Without hesitation, Brady stripped off his white vinyl apron bearing the text, *If you can't take the heat, git on out of my kitchen!* He darted out of the second-story kitchen and slid down the fire pole leading to the station's garage, where rows of tables and folding chairs had been set up to accommodate the diners. From the looks of it, every able-bodied person in Quincy's Gap was either sitting and enjoying their meal, waiting in line for a bowl of stew and a piece of homemade cornbread, or flanking the makeshift bar where cold beer was being distributed as dollar bills hurriedly exchanged hands.

"I sure hope there aren't any fires tonight," Brady heard a barrel-shaped woman with bright orange hair remark lowly as he made his way toward the bar. "I think the firemen are all going to be too drunk to drive the truck."

Her friend, a plump woman with glossy black hair and friendly brown eyes smiled and said, "I'm sure they've got some people on standby for an emergency."

Brady walked past the women in search of a Coke and then a piece of warm cornbread. As he sat in one of the few empty chairs, watching a fat pat of butter slide down the slope of moist cornbread, he wondered about what the woman with the orange hair had said. Looking around the room, he could see that every member of the Quincy's Gap Volunteer Fire & Rescue Station had a red plastic cup in his hand. Ruddy cheeks, twinkling eyes, and hearty belly laughs indicated that the members of Station Seventeen had consumed a goodly amount of beer. With a start, Brady realized that he might be the only one capable of driving the truck and he had never driven it before.

As he bit into his homemade bread and

then paused to lick a rivulet of butter from the back of his hand, a cute blonde seated at the other end of his table smiled at him. He returned the smile, forgetting all about his concerns about being the only sober fireman in Quincy's Gap. When the girl coyly waved him over to join her using only her index finger and a subtle wink, Brady leapt to obey.

James Henry had the great misfortune of being stuck in line behind three of the most fearsome women in Quincy's Gap. He had arrived late to the Brunswick stew fundraiser as his father refused to let him leave until James sat down with him and looked over a brochure containing a palette of roofing materials. Ashamed to admit to Jackson that his savings were soon to be nonexistent after enrolling in Witness to Fitness, James pretended to have great interest in the brochure until his father told him that he had already hired a roofer and that the job was slated to begin next week. Panicking, James abruptly stood and informed his father that they would need to hold off on the roof work a little longer and then, like a coward, he grabbed his windbreaker and bolted out the back door without further explanation.

"The roofer's comin' on Monday!" Jackson bellowed after him. "And he's gonna want a deposit!"

As James drove through town, his growling stomach and the wish to sit and eat next to someone he liked caused him to practically skid into one of the library parking spaces. The lot, which was across the street from the firehouse, was almost completely full. Trotting across the asphalt, James couldn't help wondering how the Shenandoah County Library could ever host an event that would cause such a full lot and raise funds for his beloved branch.

Winded, James burst in through the side door of the firehouse, darted in front of a family of six, and purchased a food ticket from one of the fireman's wives.

"Hey! That fat man cut us!" one of the children behind him whined and his parents shushed him, but not before James felt his face grow warm with embarrassment.

It turned out that James got no closer to getting his food by cutting in front of the dawdling family. In fact, the line was at an utter standstill. James stepped to the side to see what the holdup was all about. Apparently, an elderly couple insisted upon hearing each and every one of the stew's ingredients before they would accept their bowls.

"I'm very allergic to certain foods!" the woman declared. "I *could* go into cardiac arrest."

"And I simply cannot eat eggs!" her husband croaked while shaking his cane at the fireman serving the stew.

"Ah . . . I don't think there are any eggs in there, sir." The fireman looked around for help, but the only other fireman in sight was serving the cornbread and he shrugged his shoulders helplessly.

The fireman pushed a bowl of stew underneath the old woman's nose. "Ma'am, it's mostly chicken, corn, beans, onions, and tomatoes and stuff. There's nothin' bad in there."

"What kind of *stuff?*" the old woman demanded suspiciously.

"You know, like spices."

Fortunately, Mrs. Emerson, the minister's wife who had been so upset over Chilly Willy's T-shirts, stepped in and coaxed the couple into accepting their bowls of stew.

"You just have to know how to handle people," she said proudly to her companion in line as the older couple shuffled off to find seats. Mrs. Emerson's companion turned out to be Savannah Lowndes.

"Well, I wish we could *handle* some of this town's more pressing problems, like that wretched ice cream store."

"We could always pray that our townsfolk get tired of ice cream and that man has to move to Richmond," Mrs. Emerson responded with a deadpan look. "I'll ask the other folks in my Youth Leadership Group to pray with me."

"Excuse me," a third woman stepped toward the two middle-aged matriarchs. James tried to shrink backward in line as he recognized the heavily made-up stick figure belonging to Ronnie Levitt.

"Hi!" she chirped. "I'm Veronica Levitt, the proprietor of the new Witness to Fitness and I *completely* agree with you ladies."

Mrs. Emerson and Mrs. Lowndes smiled widely. "Welcome to our delightful berg, my dear." Mrs. Lowndes drawled.

"I just wanted to say, that when *my* business becomes a success around here, no one will feel the need to visit that little old ice cream shop." Ronnie lowered her voice conspiratorially. "People trying to eat healthy foods shouldn't be buying frozen custard, if you see what I mean. I vow to make Quincy's Gap a happier, healthier place!" James half expected her to shake a pair of pompoms as she uttered this passionate oath. "I might just have to design my own T-shirts. I don't think Willy's are very attractive, do you? And he's bought enough to outfit the *entire town*."

"Those shirts are entirely reprehensible!" Mrs. Emerson declared.

Mrs. Lowndes smirked. "Indeed. It looks like we'll just have to *make certain* your business succeeds where *his* does not. We women will stick together and take care of this little problem ourselves."

"Yes we shall," Mrs. Emerson said, puffing out her chest like a bullfrog. Then she turned to receive her stew and the three women moved off to find a seat together, whispering in tones too hushed for James to hear over the general din within the garage.

James had just gotten his own steaming bowl with a side of cornbread when Bennett appeared from out of nowhere and asked James to join him and a new co-worker of his at a nearby table. Relieved to have someone to sit with, James wove through the rows of satiated diners where two seats had been saved by the strategic placement of one of Bennett's letter bags. Across from the two empty chairs sat a man in his late thirties whom James had never seen before. When Bennett moved his bag, the man looked up and gave James a reserved smile.

"Carter, this is my good buddy James

Henry. James, this is Carter Peabody. He just moved here and has taken over Pat Salisbury's route. Pat retired last week."

"Nice to meet you, Carter." James felt immediately comfortable in the presence of another shy soul. Of course, Carter had the looks of a weathered surfer, right down to the sun-streaked hair and freckled nose. He seemed to be of average build with a hint of a paunch, but overall, James was certain women would find Carter very appealing. Perhaps his bashfulness was just a pretense. James cast sly glances at the newcomer as he ate his stew and Bennett warned Carter about the nastier canines on his new mail route.

"I like dogs," Carter responded simply after Bennett was finished. "Especially big ones, like the K-9 units on the cop shows. I've got a Border collie named Sergeant."

"If you like big dogs, then you've got to meet our friend Lucy," Bennett said. "She's got three of the most terrifying German Shepherds you've ever laid eyes on."

Carter's eyes gleamed. "German Shepherds are the most common breed used as police dogs. The New Jersey General Assembly actually tried to get a law passed to treat them the same as the human officers . . . so if someone were to shoot down a

K-9 officer it would be the same as shooting a man! Isn't that cool?" When neither James nor Bennett looked suitably impressed, Carter looked down at his bowl. "I visit a website about citizens who capture criminals. I guess it's kind of a weird hobby, huh? Still, maybe your friend Lucy wouldn't find it so strange. I'd like to meet her sometime."

James almost choked on his cornbread. He didn't want Bennett introducing Carter to Lucy. Why, she might fall in love with him and where would that leave James?

"Have you seen her?" James asked, trying to sound nonchalant.

"She was here earlier." Bennett took a swallow of beer. "I saw her talking in a kind of serious way to Sheriff Huckabee."

James looked around the room in hopes of spotting Lucy so that he could finally arrange a time to talk to her privately, but he didn't see her. As his eyes wandered over the rows of townsfolk, they came to rest on a young man holding a cell phone to his ear. An attractive blonde was sitting next to him, and though she seemed to be batting her eyelashes and bumping her shoulder into his in order to get his attention, the man stared straight ahead with a look of horror spreading across his face.

Suddenly, James felt goose bumps erupt up and down his forearms. He stared as the young man snapped his cell phone shut, jumped up from the table, and headed directly toward where James watched in agitated fascination.

"Chief!" The young man urgently plucked the sleeve of a man seated behind James. The older man, who was deep in conversation with his tablemates, ignored his fellow firefighter at first, but the young man persisted. "Chief!" he said loudly. "There's a fire!"

"Where, Brady, in the kitchen?" The chief and several of the other firefighters laughed and took fresh swigs of beer from their cups.

"No, sir. It's the Polar Pagoda. That new ice cream place. It's burning like crazy!"

The chief swung around to face Brady. "How do you know? We haven't gotten a call."

"My little brother just rode by there on his bike. He called me on my cell. The 911 call will probably come any second now, sir. We should get ready!"

Chief Lawrence looked down at his beer cup and then back at Brady. "You sure your brother ain't just messin' with you, rookie?"

"No, sir. He's a good kid." Brady fidgeted anxiously with his cell phone. "And there's more, Chief!" he added, his voice rising a notch.

"What?" the chief demanded crossly, his eyes sweeping around the crowded room as he absorbed the possible problems of their situation.

"My brother said . . . well, he said he saw someone inside."

At that moment, the alarm sounded.

# FIVE:
## CHERRY COLA

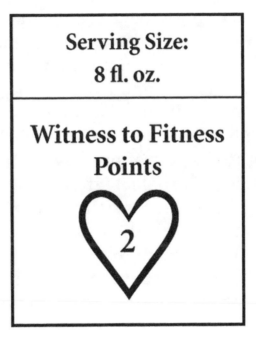

**Serving Size:**
**8 fl. oz.**

**Witness to Fitness**
**Points**

2

As pandemonium erupted around him, James grabbed onto Bennett's elbow and shouted, "Let's go!" over the roar of the alarm.

Several firemen were shouting at a group

of slow-moving patrons who had thoughtlessly parked their cars in front of the station house's garage doors. It became quickly apparent that at least half a dozen firemen were perfectly sober as they expediently gathered their equipment and prepped the truck for an immediate departure. James couldn't believe how little time it took before they were boarded and, with set expressions on their faces, clearly prepared to face whatever danger lay ahead.

"You're blocking our truck!" Chief Lawrence roared at a flustered woman who squeaked and dropped her car keys onto the pavement. "Hurry, woman!" he yelled again, pulling on his jacket and helmet while signaling to the rest of his crew to board the truck. "Let's go, rookie!" the chief beckoned to Brady from across the garage as the young man struggled to free himself from the grip of a petrified matron while simultaneously attempting to pull on a pair of flame-retardant boots. Meanwhile, Chief Lawrence gesticulated wildly. "Come on, son! You're drivin'!"

James, Bennett, and a bewildered Carter threaded their way toward the front of the stationhouse, where a knot of townsfolk blocked the exit as they dallied with coats, hats, and gloves. Looking around, James caught site of Chilly Willy, calmly finishing his stew and watching the excited crowd with a look of bemusement. At that moment, one of the young firefighters placed a hand on Willy's shoulder and gave it a wordless squeeze as he dashed for the fire truck.

The fleeting touch, which seemed to carry a mixture of pity and hope, alerted Willy as to the source of the fire. Observers cast Willy sorrowful glances as they realized that the popular and jovial newcomer might be facing a tragic beginning to his life in Quincy's Gap. After the young man moved away, Willy dropped his spoon and jerked upright, his eyes trained woefully on the wailing truck as it inched out of the garage, still impeded by an old pickup that was slowly backing out of the driveway by an extremely short driver who seemed to have a serious distrust for his rearview mirror.

James felt a deep instinct to call out to the man, to offer his sympathies, but knew that his voice would never be heard over the clanging of the alarm. As the yellow fire truck, newly washed and polished to a lacquerlike shine, burst out of the garage bay, Willy pushed his way through the crowd and out into the parking lot.

As James, Bennett, and Carter headed for Bennett's truck, which was actually a retired mail truck repainted a plain white, they spotted Willy in the parking lot next to the station. Apparently, his car had been parked in by an SUV the size of an Army tank.

"Willy!" James called out. "Come on! We'll take you!"

Willy nodded gratefully and hustled into the back seat of the tiny truck. As Bennett started the engine, he switched off the radio and the foursome drove in weighted silence down Main Street. As they crested the hill leading to West Woods Shopping Center, where the Polar Pagoda was located, they could see a thick trunk of smoke spurting into the night sky. It reminded James of a tornado's funnel, except that it churned in one place, like a storm intent on damaging a single target of wood and nails and concrete.

It took several minutes to reach the top of the rise as most of the participants of the fundraiser dinner had made their way to the scene of the fire. A long line of red taillights cruising past the burning structure on the end of the strip mall caused Bennett to swear with agitation and disgust.

"Vultures!" he spat, swerving around a red sports car that had pulled off on the side of the hill in order to get a better view of the action.

"It's just what folks do," Willy muttered, his eyes never leaving the aggressive orange and vermilion tongues of flame as they burrowed into the pagoda's new beams of wood and darkened the fresh coats of red and green paint into irregular, blackened shadows.

James didn't know what to say. He was torn between pity for Willy and the guilty thrill of watching the avaricious fire eat away at the little ice cream shop at a tremendous speed. A strong spring breeze wafted ashes across the parking lot and as Bennett turned the truck toward the conflagration, splinters of charred wood and debris still lit with devilish sparks landed on his windshield.

"And here I thought I was safe from disasters," Willy said as he got out of the car and stared at his ruined business. James followed his gaze, noticing that the firemen were doing all they could to control the blaze, but the roof had already collapsed inward and great coughs of smoke emitted from the gap left open to the night air. An arc of water rained onto the burning structure, and several other firemen began taping off a perimeter around the building in order to keep the crowds at bay.

Willy, James, Bennett, and Carter watched

in silence as the flames were finally drenched into feeble sparks. Thick smoke spread outward like a gray fog, covering the parking lot in a gossamer layer of ash. James could feel it coating his hair and skin like a dusting of gritty sand sticking to damp flesh. Willy opened his palm in order to catch some of the minute particles that once represented his entrepreneurial dreams. From where they stood in the parking lot, on a slight rise above the bustling firemen, the men noticed the arrival of two brown patrol cars. The strip of red and blue roof lights blazed, but the sirens had not been activated. Three men hopped out of their vehicles and began to confer with the exhausted firemen. James recognized Sheriff Huckabee and deputies Keith Donovan and Glenn Truett.

Two cars pulled up next to Bennett's truck. James recognized Gillian's environmentally friendly hybrid as well as Lucy's dirty Jeep. Gillian, Lindy, and Lucy approached the dumbstruck group of men. James was delighted to see that Lindy appeared to be carrying a six-pack of soda. He felt like he had swallowed a mouthful of chalk and couldn't wait to wash away the layer of grime that coated his tongue.

"We saw y'all up here from the other end

of the lot. Thought you might be a bit parched by now so we ran out and got you some cherry cola," Lindy said softly, handing each of the men a cold can. Bennett thanked her and awkwardly introduced the three ladies to Carter.

"Thank you kindly," Willy raised his can to his lips and took a deep swig. He seemed to shake off the trance he had fallen under while watching the fire. "Nothin' like a little cherry cola to bring things to light again. I reckon it's not all as bad as it looks. I've got cherry cola, some new friends, and I've got a good insurance policy."

"I'm glad you have your sense of humor intact." Gillian put her hand on Willy's forearm and smiled.

James stared at the charred structure that had promised to be a bustling ice cream parlor. The building looked like a whale beached on a square of ebony sand, long decomposed with a rib cage of black beams jutting up into the night air. Suddenly, he remembered what Brady had said about someone being trapped inside. As unobtrusively as possible, he pulled Lucy aside and shared what he had overheard the fireman report to Chief Lawrence.

"Didn't you tell me that old Pete Vandercamp was going to be working the weekend shifts?" Lucy asked, gripping James by the hand.

James looked down as her soft fingers locked onto his. He covered her hand with his free one and tried to reassure her. "Yes, but it was just a kid on his bike reporting what he thought he saw. Maybe he was wrong. After all, it would have been getting dark by then. Could have just been a shadow. It could be nothing — a trick of the light."

"Maybe, but I doubt it." Lucy turned and pointed at the patrol cars. "After all, the Sheriff's here," she said worriedly as she gazed at the smoldering building. "Oh, James. I know Pete wasn't the best of men. He drank and swore at us when we were kids and had always made lewd comments to all the pretty women in town, but no one deserves a horrible death like that. I truly hope they don't find anyone inside."

James put his arm around Lucy's shoulder but could think of nothing to say. He believed that the boy had probably seen someone and that someone would most likely turn out to be Pete Vandercamp. From where he and Lucy stood, slightly above the perimeter of tape, they watched the Sheriff pull on a pair of firemen boots and follow an agitated Chief Lawrence into the remains of the Polar Pagoda.

"I'm going down there," Lucy announced.

"Wait!" James held her firmly by the arm. "You might not want to see what they find *if* they do find something. It might look . . ." he trailed off as he noticed the others staring at him.

Gillian appeared next to James and crossed her arms over her chest. "What are you two whispering about?" she demanded.

Willy gazed at James and Lucy and then his jaw grew slack. "Do y'all know why Johnny Law is here? Is there more bad news? There talk of arson or somethin'?"

James decided that Willy deserved honesty. "There may be . . . um . . . someone might have been inside. Caught in the fire. It's not certain, Willy," he said as gently as he could.

Willy shook his head emphatically. "No way, man. Nothin' in there could have burned fast enough that . . ." he paused, ". . . Pete would have gotten out. He's no nuclear physicist, but he's got a survival instinct, same as the rest of us."

"You're probably right," Lindy assured him, but her round eyes betrayed her fear.

"What's that the Sheriff's got in his hand?" Carter asked quietly, speaking for the first time.

Lucy peered through the dark as Sheriff

Huckabee moved into the strong beam cast by the lights of the fire truck. "Those look like our standard plastic evidence bags. I can't quite tell what's inside."

"From the long neck and the fact that they look like they're made of glass — see how the lights are reflecting on the surface — I'd say they're liquor bottles. One in each bag," Bennett mumbled.

"Didn't Pete drink Wild Turkey?" Lucy turned to James. "Remember all the empty bottles he kept in his car when we were in high school? You couldn't pass him in the hall without breathing in whiskey."

"Yeah." James nodded, a queasy feeling spreading throughout his stomach.

"Well, one's a Wild Turkey bottle but the other one isn't. That's Gentleman Jack, for sure," Carter stated authoritatively.

Everyone looked at the new mail carrier with surprise. "Gentleman Jack? Do you mean Jack Daniels?" Lindy asked and Carter silently nodded. "How can you tell *that* from this distance?"

Carter shrugged. "Used to work at a liquor store. I could tell you what most bottles are without the labels and those two are easy ones. The labels have both turned completely black, but the shape is still obvious to me. Weird . . ." he trailed off.

"What's weird?" Bennett prodded.

Carter jerked his shoulders again and glanced shyly toward the Sheriff. "It's just that most folks don't mix their whiskeys, you know. They stick to one brand pretty loyally."

"Don't look at me!" Willy threw his hands in the air with a sound that was part sob, part laugh. "I'm from a dry, Baptist household. I wouldn't know whiskey, good *or* bad, from cough syrup, and neither one of those bottles is mine." He watched as an ambulance pulled into the parking lot. "Oh Lord, please tell me that poor man didn't drink two bottles full of that damnable liquor while he was on the job tonight."

Lucy touched Willy's arm as two paramedics unloaded a gurney from the back. By this time, most of the onlookers had dispersed. The fire was out and a sudden chill had appeared in the air. A few teenage boys sat in the rear of a pickup, but eventually, even they grew tired of the scene and motored noisily out of the lot and onto the street leading back to town.

Lucy squeezed Willy's arm with a bit more pressure, trying to lead him away from the scene. "Come on Willy, let's get you home."

"I know you're tryin' to spare me pain, friend, but I gotta know." Willy gently shook off Lucy's arm and appealed to the others. "I've gotta go down."

James understood. "Then we're coming with you."

As the group of seven approached what was left of the Polar Pagoda, Deputy Keith Donovan raced over to them before they could all duck under the yellow tape.

"Whoa there, folks," he said, holding up his hand like a traffic director. "That tape is there to keep civilians like yourselves safe from harm." He looked directly at Lucy as he said this, deliberately taunting her for being an administrator in the Sheriff's Department and not a bona fide member of law enforcement.

"This is *my* place," Willy said calmly and stepped over the tape. "I need to know what's happened here."

"We'll inform you in due time." Donovan stepped in front of Willy and ran a hand through his unkempt orange hair, which was flecked with ashes and other debris. "Damn!" he yelled, shaking his head violently as black flakes flew onto his shoulders and trickled down the front of his uniform. As he focused on dusting himself off, Willy walked briskly past him and approached Sheriff Huckabee.

James could hear him politely introducing

himself before the Sheriff could utter the slightest protest over his presence within the restricted area. The sheriff's face was unreadable, but he shook Willy's hand in apparent sympathy and then pulled him farther away from James and the others and began to talk in a hushed tone as he gestured between the ambulance and the ruined building. As James watched, Willy suddenly covered his face with his hands and moaned loudly. Sheriff Huckabee gazed at him with compassion and patted him awkwardly on the back.

Spotting Willy's friends, Huckabee's walrus-like mustache suddenly flared in anger and he bellowed at Donovan. "Get them out of here, Deputy!"

Although Keith Donovan did his best to push and shove the remaining six onlookers back beyond the tape, most of them, including James and Lucy, caught a clear glimpse of the gurney as it was wheeled to the silent ambulance. A figure lay unmoving under a thin shroud. James stared at the form, which was completely covered beneath a white sheet that had a sickly yellowish tinge below the headlights of the truck.

"What happened, Keith?" Lucy asked Donovan quietly. "Is it Pete?"

"Oh, come on, Lucy," he answered crossly

instead. "You'll stick your nose into everything soon enough. I'm sure you'll have read every single one of *our* reports and tell *all* your friends here every tiny, little detail by noon tomorrow."

Lucy's brow clouded. "Well since I have to *type* the reports, I guess I *will* be reading them, but it doesn't take a *deputy* to know that Pete was scheduled to be working in that ice cream shop tonight. If it's not Pete, then who is it?"

Her taunting succeeded in confirming their worst fears. Donovan gave James a final shove directly into the tape and spat, "So it's Pete. Good for you, Miss I-Went-To-College. But since *you* can't get near the scene, bein' it's a *crime* scene, I guess *you* won't be figurin' out how exactly Pete met his fiery end, now will you?"

"I guess I'd have to start by wondering if he drank all of the contents of those two whiskey bottles you brought out as evidence," Lucy said, using a mockingly innocent tone.

Donovan's freckled white skin grew mottled with anger. "I've got work to do! Why don't you and your friends go hang out at the Shoney's buffet and let the rest of us do our jobs?" And with that rejoinder, Donovan stalked away.

The group watched as Donovan began to confer animatedly with Sheriff Huckabee. As they spoke, the paramedics slammed the rear door of the ambulance, asked Huckabee to apply his signature to a document on their clipboard, and then drove off. The ambulance wheels crunched over small pieces of wood and dark shards of broken glass, and then glided silently through the empty parking lot and out of view over the top of the hill. Huckabee followed the departing vehicle with his eyes while pulling roughly on his mustache, then he sighed loudly, checked his watch, and gestured toward Willy. After placing a kind hand on the man's shoulder, Huckabee steered him over to Donovan's car and opened the passenger door for him. He then gesticulated at Donovan, indicating that the deputy should chauffeur Willy back to his car. Before sliding into the patrol car, Willy looked up at his new friends and gave them a small wave accompanied by the best smile he could muster. They all waved back, but none could force smiles to their own lips.

"It's getting late." Gillian glanced at her watch. "I've got a toy poodle coming in at eight tomorrow for the works." She sighed. "I wish there was something we could do for that poor man."

"Yeah, poor Willy." Lucy gazed at their new friend as he faced forward inside the sheriff's patrol car. "What's he going to do now?"

"Lord only knows," Bennett sighed. "He'll have to find somethin' to do to keep him on his feet until his place is rebuilt. Come on, men. Mondays are always busy at the post office. The mail never sleeps, so *we'd* better."

Lindy gave everyone a quick hug as she and Gillian turned to leave. "I wish our last night out before the diet starts had been more uplifting. We must tell Willy we'll all help him in any way we can. See y'all at tomorrow's Witness to Fitness meeting. At least we get to see Ronnie. She's so sweet! She's sure to cheer us all up!"

"Yeah, see you then," James mumbled miserably. He didn't think he could stomach Ronnie's chipper demeanor after such a sobering evening. He watched as the rising smoke began to dissipate and mingle with a group of silvery clouds high above them. Stars winked in and out of the gray veil as if too shy to allow themselves to be seen.

*Life can change so quickly,* James thought, reflecting on his own life and Willy's recent tragedy. He thought of Pete and what his dreams must have been when he was a young man. No one planned on being a drunken janitor, so what had happened? Did he fail to pursue a higher education? Was he afraid to take risks and therefore ended up living from bottle to bottle as he searched for just enough part-time work to keep the wolves at bay?

James turned to watch Lucy's form recede toward the other end of the parking lot. Suddenly, he was overtaken with the desire to connect with her.

He glanced over at Bennett who was unlocking the door to his truck. "You coming James?" he called as he hopped in.

"No. Go on without me," James answered and then clumsily jogged in Lucy's direction. "Lucy!" he shouted. She stopped and pivoted, her face a mixture of alarm and curiosity.

James panted as he caught up to her. "God, I hate running." He put a hand over his aching lungs. "Man's body just isn't designed for that kind of exercise. Listen. Could I . . . ?"

Lucy looked at him with a small measure of impatience. "It's pretty late, James."

"I know, I know." James inhaled a gulp of foggy air. "Could you give me a lift back to my car?"

"Of course." She nodded and James was

grateful she hadn't asked why he wasn't riding back with Bennett and Carter. The inside of her car still doubled as a trash receptacle. James remembered that the last time he had ridden in it, the passenger seat had been entirely covered by used napkins, clothing catalogues, old newspapers, gum wrappers, and paper bags. Lucy swept the debris into the back seat as James sat down, nudging aside a few soda cans as they rolled around his feet.

They pulled onto the main road and James knew that he only had a few, precious minutes with Lucy, as it wouldn't take long to reach the library lot. To James, it seemed as though he had parked the Bronco on a completely different night. He shared this thought with Lucy.

"You just never know what's around the bend," she agreed, shaking her head.

James gathered up his courage and spoke what was on his mind. "Lucy, I just wanted to ask you . . . I . . . um . . . if you would have coffee with me after work on Tuesday."

Lucy's face lightened up. "Of course I would. Any particular reason?"

James felt encouraged by her warm smile. "I need to talk to you about . . . well, about a couple of things."

"Sounds good," she nodded and then

glanced at him sideways while flashing him one of her dazzling smiles. "If you beat me there, I'll take a mocha latte."

"That's probably not going to be on our diet," James laughed as they pulled up next to his Bronco.

"Ugh, that's right." Lucy frowned, putting the Jeep in park as the engine idled. "Okay, a decaf with skim then. I guess I have to get used to making some sacrifices again. I hope this all works out for us, James."

James didn't know whether she was referring to their diet plans or to something more important, such as their relationship. "I hope so, too," he answered as he got out of the car.

As he drove toward home, Lucy's smile temporarily banished all thoughts of the fire and of poor Pete Vandercamp. In fact, James was already dreaming of how he would look after losing twenty pounds, of a successful date with Lucy on Tuesday, and after that, perhaps a whole new future.

# Six:
## Turkey Sandwich on Whole Wheat

| Serving Size: 1 sandwich |
| --- |
| **Witness to Fitness Points** |
| 6 |

James took a bite of his sandwich and frowned. Two slices of fat-free turkey along with lettuce, tomato, and mustard on whole wheat wasn't too exciting and he had a hard time enjoying any sandwich without adding his customary three creamy slices of American cheese. He was crossly examining the sliced Granny Smith apple and microscopic packet of sugar-free chocolate cookie wafers he planned to have after wolfing down his sandwich when Scott Fitzgerald, one of the library's four staff members, entered the break room.

"Looks healthy, Professor," the lanky young man in his mid-twenties said as he grabbed a brown bag from the fridge. Pushing his horn-rimmed glasses farther up his thin nose he examined his boss's fare while pulling out an enormous hoagie filled with salami, pepperoni, and several slices of mozzarella from his own lunch sack. James glanced at Scott's loaded sandwich, large bag of sour cream and onion potato chips, and package of Hostess cupcakes with envy.

"So how's the new diet working out?" Scott asked, brushing aside a sandy-colored lock of unruly hair from his forehead before taking a gargantuan bite of his hoagie.

"I've really just started," James answered once his own mouth was empty. "We've got our first exercise class tonight."

"Yuck. I hate exercising." Scott took another bite and a trickle of vinegar ran down his angular chin. He chewed feverishly, as if someone intended to steal his food and then hastily swallowed. "Guess Francis and I are pretty lucky, having the metabolisms we have. Shoot, we *try* to gain weight but never seem to be able to." Scott paused, unaware that his boss was glaring at him. "Did you get a load of the new Robert Jordan book? Almost eight hundred pages! I can't wait to get it home. I'll probably stay up all night tonight. Francis won't even notice 'cause he's got the new Neal Stephenson to keep him busy."

James couldn't help but grin as Scott rambled on about his and his twin brother's recent reads in the science fiction and fantasy realms. Even though they were named after a famous twentieth century American author, Francis and Scott Fitzgerald had little interest in classical literature. They were savvy mathematicians, quick at solving complex logistical problems, and were compulsively organized. James enjoyed working with them more than any of the professors from his former department at William & Mary. For one, the twins were the most enthusiastic employees he had ever seen. They worked tirelessly and were completely devoted to seeing that every patron's needs were met. In addition, they were continuously dreaming up new schemes on how to improve their library branch. However, not even the sharp-minded twins had been able to come up with a fundraiser idea that would allow for the purchase of several new computers, which were so desperately needed.

James polished off his thin cookies and was silently wishing three more bags of them would materialize out of thin air when Francis burst into the staff room.

"Professor!" he whispered urgently, jerking a thumb over his shoulder. "Things are getting a little hairy at the computer terminals. Mrs. Hughes claims that Mr. Tuttle has gone way over the thirty-minute allotment but Mr. Tuttle refuses to budge. She's threatening to sit right down on his lap if he doesn't move. I tried to intervene but . . ."

"That's all right, Francis. Why don't you have some lunch and I'll handle this."

Clearly relieved, Francis strode over to the fridge and pulled out a lunch bag twice the size of Scott's. "We've just *got* to come up with a stellar fundraiser idea, bro. I can't take this kind of conflict," James heard him say to Scott.

James couldn't agree more. The computers had become more and more popular with patrons of all ages and there was rarely a time during the library's working hours when someone wasn't anxiously waiting for one of the two PCs. And thirty minutes didn't turn out to be very long when it took each of the archaic hard drives several minutes to complete even the smallest of tasks. The result had been friction among the patrons. The Shenandoah County Library was a place meant for peace and quiet discovery, not for patrons pacing with impatience or getting into heated arguments.

Out in the nook between fiction and nonfiction where the two computer terminals were set up, Mrs. Hughes stood with her hands resting on her formidable hips and a deep scowl wrinkling her face. She was normally a cheerful, pleasant lady, and James always tried to get in her checkout lane at the Food Lion as she was the speediest cashier and bagger in Quincy's Gap. She could process and pack a week's worth of groceries in under three minutes.

Mrs. Hughes latched onto James's fleshy upper arm. "Oh, Professor! Thank the Lord you're here! I'm trying to bid on an online auction and Mr. Tuttle here won't get off this machine. I've been timin' him since I came in and it's been well over forty minutes since he first got on."

Mr. Tuttle, a small, balding, middle-aged man with a pasty complexion turned a pair of narrow eyes upon James. "Hey, I'm lookin' for work here. Isn't that a bit more important than somethin' this woman wants to go shoppin' for? I got a pile a bills at home high as the Appalachians, so I need more time on this here computer."

James indicated a sign hanging over the two computers. "You know there's a limit, Mr. Tuttle. You'll have to relinquish your machine until Mrs. Hughes has had her thirty minutes."

Mr. Tuttle slammed a fist down next to the keyboard. "Damnation, man! I've been out of a job for three months and I can't even use my own library's computer to look for a new one? What kind of public works joint is this after all? I paid my taxes like everyone else." He stepped away from the computer and gesticulated angrily at a spinner rack containing romance novels. "Instead of buyin' that trash, why don't you spend our tax money on gettin' some more computers in here?"

As James opened his mouth to reply, a man with a briefcase tapped on the shoulder of the young woman using the second computer. James recognized her. It was Amelia Flowers, daughter of Megan Flowers, who owned the Sweet Tooth, the town's only bakery. Amelia worked for her mother part-time and also attended classes at the community college. James knew that she was interested in fashion design.

"My turn, missy." The man plunked his briefcase down on the floor next to Amelia's cavernous book bag.

"One sec. I just need to print this article," Amelia replied without looking up from the screen. She continued typing as Mrs. Hughes slid into the empty seat next to her.

"Why, hello Amelia. You doin' work for school?"

"Hi, Mrs. Hughes. Yeah, I got a paper due for my History of Fashion course and the books here aren't as up to date as some of the articles I found on this awesome web-site."

"How nice, dear. I know your mama is awful proud of you for goin' to college and all." She tapped on the computer screen. "*I'm* gonna bid on a Petal Princess Barbie doll for my granddaughter. She's been col-lectin' them since she was five and her ninth birthday's comin' up."

"That's just great, ladies," the man with the briefcase said acidly. "But I've got some stock prices to check and I'm on my lunch break, so if you don't mind, I'd like to have my turn."

At that moment, the printer jammed in

the middle of the ten-page task it was performing for Amelia.

"Sir," James held out a pacifying hand to the agitated male patron before he tried to physically remove Amelia from her chair. "Let me just fix the printer and then it will be your turn next. Amelia? Is this article all you needed to print?"

Amelia nodded at James. "That's all, Professor. Thanks." She then cast an irritated glance at the man standing over her shoulder and added, "I couldn't work in this *hostile* atmosphere anymore anyway."

James tugged at the crumpled piece of paper blocking the printer. It ripped into several raggedy pieces but finally tore free. He then reset the print job and sighed with relief as the machine reluctantly resumed working. Noticing that his hands were now covered with smudges of black ink, James apologized to all his patrons for their inconvenience at having to share two computers and then headed to the restroom to wash up.

Francis was already in the men's room as James entered. The twin was rubbing his glasses absently, his eyes staring at the mirror without actually absorbing any of the details of his own reflection.

"Lost in thought there, Francis?"

Francis started and dropped his glasses in the sink. Without bothering to dry them off, he shoved them onto his face and turned to James. "I've got it, Professor!" he exclaimed happily. "I know how we can raise the money we need for the computers."

James began scrubbing his hands with pink liquid soap. "That would certainly be nice. If Mrs. Hughes doesn't get that Barbie for her granddaughter before her thirty minutes are up, I think she and Mr. Tuttle are going to come to blows."

Francis screwed up his lips in thought. "I'd have to bet on Mrs. Hughes to win that fight. I've seen her toss twenty-pound watermelons into people's carts like they were bags of cotton balls."

"Your idea, Francis?" James reminded him.

"Oh, right! Well, Scott came up with half of it. Anyway, we thought the library should host a Spring Fling."

James was unimpressed with the title. "Like last year's Spring Book Drive & Bake Sale? The library only made a couple hundred dollars from that event."

"That's because *you* weren't here, Professor. You've got more *vision* than our former employer. *This* Spring Fling would be a cross between a book drive and a county fair. We could have it at the beginning of next month, when the weather is so nice." Francis opened the door and James followed the exuberant young man out of the restroom and behind the circulation desk. Francis drew out a piece of paper with a flourish. "Here, I made a quick sketch of how we could arrange things in that empty field behind the strip mall. It worked so well for the benefit last fall and we don't need to pay anyone to use it — we'd just need to get permission from the mall owners to allow for parking and we're good to go."

James leaned over the drawing and tried to decode Francis's scraggly handwriting. "Does this say 'Pig Race Course'?" he asked incredulously, pointing to a wobbly oval in the center of the paper.

Francis beamed. "Sure does! We could have two contests. One could be a pig race. That'll appeal to a lot of folks, including men. It seems like we always have women at our events, but rarely men or children. Now, if we get some carnival rides and food booths like they've got at the state fair, we can attract a huge crowd."

"Then we'd have to charge admission." James frowned, concerned over the logistics of such a large event.

"Yes, sir. We'd also charge for people to

enter the pig race and the Ladies' Hat Contest. The winners would receive cash prizes. Scott and I think the cash will encourage more folks to enter."

James looked at Francis in surprise. "Ladies' Hat Contest?"

"Well, we haven't worked out the details of that one yet, but it's a bit different than the usual boring bake-off. Megan Flowers would win any baking contest we held anyway."

James agreed on that point. "Well, we should remind folks that this event is about the library. What if it was a hat contest with a book-title theme? The ladies could parade in front of a panel of judges and then be awarded first, second, and third-place prizes."

"That's good, Professor!" Francis beamed. "Boy, if I were a lady I'd design the coolest *War of the Worlds* hat or maybe a —"

"This is a rather large undertaking, Francis," James interrupted before Francis could fantasize about the creation of a dozen hats based on his favorite works. "I think we should limit the number of outside vendors we have for the first year and see how things go. I'm sure we could get Dolly's Diner and the Sweet Tooth to set up food stalls and we could hire a few ride and game vendors, but we don't want to get too big for our britches. We could lose money if we don't sell enough tickets." James paused. "But overall, it really is a great idea. This library branch is very fortunate to have you and Scott. If we could just make enough for two more computer terminals . . ." James trailed off as he dreamed of new machinery being placed by the windows and of a row of beaming patrons applauding their arrival.

"Two?" Francis pushed the reshelving cart past his boss. "We were thinking of at least four — maybe six. We could move those paperback spinners closer to the Children's section and create a whole Tech Corner."

James looked beyond Francis to where Mrs. Hughes sat staring at a computer screen. Mr. Tuttle was close by, flipping the pages of an automotive magazine with un- necessary vigor.

"Six new computers." James mused. "That would certainly serve our patrons a whole lot better than these two dinosaurs with microchips. I'd better get on the phone with some vendors." He retreated to his office and contentedly began to sort out the details of the first Shenandoah Library Spring Fling. All afternoon, he was so busy that he completely forgot about the banana and small bag of pretzels he had brought for snack. Even when he chatted with a vendor regarding cotton candy, elephant ears, and funnel cake, his mind remained focused on improving his beloved library, not forbidden foods.

When James arrived home a little after five, he was ravenous. He had eaten the banana and pretzels in the truck right after work but still felt as if his stomach were totally hollow. He forgot all about his hunger, however, as soon as he pulled up in front of his house.

There was his father, thirty feet off the ground, tool belt strapped around his trim waist, inspecting the newly laid roof shingles surrounding the base of the chimney. As James watched in a state of incredulity, Jackson made his way over to one of the workmen who was stapling shingles around the area that had allowed water to leak into the upstairs bathroom with every rain. His father moved in that stooped half-crawl that men employ when transversing the steep slopes of roofs, and James could not believe the older man's limberness or the camaraderie he displayed in slapping the other man heartily on the back. Soon, the two men were laughing like old friends. James hadn't heard his father laugh aloud in such a manner for years, and he smiled at the deep and refreshing sound. Jackson spied his son on the ground below and, after waving, headed for the metal ladder propped against the side of the house.

He climbed down like a man half his age and beckoned for James to follow him into the kitchen.

"Lookin' good, isn't it?" Jackson asked, his cheeks rosy with exertion and his eyes sparkling with pride.

"Sure does, Pop. Did you . . . were you working up there the whole time with those guys?" James asked, barely recognizing the invigorated person standing before him.

His father turned, filled a glass with cold tap water, and then drank the liquid down in three gulps. Slamming the glass triumphantly on the counter, he puffed out his chest and exhaled happily. "Next I'm gonna do somethin' about this kitchen. It's a mighty big disgrace. Your mama was all set to rehaul the whole room, but I kept frettin' about the cost." Jackson looked down at the stained and peeling linoleum flooring. "If I woulda known, I'd have given her the finest kitchen in all of Virginia." He looked up at James, his fuzzy eyebrows shooting high on his forehead. "But now it's you and me, boy. We gotta make this place the kind of home men would be proud to live in."

James didn't want to put a damper on either his father's fluidity of speech or his enthusiasm for home improvement, but he squirmed in his shoes and mumbled, "We just don't have the money for a new kitchen, Pop. I don't even know how we're going to pay for the roof. I had planned to talk to Hugh Carmichael over at Shenandoah Savings & Loan sometime —"

"We've got the money, son," Jackson said and then cackled. "We just gotta decide on cabinets. I'm partial to wood ones with a walnut stain. Nice and manly." Jackson spread out a few wood samples and then dumped out a bag of granite chips onto the countertop. "This granite stuff is what folks are doin' now, but it looks too darn shiny to me, like somethin' those weirdos out in California would like. I'm liable to think there's nothin' wrong with good ole laminate."

James glanced at the array of materials and then again at his father's face. Ten years seemed to have melted off of the old man's visage in the single day he had spent laying roof shingles in the temperate spring air. "I won't pry about the money, Pop. If you say we've got it, then I'll believe we do. Even though it worries me a bit, I trust your judgment." Jackson nodded in appreciation and James was relieved that he had said the right thing. "And I prefer the laminate as well. Neither you nor I are exactly gourmet chefs so I don't think we need granite or fancy appliances for that matter. If we can update the fridge and the stove and replace the floor, that'll do."

"No, sir!" Jackson shook his head. "We're gonna get new cabinets, new appliances, new counters, and I'm puttin' in a dishwasher. You've got better things to do than wash up after our every meal."

"Oh, I don't mind." He actually enjoyed the quiet moments spent scrubbing up each evening.

"Well, *I* don't have time for it, and once you get yourself a girl, you won't, either." Jackson eyed his son. "Weren't you sweet on someone from your Sunday night . . . uh . . . club?"

James felt himself reddening. "I don't know, Pop. I think I messed up with her. With Lucy, I mean."

"How's that?" his father asked as he refilled his water glass and took a seat at the kitchen table. James, half wondering if he was dreaming, sat down across from his father and told him all about his feelings for Lucy Hanover. Jackson listened carefully, staring at the strewn pile of samples and brochures, until James was done.

"So you've got another chance. When you see this girl tomorrow, you tell her you were a chicken before and now you're not. You gotta go after her, James, or someone else is gonna snap her up like a bass in the lake. You ain't too young, my boy. If you wanna start any kind of family with a good woman then you'd better get in gear." Jackson paused. "Can she cook?"

James laughed. "She's not bad, I guess. She's a horrible slob, though."

"I don't know what the world's comin' to," Jackson grumbled with a trace of his usual gruffness. "There was a time when women cooked and cleaned and sewed and were damned proud of it. What's a man supposed to do these days?"

"Things are more equal now, Pop. Men and women share in the household stuff. A lot of women are working outside of the home. They want their own careers and don't have time to wait on others."

"What a bunch of crust." Jackson frowned. "Maybe you shouldn't show up for that coffee date after all."

"Hello, my friends!" Ronnie chirped that evening at the Witness to Fitness meeting.

"I'm sorry I'm all sweaty, but Dylan was practicing his workout on me before you all showed up." She patted the light sheen of perspiration on her brow with a purple monogrammed towel and took an infinitesimal sip from a water bottle. "But don't worry! He's going to go much easier on you! You are going to have *so* much fun in there!"

James saw Lindy throw Lucy a look of panic and his own stomach lurched at the thought of bouncing around in front of both friends and strangers.

"Let's get the icky money part out of the way first, shall we?" Ronnie beamed at the group of nervous people waiting to enter the exercise room. "Now, I've got all of your entrées packed up and ready to go home to your freezers. Phoebe and I will accept cash or checks for this week's meals and for the three required exercise classes. But before we do, why not give yourselves a hand for being here tonight? Come on! Let's hear some noise for your courage and determination." She began clapping loudly and a few others tentatively joined in. "Good for you, I say! Way to go, all of you!"

James reluctantly clapped when Ronnie turned a luminescent smile in his direction. Within moments, the twenty people gathered around the cubicles were rifling through purses and digging in wallets in order to cheerfully pay for their first week at Witness to Fitness. James blanched when he saw the actual total. Each meal was almost ten dollars and did not include the salad or light dessert that should accompany a complete Witness to Fitness dinner. At almost $500 per month, James prayed that he would truly make amazing progress in only six weeks or he wouldn't have much spending money for the upcoming summer.

No one else seemed overly concerned with the cost, though James knew that with the exception of Gillian, who owned her own pet grooming business and was a partner in a second business involving luxurious pet houses, the members of the Flab Five could not easily afford the high cost of getting in shape.

When all had paid, Ronnie ushered them into the exercise room and closed the door behind them, as if to signal that there was no turning back from here on out.

"Here comes our star instructor!" Ronnie cheered for Dylan, her expression filled with an intense adoration that clearly went beyond friendly admiration for a co-worker. James wondered if Dylan had any idea that his boss was infatuated with him.

"Howdy, folks!" the object of Ronnie's

longing called out, bounding from the back room in a pair of tight black track pants with silver stripes running up his muscular legs. "Now, I know you're all nervous, but there's nothing to fear. I promise to take it slow while you get used to our routine. Help yourself to a mat and let's get moving!" He put his hands on his narrow hips and took several deep breaths as his pupils grabbed one of the blue exercise mats stacked in the far corner of the room and hustled back to their places.

Dylan seemed pleased by their eagerness. "Let's begin with some simple stretches," he said. "First, let's reach down and touch our toes."

James made a pitiful attempt to reach his toes, but he didn't succeed in getting beyond his kneecaps. Casting a sideways glance at Lindy, he noticed that she hadn't progressed much farther.

"I haven't touched my toes since Junior High," she whispered unhappily.

"I never could," James whispered back as Dylan leaned to the side and explained that they would now stretch their oblique muscles.

"Okay, folks! Lookin' good." Dylan led them through a few more standing postures then slapped a rubber mat on the floor and hopped onto it. "Now how about we hit the floor and work on our legs?"

James struggled to touch the knot in his sneaker's laces in order to loosen up his leg muscles, but he absolutely could not reach his shoe. Straining mightily, he brushed his fingers along the cuff of his white sock, sat up, shrugged, and looked over at Lindy. She was leaning miserably forward, her lips clamped together in determination. In the mirror, James spied Gillian and Bennett, who had successfully managed to touch their shoes and a frustrated-looking Lucy who had also settled for grasping her ankle.

Dylan suddenly shifted his position. He had been practically folded in half on top of his left leg when he languidly raised his head, drew both feet fluidly toward his crotch, and exhaled loudly. "Okay, let's get our legs in the butterfly position and give a *good* stretch to those inner thighs."

Several of the men groaned as they attempted to replicate Dylan's position. James could barely fold his legs at all, let alone pull his feet that close to his protruding belly. As he stared at his dirt-splattered sneakers with their frayed laces, his mind wandered to Jackson's recent attitude of carefree spending. Where *was* the money coming from?

"Hey Lindy," James whispered, trying to focus on anything other than the sharp pain that had begun to streak up his legs toward his groin.

"Yeah?"

"Do you remember when you told me your mother was going to contact my father about putting some of his paintings in her D.C. gallery?"

Lindy looked startled by the question, but she gladly ignored the next stretch and inched closer to her friend. "Sure. Your daddy's work is amazing. It's a lot like Audubon's. He's very talented." She hesitated. "Wait a minute. Do you mean that you don't know?"

James ignored the woman to his left as she tried to shush him. "Know what?"

Lindy's jaw dropped. "Oh my stars, James! Every single one of his paintings sold during my mother's winter show. He made a ton of money."

James couldn't believe his ears. "What's a ton, exactly?"

Lindy inched a little closer and whispered. "Over twenty thousand dollars. My mother sold a total of fifty paintings and got top dollar for an unknown artist. Even after her commission, she was able to send your daddy a pretty nice check." Lindy stood as

Dylan kindly commanded them all to rise. "I can't believe he didn't tell you. He should be so proud! There are, like, two dozen standing orders for future works, too."

James began Dylan's exercise routine in a stupor. Twenty thousand dollars!

"We're going to burn some fat with some leg lifts, folks." Dylan turned up the volume on his CD player and loud techno music with a chaotic rhythm reverberated throughout the room. "This song ought to get you in the mood to LIFT, and LIFT, and LIFT, and . . ."

James felt like his thighs were on fire. How could one of his limbs be so heavy? After ten lifts per side, he didn't think he could raise even his foot off the floor. He felt the extra flesh on his belly, thighs, arms, and chest shaking and flailing about as if it were becoming detached from the bone. Glancing around in the mirror, he noted that everyone else's bodies looked the same. Red faces were streaming with moisture, sweatshirts were stained with sweat, and people bent down to tie shoelaces every few minutes as an attempt to catch a prolonged breath.

"Stay hydrated, folks!" Dylan called in between jumping jacks. "Hang in there! We're halfway done!"

*"Halfway?"* James panted to no one in particular. His chest was tight and he had a sharp pain in his side. Sweat dripped into his eyes and his body felt as heavy as an anchor. He didn't think he could take another step, let alone raise his arms high above his head and wave them left and right.

"Trees in the wind!" Dylan shouted. "Wave those arms, folks!"

In the mirror, James saw Lucy behind him and off to his right. She was struggling, but still managing to weakly imitate Dylan's moves. She caught James watching her and gave him an exaggerated eye roll accompanied by a quick smile.

Wanting to appear as capable as Lucy of grimly following through to the bitter end of Dylan's routine, James raised his elbows slightly above his waist and tried to follow the instructor's energetic sidestepping motions. As James held up his leaden arms and shuffled to the left like a zombie, the lights in the room seemed to gradually grow brighter. He gazed at the ceiling as the dozen tiny spotlights flared out like Christmas tree stars. The pounding beat of the music changed, too. Suddenly, James could barely hear it at all. His head filled with a pleasant feeling of emptiness and a curtain of darkness fell before his eyes.

"James!" Lucy shouted, bending over him. James looked up at her from his vantage point on the wooden floor.

"Are you okay?" Gillian's face appeared among the ring of faces that were encircling and gazing down upon his sweat-slicked body. "I think you need some water."

"I agree. Let's give him some room, folks." Dylan waved the small group back and knelt beside James. "Y'all grab yourselves a mat and we'll do some cool down stretches in a second. Our friend will be just fine."

The members of the class hesitated and then gratefully positioned their mats and sank down onto them. No one even pretended to stretch. A few people even lay prone on the mats, their chests rising and falling rapidly. Lucy was the last to sit down and even after she did, she continued to stare in James's direction, a look of concern on her flushed face.

"Did I faint?" James asked the younger man in a horrified whisper.

Dylan nodded briskly. "Don't be embarrassed, though. You were just working really hard and you didn't hydrate enough. Here, take some slow slips of this."

James refused to allow Dylan to hold onto his head as he propped himself up on his right elbow and drank some tepid water.

130

"Better now?" Dylan asked kindly as James moved himself to a sitting position.

"I'm all right. Sorry to interrupt the class." James slouched over to where the stack of blue floor mats were kept and pulled one to the very back of the room by the door. As Dylan led the class through their final stretches, he reiterated the importance of drinking water throughout his classes. James was completely mortified and avoided the eyes of all his friends as they attempted to meet his in the mirror. He knew they meant well, but he was too humiliated to accept their sympathy at the moment.

The second the class ended, James hustled out of the room as fast as his numb legs would carry him and did not even bother to replace his exercise mat. He grabbed his bag of entrées on the way out and only felt like pausing to slug Ronnie. As she handed him his food, she clapped him repeatedly on his sweat-soaked back and oozed, "Don't *you* have a healthy glow?" Then she winked at him flirtatiously and exclaimed, "Why Mr. Henry, I swear you look thinner already! See you Wednesday!"

# SEVEN:
## ALMOND BISCOTTI

**Serving Size:**
1 cookie

**Witness to Fitness Points**

2

James settled himself in a booth at Dolly's Diner fifteen minutes before his scheduled meeting time with Lucy. This booth had become a favorite of James's as the paneled walls above it were decorated with coconut shells, a grass skirt, a grouping of colorful leis, two small tiki torches, and a large poster of an azure sea bordering a strip of gleaming, pale sand with a tag line reading, *Need a break? Paradise is waiting for you!* James always felt agreeably transported when he ate beneath the island relics. It was as if he only needed to step into the poster in order to find respite from the long winter days living in a small town enclosed by mountains. Now that spring had come to Quincy's Gap, James sat in the booth dreaming of a vacation in paradise, he and Lucy strolling hand in hand on the stretches of pristine sand.

"Coffee, hon?" Dolly asked, jiggling a chewed pencil between her thumb and index finger. She always carried the pencil but never used it to take an order, as her memory was flawless.

"Please." James smiled at the busty, middle-aged proprietor and issued a quick wave to her husband, Clint, who had just emerged from his domain in the kitchen in order to refill his soda glass. Dolly placed a tiny creamer filled with half-and-half in front of James and gave him a thorough inspection as he stirred a packet of artificial sweetener into his coffee.

"You do somethin' different with your

hair, Professor?" she asked, in no hurry to move away and check on her other customers.

James absently touched a nutmeg-colored strand and then shook his head. "No, ma'am. Um, do you have skim milk, Dolly? I've joined that new Witness to Fitness program and I don't think I can afford to waste any food points using half-and-half in my coffee."

"Sure do, hon. Back in a flash." Dolly hustled off to the kitchen and returned with another metal creamer. Putting a hand on her hip as if to signal the commencement of a casual chat, Dolly asked, "So what do you think of that Ronnie Levitt girl? She's a cute little thang if you like your women with no meat on 'em. That girl's a walkin' celery stick if you ask me. But you men can see things different, can't you?" She raised her brows as if daring James to argue and her blue-and silver-tinted lids twinkled beneath the overhead lights.

James shrugged. He didn't dare tell Dolly how he truly felt about Ronnie or his feelings would be spread around town faster than the winter flu. "A bit too perky for me," was all he could manage without fully giving away how irritating he found Ronnie Levitt.

Dolly frowned. She disliked terse answers. She lived and breathed for gossip and for the opportunity to play matchmaker with any of Quincy's Gap singles. James continuously disappointed her attempts on both fronts. He had had many a meal interrupted while Dolly introduced him to one unattached female after another. Most of the time the women looked equally mortified to have been led over to his table like mares about to be given over for use on a stud farm.

Suddenly, Dolly's sharp eyes spied a new victim approaching the front door. "Oh! Here comes Lucy Hanover. Well, I'll be plucked and strung up like a chicken! She's all gussied up! I wonder who she's gotten so dolled up for?" Her large head pivoted back and forth as she examined the customers seated around her. "Hmm. Maybe it's . . ." she mumbled to herself and rushed off to take up a more favorable viewing position from behind the counter.

James was relieved that he had chosen to sit with his back to the entrance. He was nervous enough as it was and didn't need to compound his anxiety by watching out for Lucy's arrival. He had no idea how he was going to begin to tell her how he felt. The brightness of the diner seemed to induce loud conversation, not the whispered endearments he had planned upon. And when Lucy finally slid into the opposite side of his booth, James regretted his choice of seating. He wished he had been prepared for her dramatic change in appearance from a long way off.

She had clearly just had her hair done for her thick, caramel locks were neatly sheared and angled into an attractive bob that framed her soft chin perfectly. She wore a shade of pale red lipstick and a kind of dusky, frosted shadow that made her cornflower-blue eyes larger and more luminous than ever. Her indigo blouse had a deep neckline and she wore a silver cross on a long chain that dangled flirtatiously above her generous cleavage. A faint waft of floral scent floated across the table and James had a pleasing sensation of breathing in a cluster of dew-covered wildflowers.

Before James could speak, Dolly hurried over to the booth as fast as her two rubber-shoed feet would allow, the ends of her apron strings trailing out behind her plump bottom like a kite's tail. "Lucy, darlin'! Don't you just look a picture! Isn't she stunnin', Professor?"

James nodded dumbly. He cast a shy grin in Lucy's direction and then began to carefully study the surface of his coffee cup as if he were an augur.

Dolly's eyes shifted eagerly from Lucy to James as she took Lucy's order for coffee. "I'll just leave you two alone," she whispered conspiratorially after placing a cup and saucer delicately on the table.

Lucy watched her move off and then giggled. "Dolly is somethin' else, isn't she? She's probably got every booth bugged so she can catch up on all the latest news."

James laughed in agreement and immediately felt the tension drain from his clenched shoulders. "But she *is* right about you. You do look . . . great," he stammered.

"Thanks. The sheriff sent me to Waynesboro this morning to pick up the specialist's report on the Polar Pagoda fire. Our only fax machine is busted again. So I decided to visit a friend of mine who just opened up a beauty shop there before headin' back. I could have returned with a purple mohawk and the guys in the office would never have noticed! They're all obsessed with the upcoming Law Enforcement Bowling Tournament!" she snorted.

"Who's the specialist?"

"A fire investigator sent out by the company insuring Willy's business. Chief Lawrence met him at the scene after we had gone. I guess the two of them collaborated in order to figure out what happened."

"A fire investigator," James said thoughtfully. "Wow. Did you get to read any of his report?" James asked, his curiosity distracting him from the personal topic that he had meant to discuss.

"Of course! I read the whole thing while Cindi was workin' on my hair." Lucy gave James a tender look. "You *know* I can't resist knowing as much as those chauvinistic deputies I have to work for."

"Oh, it won't be too long now before you're working right alongside them, Lucy."

Lucy's smile lit up her face. "It's nice to have your confidence in me, James. You are so sweet." She reached across and brushed his hand with her fingertips. James felt his heart quicken in his chest. "Anyway, both this investigator and Chief Lawrence ruled that the fire was a case of arson!" Lucy's eyes danced with excitement.

James took a sip of coffee and grimaced at the thin, foreign taste of skim milk where his thick and creamy half-and-half should be. "Was it caused by some kind of negligence on Pete's part? Can you tell?"

"Negligence is strongly implied in the report. Looks like whiskey was spilled all over the back of the shop, especially around the cardboard boxes where the T-shirts were kept. Somehow this specialist could follow the trail of the fire and discover its source. Pretty cool, huh? There were also several cigarette butts, Pall Mall Lights I think, in the same area. So I guess Pete was just hanging out, drinking *and* smoking his whole shift long. Guess he didn't get too many customers that night or someone would have noticed he was drunk."

"Everyone in town was at the Brunswick Stew Dinner. That's why he had so little business." James paused and frowned. "But I always remember Pete as a chewing tobacco man. Have you ever seen him smoke?"

"No, but who knows what the man did in private?" Lucy shrugged. "It seems strange to me that so much whiskey was spilled, though. I can't see Pete accidentally knocking over a perfectly good bottle of booze, you know? Still, there's a medical examiner who specializes in burned . . . um . . . cadavers coming all the way from Richmond to examine the body."

"You kids need a refill?" Dolly asked, appearing in front of James and Lucy like a magician and causing them both to start, sloshing coffee into their saucers. "I've also got these low-fat almond cookies for you to nibble on. Got some Italian name. Clint's been experimenting with some healthy sweets to add to the dessert menu. Lemme know what you think." She poured more steaming coffee into their cups, checked the level of milk in the creamer, and stood hovering over them for a good five seconds.

James picked up one of the two biscotti and took a bite, figuring that Dolly was going to stand there until he did. The crunchy almond flavor was a pleasant accompaniment to the coffee. "These are good, Dolly. Clint's got a winner. He can serve them to all the folks on our diet."

"Well, I hope we don't have to change our *whole* menu on account of this Ronnie person. Ain't nothin' wrong with some good ole Southern cookin' once a day. My Grammy lived to be over a hundred and she ate fried chicken with biscuits and gravy every single day of her life!"

"No one could run you out of business," Lucy assured the flustered proprietress. "There's no diet in this world that could keep me from your meatloaf or blackberry pie."

Dolly smiled, pacified, and went to refill the coffees of her other patrons.

"And speaking of our diet," Lucy turned back to James, "we are all saving our baked ziti to eat at Gillian's house this Sunday. We figured we'd still make a salad and a dessert and eat together even though we're just heating up a frozen dinner."

"I'm glad." James dusted biscotti crumbs from the table and onto the floor. "I'd hate our dinners to end just because we all joined Witness to Fitness." He hesitated and then decided that there had been enough small talk and it was now time to come to the point with Lucy. "Besides, I especially look forward to seeing you —"

"Professor Henry! How lucky to have run into you!" Murphy Alistair popped up in front of them and dropped a notebook onto the surface of their table with a decisive thwack. "I called you at the library but you had already left. I'm dying to get the scoop on your first Witness to Fitness class." She looked expectantly from James to Lucy. "Oh. Am I interrupting? I can just sit down at another booth until you're ready to talk, James." She made a slow move to recollect her notebook.

"That's okay," Lucy said with what James recognized as false sweetness. She eyed Murphy's form-fitting blouse and ironed jeans with barely concealed envy. "I see Carter Peabody's just come in. I think I'll go say hello." She gathered her purse and left

141

some money for the coffee as James struggled to find his tongue. "See you," she said to James, her face clearly reflecting her disappointment in him and scooted out of the booth.

James opened and closed his mouth like a frog searching for flies. He knew he should send Murphy away and tell Lucy what he had come here to say to her, but the sudden presence of another woman, especially one with such a forceful personality as Murphy, had thrown him completely off balance. Before he could even say goodbye, Murphy had taken Lucy's place in the booth and Lucy had greeted Carter loudly as he settled onto a stool at the diner's counter. Carter looked slightly taken aback by Lucy's effusiveness, but then he issued a brief, yet sincere smile that momentarily transformed his plain features into a warm and handsome visage that any woman would enjoy gazing upon. James scowled as he watched them.

"So." Murphy uncapped a ballpoint pen and turned to a fresh sheet of paper in her notebook. "How was your first class?"

James answered Murphy's questions as succinctly as possible, hoping to give her the information she needed and then reclaim his alone time with Lucy. He praised

Dylan's teaching abilities and described some of the more difficult portions of the workout without mentioning his own collapse. Murphy scribbled away and nodded vigorously, encouraging James to share even mundane details such as the music used and what outfits most of the dieters wore to class. As James spoke, he continuously cast sidelong looks in Lucy's direction where, to his dismay, he saw her order a fresh cup of coffee. It looked at though she was telling Carter an animated tale as she gesticulated dramatically and laughed noisily. Carter seemed quietly amused and James couldn't help but wonder if Lucy was putting on a show to get his attention as he sat talking to Murphy. If so, she was entirely successful.

"Professor? Woo-hoo!" Murphy waved a hand in front of his face. "I was asking you how your first meal tasted."

"Not great," James replied quietly without really thinking that hundreds of local readers would soon read all about his opinion of Witness to Fitness. "It was kind of a rubbery chicken with sautéed vegetables and tasteless noodles. I'm not much of a vegetable fan, though," he added guiltily.

"You don't have to backtrack." Murphy assured him. "You're paying good money for this stuff. What did you say?" She consulted her notes. "Around ten bucks a pop for these dinners? They should be filet mignon and lobster tail dinners for those prices. Don't you think the cost of this program is a bit steep?"

James nodded. "I do. That's why I really hope it works. Once the money is gone, it's gone. There are no guarantees with Witness to Fitness."

Murphy grinned triumphantly and jotted down his last sentence word for word. Closing her notebook, she said, "We'll do a follow-up after your first weigh-in. Maybe we could meet here again next week."

James glanced over at Lucy once more. She said goodbye to Carter and without looking over at James, rapidly left the diner. James was debating about whether to follow her out when Murphy signaled to Dolly.

"You ready to order somethin'?" Dolly asked, acting put out because Murphy hadn't wanted anything to eat or drink when she first arrived.

"I'm feeling like a bacon cheeseburger, fries, and a chocolate shake." Murphy patted her flat stomach. "I had some store-bought sandwich for lunch and it didn't do the trick. Not like your Clint's food, Dolly. You two know how to send people home with full stomachs."

Dolly beamed. "Ain't that the truth? Be right back, sugar. I'm gonna make your shake extra thick so you won't starve before that burger comes."

"You knew just what to say to Dolly." James wryly congratulated Murphy. "Look, I'd better be going."

"Sure you don't want to join me?" Murphy inquired, giving James that same flirtatious smirk she had used at Chilly Willy's Grand Opening. "I'm sure Dolly could fix you some kind of egg-white omelet or something."

James couldn't tell whether the attractive reporter was teasing him or not. He flushed. "Um, I've got a ten-dollar frozen dinner awaiting me at home, remember?"

Murphy shrugged. "Well, maybe after six weeks have gone by and you've slimmed down, you can take me out for a celebratory meal. What do you say to that, Professor?"

James stood up as Dolly arrived with an enormous malt glass filled with a rich and thick chocolate shake, complete with a miniature mountain of whipped cream and a plump maraschino cherry on top. He almost groaned as Dolly slid the glass, a napkin, and long straw in front of Murphy. Instead, he issued both women a brief wave and fled the diner. He drove home to a frozen meal of Salisbury steak in mushroom sauce and an evening of watching game shows with his father. Neither his food nor his entertainment succeeded at driving away the memory of his failure to connect with Lucy or of the alluring vision of a tall and creamy chocolate shake.

Having attended two more exercise classes, the members of the Flab Five were full of complaints about a myriad of bodily pains when they got together Sunday night at Gillian's. Gillian lived in a large and immaculate Victorian filled with a mixture of antique and comfortable modern furniture. James was admiring the patina of the sideboard in Gillian's dining room when her cat, the Dalai Lama, entwined himself around his legs and howled. James bent over and scratched the tabby behind the ears. The trim feline cocked his head for more until James's hand was covered in brownish fur.

James walked stiffly back into the kitchen, wincing over his sore muscles. His friends were gathered around the counter pouring themselves glasses of diet iced tea from a large pitcher. Thin slices of lemons were perched around the rim of each tall glass.

"Your legs hurtin', huh man?" Bennett asked, noticing how James was near to limping.

"Killing me. It even hurts to drive." James accepted a glass of tea from Lindy.

"At least you two don't have to worry about bras." She mimed cupping her large breasts with her hands. "I'm going to have to buy something made out of steel if I'm going to survive the next few weeks of that class."

Everyone laughed. "*I* feel like I am actually *exorcizing* negative toxins by sweating so much." Gillian turned on the oven. "I *really* think the positive energy of Dylan and Ronnie is starting to have its effect on me. I'm actually looking *forward* to our weigh-in on Monday."

"I like Dylan a heck of a lot better once class is *over,*" Lucy stated. "He's a hottie, that's for sure, but he makes us work so hard that I find myself hating him somewhere between our leg lifts and tummy crunches."

James smiled at her, relieved that she didn't have a genuine crush on their instructor. Since Tuesday, he had been so busy arranging the details for the upcoming Spring Fling that he hadn't set aside time to call Lucy from work following their brief meeting at the diner.

He longed to just stop by her house and profess his feelings to her, but somehow he never got further than daydreaming about it. And at home, he and Jackson had spent every evening making plans for a new kitchen. James was so thrilled by his father's exuberance that he didn't want to do anything that might influence him to backtrack to his former state of gruff detachment. Even when James cautiously inquired about his artistic success, Jackson mumbled something about the private nature of his work, but not in the same, snappish manner that he would have used a matter of months ago. He simply made it clear that his paintings were not a subject open for discussion.

However, Lindy was more than happy to tell the supper club members all about James's ignorance in regard to his father's astounding sales.

"So how did you think the old man was gonna pay for that new roof?" Bennett asked as he dribbled a light Italian dressing onto his salad.

James shrugged, smiling. He didn't mind being the butt of a joke. "I was pretty panicked about it. With the cost of Witness to Fitness, I don't have a lot of extra cash on hand."

"Speaking of extra cash," Gillian said, waving a forkful of salad in the air. "I talked Willy into working with me and Beau Livingstone selling Pet Palaces. Beau has had so many custom orders since Christmas that he hasn't been able to focus on sales or balancing the books. Normally, I do the accounting, but with those two major horse shows, I've gotten behind at the Yuppie Puppy. Anyway, not only can Willy work with numbers, but he's also an expert carpenter and has a whole garage filled with tools. He has been doing a great job assisting Beau put the finishing touches on our orders. See? There is a higher power orchestrating things so that we can all benefit from one another!"

"That's terrific news!" Lindy clapped. "I'm so glad to hear that Willy has a source of income these days. I can just see him designing a Pooch Pagoda! Gillian, you are truly a giving person."

"There's a Chinese proverb that says *'A bit of fragrance always clings to the hand that gives roses.'* I guess I'd just like to smell good."

"You smell better than this here ziti." Bennett frowned over the large aluminum tray, which he had just removed from the oven. "I think it's a bit burned around the edges, but that might give it some flavor."

"So this is going to taste as bad as all the other meals?" James groaned. "I've practically used up all the salt in my shaker trying to spice this stuff up."

"It's not that bad," Lucy snapped. "You men are just too fickle."

Bennett looked surprised by the hostility in her voice. Lindy, ever the diplomat, quickly changed the subject while she helped Bennett pass out plates of ziti.

"So are there any updates on the arson case?" she asked Lucy while sprinkling heavy amounts of salt and pepper on her entrée.

"I was going to save all that juicy stuff for dessert," Lucy answered, successfully diverted. "The liquor bottles were already analyzed at the state lab. Huckabee sent them both off 'cause he saw some strange-looking residue in one of them. Must be a slow time for the crime lab because normally we'd have to wait weeks for these kinds of nonpriority results. Turns out one of the bottles was coated on the inside with something that shouldn't have been in there."

Lindy swallowed and gazed at Lucy in confusion. "So it was, like, defective?"

"No." Lucy paused for dramatic effect. "It

had traces of a drug called diazepam. That's the generic name for Valium."

"Lord have mercy!" Bennett exclaimed. "Was ole Pete tryin' to kill himself or what?"

"I don't think he'd dump Valium into his whiskey if he wanted to do that. He'd just swallow the pills first and then take a drink," James argued.

"The man drank, smoke, *and* abused drugs. The poor soul is probably better off in whatever plane of existence he's gone on to now anyhow," Gillian sighed theatrically.

James scowled with impatience. "But he *didn't* smoke. He used chewing tobacco. I rarely saw the man without a plug. He even had one that day we all officially joined Witness to Fitness."

"I didn't realize you knew all about him, James," Lucy said testily and then turned back to the rest of the group. "In any case, office gossip is that the blame is being laid on Pete's door and because the insurance company isn't wild about rebuilding, they are putting all the onus on Willy for hiring Pete as an employee."

"That's a load of bull." Bennett stabbed a noodle angrily. "Willy didn't know all of Pete's bad history. The man worked at the high school for over twenty years, so he had an employment record. I'm sure Willy hired

151

him based on that."

"But who knows how clean it was," Lucy said. "If James and I knew he was a drunk back in high school, everyone else must have known it, too."

"This whole thing feels real funny to me." Bennett stroked his toothbrush mustache thoughtfully. "Maybe someone *gave* a tainted bottle of whisky to Pete. You know, with the drugs in it."

"But that would mean . . . You think someone tried to murder Pete?" Lindy was astonished.

"Or ruin our poor, dear Willy," Gillian offered. "Maybe someone else started the fire and Pete was just *too* far gone to escape. Remember how angry Savannah Lowndes was over the whole architecture issue?"

"Or Mrs. Emerson and her youth group over those T-shirts?" Lucy added.

Bennett uttered an exasperated moan. "Come *on,* folks. You don't think a group of God-fearing middle-aged women slipped Pete some drugged liquor and then burned down Willy's store, now, do you?"

"No," Lucy admitted. "That does sound far-fetched. It must have been Pete all by himself."

As the group cleared away the dishes and loaded Gillian's dishwasher, James debated about whether or not to share the altercation he had witnessed between Pete Vandercamp and Ronnie Levitt outside of Witness to Fitness. As Lindy passed out chilled cups of fat-free strawberry mousse, James decided to speak up.

"I *did* see an odd thing happen between Pete and Ronnie," he began and then quickly explained what he had witnessed through the window.

"So you didn't actually hear anything that was said between them?" Lindy asked skeptically.

James looked at his mousse sheepishly. "Pete felt sure he had seen Ronnie on TV. That seemed to bother her and then, when they went outside, I could *tell* that she was really upset. She threatened him. It was all in her body language."

"I dunno, friend." Bennett shook his head. "You're a smart man and I'm not doubtin' your power of observation, but she seemed her spunky little self when she came back inside."

"Plus, why would Ronnie do either Pete or Willy any harm?" Lindy asked. "She's just as sweet as can be and really, if you think about it, the Polar Pagoda wasn't genuine competition for her. If it did well, Ronnie would just gain more customers!"

"I think her niceness is put-on," James insisted. "I saw her mask slip a little that day and I just do not trust that woman."

"James, darling." Gillian reached over and patted him patronizingly on the back. "I think our little adventure in helping solve a murder last fall has gotten your imagination a *little* too fired up. Maybe you're unconsciously stressed and the tension is affecting your rational judgment. I have a wonderful antioxidant red tea that could restore your balance and give you clearer *vision*."

James clenched his fists underneath the table but kept his voice calm. "Thank you, Gillian. I don't think I need any tea. I was just sharing my experience from that day. I'm sure you're right and there was nothing to it."

Lucy had remained silent during the entire exchange. James could feel her carefully studying him, but he couldn't tell what she was thinking as her face remained impassive. Suddenly, she shifted her gaze to Bennett and propped her elbow on the table, "So it seems like Carter has settled into Quincy's Gap quite nicely."

"Yep. He seems to like the quiet life we offer here. What with murders and arson and all, who wouldn't?" Bennett snorted in amusement at his own sense of humor.

"Well, do you happen to know," Lucy began, her eyes sliding away from Bennett's to issue James a fleetingly brief but challenging look, "if he's got a girlfriend?"

# Eight:
# Butter Rum
# Life Savers®

Serving Size:
2 candies

Witness to Fitness
Points

0

"You've lost four pounds!" Ronnie squealed and then jumped up and down on the balls of her narrow feet. "I am *so* proud of you, James! Aren't you just *thrilled beyond be-lief?*"

James stared at the glowing red digits of the scale, which usually cast its numbers in an accusing and sinister crimson. Today, however, they glowed with the bright cheerfulness reminiscent of balloons or dimestore gumballs. James felt a surge of happiness and glanced down at Ronnie who was gazing at him expectantly. Perhaps he had been wrong about her. Maybe she *was* as sincere as she pretended to be.

"This is a good start," he admitted, allowing a small smile to creep onto his face as he answered her. He stepped off the scale and reluctantly watched the lit numbers disappear. "Has everyone else done well?"

In reprimand, Ronnie nudged James in his doughy side with a sharp elbow. "Your only competition is with *yourself,* mister. Now, why don't you settle up with Phoebe for this week's meals and then get a head start on your stretches before class starts." She prodded him in Phoebe's direction and beckoned Bennett toward the scale.

"I hear Dylan's added a few more maneuvers to tonight's routine," Phoebe teased as she accepted payment from James and another dieter. "Says he doesn't want you folks to get bored."

"Bored?" the woman next to James huffed. "I'm too busy tryin' to stay alive to fret over bein' bored."

James nodded in agreement. "Besides," he added, "I'd rather have more variety in regard to these Witness to Fitness meals." He frowned as he looked over the menu for the upcoming week. "This is hardly different from last week's menu."

Phoebe held up her own copy of the menu and studied it. "I noticed that, too," she said in a kind, but slightly distracted manner, running her long fingers through her blue-black hair. "I'll talk to Miss Levitt about spicing things up a bit. Still, I'm glad to see that both of you made progress this week. Congratulations."

James and the woman smiled shyly at one another as they shared a moment of dieting kinship, and then James entered the exercise room in order to catch up with the other members of the Flab Five. The ladies had already been weighed in by Dylan and were now feverishly stretching as they sat on their blue plastic floor mats.

"Did you lose anything, James?" Lindy called out as she reached her hands out over her knees and attempted to grab the shoelaces of her left sneaker.

"Yes. And how about you?"

"Everyone did!" Gillian announced happily. "Our *whole* supper club has had success. Oh, the stars must have been *perfectly* aligned the day you and Lindy ran into the wonderful Ronnie at that superstore. I believe we were *meant* to have been guided to good health by her and Dylan and Phoebe." Gillian clasped her hands together and sighed loudly with contentment. She then began to arc her body sideways with her arms held aloft over her head as if she were exhibiting some kind of awkward ballet move.

Lucy cast James a look that said *I told you so* and again, he doubted whether he had completely misjudged the spunky fitness guru from the first. Before he could dwell on the idea that he had totally lost his ability to read people's characters, Dylan bounded enthusiastically into the room and for the next forty-five minutes, all James could think about was the shortness of his breath and the splintering cramp dominating the whole of his right flank.

Throughout the routine, Ronnie leapt around in the back row, encouraging those who wanted to give up by letting out energetic whoops whenever Dylan asked the class to pick up the pace. She continuously winked and smiled at Dylan when she wasn't motivating her clients. He acted as though he didn't notice her flirtatious expressions. After twenty minutes of Ronnie's clapping, whooping, and backslapping, James, on the other hand, was ready to smother her with one of the blue exercise mats.

Once class was over, James joined his friends outside as they limped over to Gillian's compact hybrid. She wanted to show them all her newly printed catalogue featuring photos of the complete Pet Palace line.

As the foursome praised Gillian on the brochure, she waved off their compliments with a flick of her hand. "We would never have had such a professional layout without Willy's help. He's really got an eye for graphic design. A man with *many* gifts indeed."

"I'm glad to hear he's doing well," Lucy said. "And speaking of Willy, I'll fill y'all in on what the deputies found when they searched Pete's house this morning for signs of any drug use."

Lindy's eyes flew open. "That's right — the Valium. Oh, do tell! What did they find?"

Lucy shrugged and frowned. "That's the thing. They found absolutely nothing suspicious at his place. Donovan even went to Goodbee's afterward and they looked up Pete's prescription record. The man never ordered any medications other than a high-

160

powered hydrocortisone cream. Apparently he had eczema, but that's it."

"So he never ordered any Valium?"

"Well, he could have gotten it at a pharmacy out of town," Lucy suggested.

A thought suddenly occurred to James. "Lucy, did the report mention whether or not the deputies found any signs of cigarette smoking at Pete's — ashtrays or empty packs or anything?"

Lucy stared at James in confusion. "I doubt it. They were looking for drugs and for the brand of booze he drank."

"Was it Wild Turkey?" Lindy asked. "You and James said that was his brand of choice."

"Yes, they found two bottles of it, partially full. One in the living room and one in the bedroom."

"But no Jack Daniels?" Bennett queried.

Lucy shrugged again. "No. Just the Wild Turkey."

"That's two things out of place at the scene then," James insisted. "Pete didn't smoke and he probably didn't buy that bottle of Jack Daniels."

"I don't know. This feels a little *weird* to me." Gillian looked at her friends. "It just doesn't add up correctly."

"Let's not get bent into pretzels over

nothin'," Bennett advised. "The man could have bought the drugs elsewhere and might have gotten some Jack Daniels just for the heck of it. What do we know?"

The five friends grew silent. A hesitant breeze tickled the treetops lining the parking lot and a dog barked from one of the houses in the newer development tucked behind the strip mall. Low stars gathered on the lip of the darkening horizon and a weak moon, blurred by a striping of gossamer clouds, hung low in the sky like a pendulum.

"Despite these new findings," Lucy began, breaking the silence. "I think something is amiss with this whole fire. I agree with you, Gillian. Something feels odd. If it was just a feeling, I might be able to let it pass, but the sheriff himself said something to me that let me know that, in *his* mind at least, this case is not closed."

"He said something to you or to the deputies and you just happened to overhear?" James asked, seeking clarification.

Lucy scowled. "Directly to me. He was leaving for lunch and he looked . . . really distracted. I asked him if everything was all right and he barely heard me. Then he kind of sat on the corner of my desk and told me that he couldn't believe Pete would have chosen to kill himself. He said that if Pete had ever planned to do that, he would have used a gun and he would have done it years ago. Apparently, he and Sheriff Huckabee grew up on the same street over in Lacey Spring. Said Pete was an easygoing, fun-lovin' guy when he was young. Married right out of high school, but his wife died before they even reached their first anniversary."

Lindy gasped. "How awful! What happened?"

"Some kind of boating accident in the Rappahannock River. She was with a bunch of friends and their boat hit someone else's. I think the girl who was driving their boat was pretty sloshed at the time. When Pete headed out to the Bay to identify her body, the local coroner informed him that his wife had been pregnant. According to Huckabee, she was going to surprise him with the news the very next day. She had made dinner reservations at a place they couldn't really afford and had a pair of knit booties in her purse."

"Pete had a wife." James felt remorseful. "I never saw him in that kind of light. He was so hostile — muttering angrily to himself while he cleaned the school. No wonder!"

"I guess some folks have the right to be angry. Pete was certainly mad at the world for a *long* time," Lucy mused as she looked up at the rising moon. "Thing is, Huckabee believes that if Pete didn't kill himself the day he identified his wife's body, then he was never going to. Why now? It makes no sense. He even asked *me* to keep my ears open regarding the whole affair. He's never asked me anything like that before. I feel like this is my chance to prove to him that I can be a more valuable part of the Sheriff's Department than I am now."

"We'll help you!" Gillian laid a hand on Lucy's arm. "We *know* you've got tons to offer that rooster house you work in, *and* we don't want Pete to pass on having folks believe he killed himself if he didn't."

"Then that means someone *else* killed him," Bennett pointed out. "But who?"

"Someone who recently bought a pack of cigarettes," James suggested.

Bennett nodded. "Yeah, *and* a bottle of Jack Daniels."

"And there's still the little matter of motive," Lucy reminded them. "Sure, he was a grumpy old man, but we'd have a high pile of bodies if all the town's geezers who hang out at Dolly's counter were suddenly murdered."

164

"We'll just have to dig deeper into Pete's past. There's got to be some clue there that could point us to a motive," Lindy insisted. "And I'd say his recent past, too. No one's bothered with him until he started working for Willy."

At the sound of a pair of clicking heels, they all fell silent and turned to see Phoebe heading their way. She took out her car keys and unlocked the creaking door of an old, sad-looking Chevy Malibu. The driver's side door was light blue while the rest of the car was a shade of lackluster silver.

"Parking lot powwow?" she asked them.

"We're drinking bottled water around the car instead of glasses of margaritas at Nacho House," Lindy answered lightly. "Plus, Gillian's new Pet Palace brochure is hot off the presses. You should see how gorgeous it is."

Phoebe peered at the open brochure. "Those are the coolest doghouses I've ever seen." She flipped to the back page where the price list was written. "I could never afford one of these for my pooch, however." She indicated her car door. "As soon as I can save a little money I'm going to have *two* silver doors on my car again. 'Night all!"

"Good night!" the five friends echoed in return. As Phoebe drove off, each supper club member promised to delve into Pete's past as well as all of the town's recent events leading up to the night of the fire. Lucy promised to sneak copies of the sheriff's reports on both the fire and the search of Pete's house to show them at their next supper club meeting.

"I'm starting the detective work right now," James pronounced.

"By doing what?" one of the others asked as they turned toward their own vehicles.

"I'm heading for the liquor store. It's the closest one in twenty-five miles and Danny has a mind for faces like a minnow trap. Nothing escapes him!" James opened his car door and called out, "Besides, my pop is fresh out of Cutty Sark and he likes to sip on it during *Jeopardy!*"

As James opened the door to his Bronco, he felt that he had forgotten something.

"My meals!" he yelped and headed back inside Witness to Fitness. The cubicle area was still lit but the exercise room was dark and empty as James entered and called out, "It's just me, James Henry. I forgot my food for the week."

No one answered so James flicked on the lights and gathered his shopping bag full of entrées. As he turned to leave, Ronnie came out of the kitchen area, a fuchsia towel draped around her neck. She put her hands over her heart as if startled and then broke out into a giggle.

"Oh my! You made me jump!"

James forced himself to look abashed, not believing for a second that she had been the slightest bit frightened. "I'm sorry."

"Well, you can make it up to me. My silly little car won't start and I'm sure it's the battery acting up again. I've got an appointment to get it fixed on Friday, but I could certainly use a sweet hero to get me home tonight."

"Sure," James replied without much chivalric enthusiasm. "Where do you live?"

"In that group of townhouses behind the post office. You know, the darling yellow ones with the green shutters and flower boxes?"

James nodded. The quaint townhouse block had caused quite a stir during the town planning meetings. The builder of the three-story town homes had promised to paint them a delicate shade of buttery yellow. Instead, he had gotten a deal on a different hue and the grouping of buildings had been covered by three thick coats of an orange-yellow so blindingly bright that groups of bees and other flower-friendly insects were constantly swarming around the area. The poor bugs apparently thought that the wooden structures were actually gigantic marigolds loaded with nectar. The fact that all the residents overloaded their window boxes with every variety of flowers during the growing season didn't help matters, either. James had heard Bennett complain more than once about having to douse himself with bug repellent before venturing out to deliver mail at the Cozy Valley Town Homes.

"I've got to swing by the liquor store on the way, if that's all right with you," James said, holding the front door open for Ronnie.

A cloud passed over her face as she locked the door to her business. "Alcohol is just empty calories, James."

Her patronizing tone instantly grated on him. "It's for my pop."

Ronnie smiled her false smile, clearly doubting James at his word. "Well, *of course* it is."

James gritted his teeth and opened the passenger door without speaking. He had always hated that derisive sarcasm.

As he parked in front of the town's only liquor store, Ronnie pulled a fitness magazine out of her cavernous gym bag. "I'll just sit tight. That's not a business I frequent."

A bell tinkled out a greeting as James entered the store. Danny Leary looked up from a book of word puzzles and issued a friendly nod. James located a bottle of Cutty Sark and placed it gently on the counter.

"You any good at word scrambles, Professor?" Danny asked, pointing at a grouping of letters. "I can't figure this one out at all. The clue is that all the words are capitals of foreign countries." He made a cough-like sound. "Shoot, I haven't been farther away than Kentucky, so it's not like I recognize too many of these, but I've got 'em all except for this one. I've been staring at this clue for almost an hour."

James turned the book so that it was facing him. He examined the letters.

ihleniks

Danny rang up the Cutty Sark and placed the brown bag to the side of the word puzzle book. James had the answer right away, but he stalled so as not to hurt Danny's feelings.

"This is a tough one, Danny. Give me a minute to stare at it some more."

Danny seemed pleased that James was stumped as well. He settled back on the stool he had sat in for over twenty years. He had long white hair pulled back into a neat ponytail and he occasionally twisted the end of it around his finger when he was working one of his puzzles. He wore steel-rimmed reading glasses low on his nose and with his open, wide face, he often reminded people of Ben Franklin.

"Nasty business about that ice cream store," James said, hoping to ease his way into getting some answers out of Danny.

"Sure was." Danny unwrapped a piece of gum and popped it in his mouth.

"Heard a rumor that old Pete Vandercamp was inside with both a bottle of Wild Turkey *and* a bottle of Jack Daniels."

Danny shook his head. "No chance. Ole Pete has drunk Wild Turkey all his life. He wouldn't touch another brand. Said it was a favorite of his father-in-law's and Pete admired that man to no end. Too bad the guy got cancer at such a young age. Pete could have used a friend back then."

"Was that when his wife was killed?" James asked, not daring to look up from the puzzle book.

"Just a year or two after that. Left Pete all alone in this world. Still, he never drank another whiskey in all the years I've known him. Ah, I mean, knew him." Danny cleared his throat. "It'd seem disloyal to his father-

170

in-law's memory."

James nodded. "Well, my pop's like that with his Cutty Sark. I guess someone must have given Pete that bottle of Jack Daniels then."

Danny seemed disinterested. "Yeah, reckon so. We sell quite a lot of Jack in here, so there's no tellin'. Never to Pete though and that's all I've got to say about that. How's your daddy doin' these days?"

"Oh, he's doing just fine, thanks for asking. I think the answer to this clue is Helsinki, but you'd better double-check."

Danny squinted at the clue and then smiled happily. "Darned if you're not right. Thanks, Professor." Danny looked beyond James toward the parking lot. "You got a lady friend with you?"

James controlled his feeling of revulsion so that it was not mirrored on his face. "She owns Witness to Fitness, that new weight-loss business. Her car battery is dead so I'm just giving her a lift home."

Danny removed his glasses and gave the woman in the Bronco a good look, but Ronnie had her face practically buried in her magazine. Another car pulled alongside James's truck on the driver's side and a group of young men jumped noisily out of each of the four doors. Ronnie looked up from her magazine momentarily as Danny watched the men make their way to the front door.

"Oh, I recognize her now," he stated matter-of-factly. "She's a pretty thing, if you like 'em skinny."

"You seen her around town?" James inquired. "She said she's never been in here."

Danny looked wounded. "Well, sure she has. Just once, a few weeks ago. I don't remember what she bought, but I remember her. You know I never forget a face and hers is a new one 'round here."

"She must just not want to come in," James said hurriedly.

"Well, shoot. Tell the gal I don't bite," Danny replied and then turned his attention to his other customers. James cast a glance back outside to see that Ronnie's visage was again obscured by her magazine. "So she was in here once," he mumbled to himself and then bid Danny a good night.

Ronnie chattered on about how much she adored Quincy's Gap as James pondered over his discovery at the liquor store. Before he knew it, they were pulling into the road leading to Ronnie's town house. Beneath the Victorian lampposts, a man slowly walked a dog on what appeared to be a very long leash. He wore a hooded sweatshirt, dark pants, and a baseball cap. He seemed to be the only person outside and in no hurry to return to his home.

"Him again," Ronnie said lowly, sinking down a tad in her seat as they passed by the man.

"You know him?" James asked, his curiosity alerted by the lack of peppiness that was customarily injected into every word Ronnie uttered.

Ronnie stuffed her magazine back into her gym bag. "He's my creepy mailman."

"Oh yeah? Why creepy?"

Ronnie gestured to one of the units on the right. "The next one's mine. I don't know why he bothers me. Whenever he has to hand me a package too big for the mail slot he stares at me." She laughed lightly. "It's not like most men don't look at me. I'm used to that. He just looks in a funny kind of way. I'm sure it's nothing. Still," she glanced backward out of the side mirror. "He doesn't live in one of these townhouses, so why is he walking his dog here?"

James couldn't think of any comment to supply to Ronnie's rhetorical question. He was relieved to see her jog into her townhouse and shut the door. What he wanted was a quiet drive home so that he could ruminate over all the details of the Polar Pagoda fire.

Reaching into his center compartment in the hopes of finding a stick of gum, James felt his hand close on a roll that felt like a sleeve of nickels, but when he drew the package into the dim interior lights he recognized the form of a Life Savers candy roll. And in Butter Rum flavor, too. His favorite.

James examined the nutritional information while backing out of Ronnie's driveway at a snail's pace. Figuring that a few candies wouldn't disrupt his weight loss progress, he eased the Bronco onto the road and popped two Life Savers into his mouth. Sucking contentedly on the candy, James passed by the man walking his dog just as the twosome moved directly beneath a pool of lamplight.

The mailman who gave Ronnie the creeps was none other than Carter Peabody.

# NINE:
## CHOCOLATE
## CROISSANT

---

| **Serving Size:**<br>1 croissant · 4 oz. |
|:---:|
| **Witness to Fitness**<br>**Points**<br><br>♡ 12 |

James was on his way to work the next day when he remembered that it was time for the monthly library staff meeting. Even the retired schoolteacher who helped out on evenings and weekends, Mrs. Waxman, came early for her shift in order to attend. It had become a habit on meeting days for James to stop by the Sweet Tooth, the town's only bakery. He enjoyed choosing homemade treats for his employees and everyone looked forward to the meetings due to the freshly baked goodies they could expect to consume while discussing improvements to their branch.

Today, James was anxious about stepping inside the famed bakery. The owner, Megan Flowers, had decorated the window with bright tissue paper flowers and whimsical kites made with construction paper. In the center of each flower, cinnamon buns and apple streusel muffins bloomed. Trays lined with fudge and butterscotch brownies covered a red and white checkered cloth and a picnic basket overflowed with French baguettes and crusty Italian Semolina bread. Chocolate-dipped sugar cookies in the shapes of ants marched around the base of the basket. James paused in order to absorb the tempting sights and then opened the door to the cozy warmth and heavenly smell that the Sweet Tooth maintained all year round.

"Good morning, Professor!" Megan greeted James affably as she dusted flour from her hands. "I was just whipping up a few loaves of raisin bread. How are you?"

James inhaled the tantalizing aromas of baked butter and cinnamon and felt the saliva inside his mouth rapidly begin to multiply. Despite the pleasant scents within the small storefront area, James noticed that Megan's shelves were unusually full for this time of the morning. By nine o' clock, her supply of breakfast Danishes, coffee cakes, and muffins were typically depleted. James noticed, too, that Megan seemed even thinner than normal. Her attractive, angular face looked pinched around the mouth and eyes and she ran her flour and butter encrusted hands over her brunette hair without even realizing she was coating herself as if greasing a pan.

"Everything all right, Megan? How's Amelia doing in school?" James asked, genuinely concerned.

Megan smiled tiredly. "She's really excelling. I am so proud of her, Professor. I mean, since all that nonsense last fall she's really come around. Works hard here and hits the books at school." She held out her hands in a gesture of helplessness and laughed. "I guess it takes a murder to straighten out some teenagers!"

James grinned, remembering how surly Amelia once was. "Well, that's terrific news.

We've got our staff meeting today so I thought I'd load up on some peanut butter cookies and maybe some white chocolate macadamia nut ones as well." James paused, his eyes feasting on all of the delectable items encased behind glass. "And I think I'll bring Pop a loaf of rye for his sandwiches and one of those raisin breads you just finished baking. He loves a slice with cream cheese as an afternoon snack."

Megan seemed delighted to fill the order. "I've got to tell you, Professor," she began as she boxed up the cookies and tied the box with red-and white-striped string. "Amelia might be doing well in school, but I'm not sure how much longer we can afford for her to attend." She sighed as she wrapped and bagged the two loaves of bread. "All of a sudden, my customers have gotten on this crazy health kick. It's like the opening of Witness to Fitness has scared them all away completely. Sure, some of them come in for wheat bread and I've started making these light bran muffins, but those two items are my big sellers these days." She dusted her hands on her apron. "And let me tell you, it's not much fun baking bran muffins all the time."

"So even people who haven't joined the weight loss center are trying to cut back on baked goods?" James was surprised. "Surely, you have plenty of regular customers who don't need to diet."

"I do!" Megan exclaimed. "Women thin as fence rails are telling me they feel guilty eating a donut once a week or even buying cookies for their kids. I don't normally resent a woman who's trying to run a successful business. But I tell you what, I resent the *hell* out of that Ronnie Levitt 'cause she's killin' mine!"

James looked at Megan's haggard face and offered her a sympathetic smile. "Well, I know of an upcoming event where *your* business will shine and I can guarantee that no one will be thinking of Ronnie Levitt or about dieting on this particular occasion." And James proceeded to discuss the details of having the Sweet Tooth as one of the major food booths at the library's upcoming Spring Fling.

Megan was delighted. "That's just what I need, Professor! We ought to have great sales that day and then hopefully my regulars will start drifting back into the store. How can I ever thank you? Here, take a chocolate croissant on the house. I know they're a favorite of yours."

James hesitated for a fraction of a second, knowing that he should refuse the treat before Megan even had the opportunity to put it in a bag, but he held his tongue. Watching her gather his purchases together, James's thoughts were already fast-forwarding to the moment when he could sink his teeth into the flaky layers of croissant crust and hit the soft, chocolate cache contained within.

The moment he was safely seated in his truck, he retrieved the pastry from the white paper bag and took a generous bite from one of the ends, baked to an appealing bronze in the oven. The rich, buttery dough caused him to sink gratefully back into his seat and then he took another bite, savoring the rich chocolate filling as it coated his tongue and nestled around his gums. Within ten seconds, the entire croissant had been consumed and James was plucking crumbs off of his shirt and popping them greedily into his mouth.

"Oh man," he moaned, thinking simultaneously of the amount of calories and fat the pastry must have contained and whether or not he should buy another one. Luckily, the strong possibility of being late for work spurred him into putting his car in drive. Licking his lips, he eased down Main Street and began to hum along with the radio. He couldn't help but note that nothing on the torturous Witness to Fitness menu had ever given him the urge to hum.

"Life is so unfair," he muttered and switched off the radio.

The first thing James did upon arriving at work was to send the members of the Flab Five an e-mail about his discussion with Danny Leary the night before. He also asked Lucy to see if the deputies had thought to collect Danny's receipts for all of his store's March credit card sales. James believed there was a slim chance that a suspect — and in his mind the primary suspect was Ronnie Levitt, though he still had no inkling what her motive was — might have charged a bottle of Jack Daniels. Lucy immediately wrote back that the receipts had been brought in and sorted as soon as Sheriff Huckabee had learned about the Valium contained in the Jack Daniels bottle. She promised to examine them when the other deputies were out to lunch.

The afternoon staff meeting was extremely productive and James was pleased to note that they were completely organized in regard to the Spring Fling. As he deliberated over whether to have another one of Megan's sumptuous peanut butter cookies, the bell at the checkout desk rang. It was a vintage brass bell once used to summon bellhops in the finer hotels, which James had purchased from one of the local antique stores for the infrequent times when he and his staff were tied up in their monthly meeting and patrons needed help. They were rarely interrupted for more than a few minutes at a time, but when James approached the checkout desk and absorbed both the ripe scents and argumentative tones of the two men waiting there, he knew he would be tied up for much longer.

"We're here to register our pigs for the big race," the first man said, tucking his hands beneath his overall straps as he rocked on the heels of a pair of dirt-encrusted boots.

The second man adjusted the straw cowboy hat on his head so that James could view a pair of deep-set eyes surrounded by weathered skin. "Don't know why you're botherin', Jake. No one can beat my Truffles, 'cept maybe her sister Jiffy Pop."

"Ha!" The other farmer bellowed and James strongly suspected it was the first time either man had stepped foot inside the Shenandoah County Library. "Your fat sow's got nothin' on my Blossom. Why, she's as streamlined as a speedin' arrow." He took off an ancient John Deere baseball hat and shook it at his fellow farmer. "And

I've got Rutabaga fit to race, too. There's no tellin' how that pig's gonna tear up a race course." He turned to James. "Shoot son, you may as well hand over that $1,500 jackpot purse to me right now."

James shushed both men even though he didn't see any other library patrons in his immediate view. "Gentlemen. I'm sure you both have fine animals who have excellent chances of winning." He smiled. "But you should also know, there are forty other pigs entered in this race."

The farmer named Jake scowled. "Well, in that case, sonny, I'll enter *both* my swine. What about you Lenny?"

"Count *me* in on two pigs, too," Lenny answered forcefully, slapping three fifty dollar bills on the counter. "At least you and me gotta beat the tar off of ole Billy Ostler, Jake."

Jake gave an irritated snap to his suspenders and harrumphed. "That rat bastard'll probably juice his pigs up on some kind of special slop before the race. 'Member how he fixed that Cow Pull a few years back?"

"Do I?" Lenny roared. "He didn't need the prize money anyhow! His daddy's about as rich as that fellow with the crazy hair . . . Trump."

James hurriedly handed both the farmers

receipts for their entries and wished them a good day, hoping that they would leave quietly. Neither man paid him any attention as they continued to reminisce about the myriad of wrongs done to them by one Billy Ostler. After they finally exited, James noted the muddy tracks left on the library carpet and clucked his tongue. Scott or Francis would soon be playing Rock, Paper, Scissors to see who would be using the carpet cleaner before opening tomorrow morning. James could only hope that the smell of manure would dissipate along with the dirty footprints.

When he returned to the break room to deliver the bad news, the twins were so elated about the entry of four more pigs that they both offered to do the carpet cleaning.

Scott whipped a tiny spiral notebook out of his front shirt pocket and eagerly turned a few pages. "Four more . . . why, that makes fifty pigs in all!"

"At a cost of $75 per entry," Francis said, sitting up taller in his chair, his eyes aglow behind the thick frames of his glasses. James wondered, for the umpteenth time, why the brothers refused to invest in contacts. They were both relatively handsome young men but seemed to prefer to hide behind black or tortoiseshell frames similar to those seen in films of the early fifties. "Even *after* we've handed out the $1,500 prize purse," Francis continued, "we've already cleared $2,250 in profit for our new Tech Corner!"

Mrs. Waxman clapped gleefully. "I've collected entry fees from forty women for the Ladies' Hat Contest as well. We'll have $500 to add to that kitty after we've paid out cash to the first prize winner. Not only that," she smoothed her heavily hair-sprayed coif of tawny hair streaked with gray and added smugly, "but Shenandoah Savings & Loan agreed to donate two bonds for us to use as runner-up prizes. One is for fifty dollars and the second's for one hundred dollars!" Mrs. Waxman giggled. "Little Hugh Carmichael might be President of that bank, but I swear he still thinks he's in my English class about to see his grade on another spelling test whenever I approach his desk. I think he'd hand out bonds to me just to make me go away."

James and the twins joined in her laughter. Their dream of bringing the library into the twenty-first century was looking more and more like a reality.

As the week went by, James felt buoyed by the realization that having cheated on his diet on Tuesday didn't prevent him from losing weight. Once again, he and his friends each got on the scale and were pleased to see lower numbers, by four or five pounds, than they had seen the week before. The exercise classes weren't becoming any easier, but at least James felt he could breathe during the workouts without his lungs turning to liquid fire.

By Friday, James was feeling less elated. He barely had the energy to make it to the end of Dylan's latest routine and he was thoroughly sick of eating the bland Witness to Fitness entrées. The other supper club members who were gathered around his Bronco after their exercise class that night agreed.

"I could really go for a pizza right about now," Bennett moaned. "The thought of eatin' that stir-fry made of rubber bands and tired-out vegetables does not make me wanna rush on home."

"Forget pizza. How about a spicy cheese and chicken enchilada?" Lindy sighed. "The Witness to Fitness Mexican Marvel dinner tasted like tree bark in red sauce. I don't think Ronnie's ever tasted real Mexican food."

"There are a few of those dinners that I just can't swallow," Lucy said. "I actually had a Happy Meal yesterday for dinner instead of that package of fettuccine and broccoli. I took one whiff of that as it came out of the oven and got right in my Jeep." She laughed. "I don't like broccoli as it is, but boy, that stuff smelled awful, like some chemistry experiment gone bad."

"I've been adding organic sea-salt to *all* of my meals," Gillian confessed. "I don't think they're bad, they just lack a sense of *soul*. So," she looked at her friends, "anyone have a report to make on Pete or the fire?"

"I do!" Lindy exclaimed. "Not a break-through on the case, but I *did* find out that Pete was kind of chummy with one of the history teachers from school. Mr. Wimple has long-since retired, but according to one of the teachers who have been at Blue Ridge High the longest, this man was the only person Pete was ever seen talking to. I guess that although he muttered to himself a lot or grumbled at students, he didn't socialize with any of the other teachers or staff."

"Where's Mr. Wimple now?" James asked.

"Wandering Springs. It's a nursing home." Lindy pulled a piece of paper from her purse. "It's over in Harrisonburg. I've got directions here and Saturday's visiting hours, but I can't go 'cause I'm going to visit my mother and daddy this weekend. Can anyone else go? Mr. Wimple might know something about Pete that we won't be able to find out on our own."

"Count me out," Bennett said. "I've got to cover for Carter. He says he's got somethin' important planned for Saturday so I'm takin' his shift."

Gillian shook her head forcefully. "*I've* got two horse shows. It'll be by the grace of Buddha that I even make it to our Sunday dinner *alive.*"

"James? What about you? And Lucy?" Lindy asked them both simultaneously.

"I can go," James answered quickly.

Lucy hesitated. "I guess I'm free, too."

"Great!" Lindy smiled. "And Lucy, did you have any inside news from the Sheriff's Department?"

Lucy shook her head. "I looked through the credit card receipts from the liquor store, but none of the customers seemed connected to Pete. There weren't too many of them, either. You know most folks around here like to pay for things with cash."

"So we're at a dead end so far." Bennett kicked at a stone with his shoe.

"I hope you and James can discover something from Mr. Wimple." Gillian slung her gym bag over her shoulder. James grinned at the sight of her orange hair paired with a neon yellow bag and her shimmering lilac tracksuit.

"We'll do our best," James replied solemnly and then an image of Lucy's filthy Jeep arose in his mind. "Oh and Lucy, I'll drive. Pick you up at ten?"

James couldn't believe his eyes when he and Lucy pulled up to Wandering Springs. The building, which resembled a miniature Monticello, had a manicured lawn and a sweeping gravel drive flanked by azalea bushes exploding in all spectrums, from delicate pinks to fiery crimsons and oranges. Mammoth magnolias and tall, thin pine trees dotted the tidy grass and a row of dogwood trees led visitors to a small parking area. Off to the side, beyond the front lawn, James noticed that the walking paths were populated by several groups of elderly residents and that a woman dressed in a kimono was singing as she stood on a wooden bridge in the middle of what appeared to be a Japanese garden. Hummingbirds and bumblebees filled the air with pleasant sounds of industry and a variety of birdhouses and feeders attracted groups of bright finches, cardinals, and blue jays.

"If this is what old age has in store, bring it on now," James murmured.

Lucy inhaled deeply. "Count me in, too. Even the air is restful here."

James glanced over at Lucy and smiled. She had seemed a bit tense and unusually taciturn during the forty-minute ride from Quincy's Gap to Harrisonburg. James had tried to warm her up by recounting the tale of the two pig farmers and though she smiled when James shared some of the names given to the cloven-hoofed racers, that smile faded away just as quickly. She also inserted Carter's name into the conversation several times, praising him for being a dog lover and musing over what was so special about his Saturday plans that Bennett had needed to cover his postal route.

It was all James could do to refrain from mentioning that Carter was undoubtedly smitten with Ronnie Levitt. Why else would the man walk his dog in a different neighborhood if not to catch a glimpse of the woman he admired? But he kept silent, not wishing to draw Lucy into an argument.

Finally, James resorted to rehashing details of the Polar Pagoda fire until they reached the nursing home. Despite the choppy beginning to their day of investigation, James felt a renewed sense of hope as they mounted the sweeping stairs leading into the brick mansion's entranceway. A willowy blonde seated at an ornately carved oak reception desk greeted them warmly when they asked if they might pay a visit to Fred Wimple.

"Oh, he'll get a kick out of talking about his days as a teacher," the blonde assured them, directing them along a plush carpeted hall that led to the back of the building. "Mr. Wimple likes to read outside before lunch, so I'm certain we'll find him, nose buried in a book, out on the sun porch."

Lucy was craning her neck as they passed large oil paintings in gilt frames and stately pieces of antique furniture. "How many residents do you have here?" she asked.

"About sixty. We keep it cozy so it feels more like a home filled with extended family than some kind of hotel or hospital." The blonde gestured gracefully as they passed an intersecting hallway. "Our dining room and kitchen are to the left and we have exercise facilities, a music room, and a media center to the right. All of our residents live on the second floor. Each room has a private bath."

"This place must cost a fortune!" James blurted out.

The blonde slowed her pace. "It's not inexpensive, no, but the people who come to live here are genuinely happy. They don't feel like they've been left here to die, but given a place where they can genuinely *live* out their golden days." She held open a heavy door leading out to a wide, sunlit porch. Several men and women were reading in wicker rocking chairs with plump cushions and a foursome were playing Hearts as they sipped on glasses of cool tea. The sound of soft jazz was being piped through speakers tucked beneath the eaves, and a gardener was carefully pruning the hedge growing alongside the porch. "Here we are. That's Mr. Wimple in the corner wearing the gray vest. Oh, and I'm Trish. Just call me if you need anything. Someone will be coming by shortly to see if any of the residents are thirsty. Feel free to try some of our homemade limeade at no charge, of course. Enjoy!"

Lucy moved forward in order to introduce herself to Mr. Wimple. He was a slim and dignified-looking octogenarian with thick, wavy white hair receding along a pink forehead. Along with his vest, he wore a pair of comfortable chinos and leather house slippers. His hands shook slightly as he turned the pages of his book.

"Mr. Wimple?" Lucy interrupted his reading using a soft voice. "We came to talk to you about someone we believe was a friend of yours," she began after introducing herself and then James. "We heard you were a friend of Pete Vandercamp's."

"Well, I can tell you one thing," Mr. Wimple said, "I was truly shocked to read about his death in the paper. You work for the Sheriff's Department you say?" he asked Lucy.

"That's right." Lucy plowed on in a direct manner. "You see, a friend of ours teaches art at Blue Ridge High. She thought you might be able to shed some light on Pete's past. That's why we came, Mr. Wimple. We aren't convinced that Pete Vandercamp's death was an accident, but we really don't want to disturb you if you'd rather not talk about it."

Mr. Wimple carefully closed his book and removed his reading glasses. He studied Lucy and James for a few moments with a pair of keen eyes from within crinkled folds of skin and then seemed to come to a decision. "Call me Fred — my teaching days are long over. So you think I might be of assistance?"

James nodded. "No one really *knew* Pete. We might have thought we did, but we just knew *of* him. You know, only the bits he showed the outside world."

Fred Wimple seemed to consider James's

words very carefully. Finally, he folded his hands together and looked James in the eye. "Tell me everything you know about the fire so I know the background a bit more. I might be able to fill in some blanks."

As Lucy filled Fred in on the details of the tragedy and the subsequent findings from the fire investigator, the Sheriff's Department, and Willy's insurance company, James found his eyes wandering to the lush and verdant gardens beyond the back porch. A muscular young man wearing athletic shorts and a tight T-shirt wheeled an elderly man down one of the garden paths. James recognized the fit form as belonging to Dylan Shane, but didn't dare wave hello. He returned his attention to the task at hand as Lucy finished her summary of the events involving Pete's death.

When she was through, Fred hailed over a middle-aged woman taking orders for refreshments and asked for three limeades. When the woman moved away, he cleared his throat and in a wobbly voice said, "Peter never smoked cigarettes and he never used drugs. I may not have seen him every day of his life, but I knew the habits that became his demons and those were chewing tobacco and Wild Turkey. And those two were enough!"

"I don't know whether you remember Danny Leary, the owner of Quincy's Gap's only liquor store, but Danny doesn't believe that Peter would ever have purchased a bottle of Jack Daniels. Would you agree?" James asked.

"Yessir. Mr. Leary had the right of it in telling you Peter would only buy one brand of whiskey. My young friends, someone else dropped those cigarette butts at the scene of the fire and someone else brought our Peter that Jack Daniels."

James and Lucy nodded. They both agreed. "Do you have any idea about who his enemies might have been?" Lucy queried.

Fred shrugged. "Peter's worst enemy was himself. He punished himself day after day for not being with Jeannie, his wife, the day she was killed. The whole world knows it wasn't his fault. Shoot, he wasn't even invited as it was just for the womenfolk, but that didn't stop him from blaming himself." Fred smiled as he accepted a cold glass of limeade from the woman who had returned with three glasses and a bowl of pretzels. "Thank you, Mabel."

When the woman moved away to serve drinks to the other residents, Fred continued. "Peter and I had a bond of loss, in a

195

manner of speaking. My twin brother was killed during the Korean War. He died trying to protect me and so I understood the kind of guilt and grief that Peter knew. Neither of us were men with many friends, but we spent some time together. I don't partake of alcohol and I tried to be a positive influence on Peter. I know he wasn't a popular man, but he never did anyone wrong."

James took a sip of refreshing limeade. He could practically feel the sugar as it slid down his eager throat. Lucy finished her own glass in four swallows and then delicately dabbed at her lips with a cocktail napkin. "Anyone could see that Pete was unhappy. That's why the authorities, with the exception of my boss, accept the ruling of accidental death."

"Yes, Peter was unhappy." Fred looked off into the distance. "But he was trying to turn things around. I saw him just a few days before the fire. He was really looking forward to working with Willy. Peter viewed him as a fellow survivor and genuinely admired the fellow. *I* saw it as Peter turning over a new leaf." Fred leaned over and clutched Lucy's forearm. "If Peter was killed, then his enemy is someone I don't know. I believe I knew all of the people Peter associated with, and there were very few of those. He was a true loner."

Lucy nodded. She clearly could think of no other questions to ask. "Thank you for your help. I'm more convinced than ever that he was murdered. We're just no closer to discovering why."

Fred leaned back in his chair, clearly wearied physically by the conversation, but his eyes remained alight with intelligence and determination. "Peter was gruff with people. I know what he was like. He said something to someone near his end and that someone became angry. Enraged. Find out who he talked to and I bet you'll find your man." He gripped Lucy's forearm. "And do let me know what I can do to help. I may be an old man, but my mind's still sharp as a razorblade."

James rose and shook Fred's hand. He and Lucy promised to keep him informed and to return to Wandering Springs if they had any new or significant information to share. On the way out, James led Lucy around the outside of the house toward the walking paths spiraling around the back gardens.

"Why are we going back here, James?" Lucy asked curiously.

"I swear I saw Dylan earlier. This must be

the nursing home where he volunteers."

Lucy immediately brightened. "Wouldn't *that* be a coincidence? You're right, there he is, reading the paper to that man dozing in the wheelchair."

Lucy and James approached Dylan and called out a greeting. At first, Dylan seemed stunned at seeing them in such a setting, but after they explained that they had come to visit Mr. Wimple, he smiled. "Fred doesn't get many visitors. His folks were really well off but money doesn't do you much good if there's no one to spend it on. It was nice of you both to spend time with him."

"Well, we wanted to question him about —" Lucy began.

"Local Quincy's Gap history stuff," James quickly cut her off. Lucy gave him a look of annoyance but before she could say anything further, the man in the wheelchair seemed to suddenly wake from his snooze. "Why hello, kids," he croaked sleepily. "You all headin' over to the ball game with my son?" he gazed at Dylan with pride.

"No, Randolph," Dylan patted the older man tenderly on the shoulder. "These folks are here to see another friend."

"Well, stop on over to our house afterward and we'll fix you some supper. My Louise just loves to cook for you kids after one of our boy's big wins. Best point guard in the whole of Miami-Dade County, yessir!"

"Thank you, sir. We'd be delighted to come," Lucy answered and Dylan winked gratefully at her.

Dylan then leaned forward and whispered, "He's got Alzheimer's, poor man. He thinks I'm his son." He began pushing the wheel-chair forward, toward the Japanese garden James had seen from the parking lot. "Phoebe is here today, too. She's been singing some Chinese folk songs for the residents." He laughed. "They think she's Japanese 'cause she's wearing a kimono. She rented it from a party store and is going to help host an Asian tea ceremony later this afternoon. The residents are really pumped. Would you like to stay?"

"We'd love to," James answered quickly, "but I still have so much work ahead of me if I'm going to be ready for the library's Spring Fling."

"Okay then, you two have a nice day. See you in class on Monday." Dylan smiled warmly and he and Randolph moved off down the path.

"Why did you lie to him?" Lucy asked angrily once they were safely in the Bronco heading back toward Quincy's Gap.

"Dylan's a stranger to us, Lucy. And to Pete. As much as I like him, we can't trust anyone."

"Oh please," Lucy sighed in disgust. "So I suppose Carter and Phoebe are suspects, too."

"Yes," James insisted. "Any stranger, including Ronnie Levitt. No one was interested in Pete's existence until that group of newcomers moved to Quincy's Gap."

"Oh," Lucy scoffed, "so next you'll be adding Willy to that list."

James scowled. "Willy was at the Brunswick Stew Dinner, along with Savannah Lowndes, Mrs. Emerson, and the rest of us."

"Well, *so* was Ronnie," Lucy said triumphantly. "I guess she's got an iron-clad alibi!" She smiled smugly. "And that leaves *Carter* in the clear as well."

"Oh good," James mumbled miserably. He drove the rest of the way in sulky silence.

# TEN:
## CORN DOG

**Serving Size:**
1 corn dog

**Witness to Fitness Points**

6

Over the next two weeks, the members of the Flab Five thought of every excuse they could in order to bring up Pete's name in front of anyone who had recently moved to Quincy's Gap. Bennett pried Carter at work, Gillian questioned Willy as he was painting a pink San Francisco Doggie Town House on the front lawn of his rented house, Lucy and Lindy divided the task of grilling Phoebe, Ronnie, and Dylan during one of their weigh-in sessions, and James even asked a few subtle questions to Savannah Lowndes and Mrs. Emerson after church let out. No one discovered anything of any use.

"All I learned is that my man Carter seems to have it bad for Ronnie." Bennett remarked at their last supper club meeting. He shook his head, perplexed. "She's not my kind of woman, but I guess some men like 'em scrawny."

"How do you know he's interested in her?" Lucy asked while violently stabbing a piece of chicken with her fork.

"Oh, he's always wondering about little details. Where'd she come from? What did she do before Witness to Fitness? Like how would *I* know?" Bennett smoothed his moustache and added sympathetically, "That boy can barely concentrate on delivering the mail. Sometimes I see him just starin' off into space when he's supposed to be sortin' letters. Shoot, I haven't seen one creature moon over another since the old hound dog I had as a kid fell for the beagle next door. Too bad they both were males," Bennett cackled.

"Ronnie's too old for Carter anyway," Lindy quickly said after noting the stormy looks Lucy was directing at Bennett.

"She certainly is not!" Gillian was miffed. "Men can date women ten years younger than they are so why can't women do the same thing? True, Ronnie might be closer to her fortieth birthday than to her thirtieth, but look how young her soul is. Plus, *women* get better and better as they age."

"Kind of like wine?" James teased.

"More like a *priceless* antique," Gillian continued. "All of that life experience only increases one's appeal."

Lindy tossed a lock of hair behind her shoulder. "Well, if I can look as good as Ronnie at thirty then I'll be happy."

"Please," James sighed. "Lose some weight if you want, Lindy. But don't end up looking like a praying mantis. At least all three of you look like real *women*."

"Why James Henry," Lindy smiled, placing her hand above her heart, "don't you just say the sweetest things?"

Later that week, James allowed Murphy Alistair to interview him regarding his current weight loss progress in exchange for some front page publicity on the upcoming Spring Fling.

"This sounds like a fundraiser to beat all fundraisers," Murphy commented as she took notes on the details of the festival. "Pig races? This is surely going to be a Saturday to remember. Sometimes all it takes is a little competition and presto! You've got a crowd. *I've* been working on my hat entry for the last two nights." She winked at him coyly. "I don't suppose I have an 'in' with one of the judges, now do I?"

James felt his neck growing warm. "Uh . . . Mrs. Waxman and two of the library volunteers are judging the hat contest. I'm going to help the twins manage the pig races. Though the closer we get to Saturday, the more I wonder what we've gotten ourselves into."

Murphy swatted the air in dismissal. "Come on, what's the worst that can happen? Even if one of those pink speed demons tries for a prison break, we can just shoot the little oinker and have fresh ham and bacon for dinner!" Murphy gave James a playful nudge. "How *are* you planning on containing the thoroughbred swine, may I ask?"

"Hay bales." James frowned. "But now I'm wondering if I ordered enough. Can pigs jump?"

Murphy laughed. "Most people only wonder if they can fly, but jump? Oh, I am *so* bringing extra film for my camera." She flipped open a notebook and uncapped a pen. "By the way," she said without looking up, "your weight loss is really beginning to show. I guess all the pain has been worth it. The question is, how much further do you plan to go on?"

James had asked himself the same thing and told Murphy as much. "I just can't stomach the idea of eating those entrées much longer. If I could make my own food, then I could stick this out, maybe even for the long run." He opened the top drawer of his desk where a package of Twinkies nestled amongst loose rubber bands and paper clips. "See? I'm starting to buy junk food again merely to allow some kind of taste sensation to return to my mouth during the day. I know that once dinner rolls around, I might as well be eating straw."

Murphy scribbled on her pad. "What if you could make your own meals, using a cookbook filled with light recipes? Would you really do that? I mean, most people don't have time to cook every night."

"I would buy some light frozen entrées if I were too busy," James replied. "But I honestly don't mind cooking. I like the way the kitchen fills up with aromas. It reminds me of my mother."

"A sensitive man with a multitude of talents." Murphy nibbled on the end of her pen and stared intently at James. "I can't believe Dolly hasn't gotten you married off yet."

James noted the glint in Murphy's eyes, which shifted from gray to green beneath the fluorescent lights, and hastily changed the subject. He leaned closer and whispered conspiratorially, "Listen, Murphy, there's something truly odd about the Witness to Fitness meals."

"Aside from their bad taste?" Murphy's eyebrows rose up her forehead.

"Yes." James hesitated and then decided to take the plunge. "I think they're the same as all the other frozen entrées from the grocery store. You know, like Lean Cuisine and Smart Ones?"

"As in they taste the same?"

"No, as in they *are* the same. I think Ronnie is just repackaging them in foil containers." He watched as Murphy absorbed what he was implying. "For example, she gave us this ziti entrée again this week. We've had it once every week. Well, I bought one of the ziti entrées from Food Lion's freezer section and I believe they are identical."

Murphy absorbed this information hungrily. "That would be a case of fraud if that were true. Especially with what you are being charged for meals." She suddenly slammed her notebook shut, jumped out of her chair, and pulled a large black satchel over her shoulder. "I'd better check this out right away. This could be a *big* story."

James also rose and stood, shifting back and forth uncomfortably on his feet. "But what if I'm wrong?" he worried. "I don't want to damage anyone's reputation."

Murphy smiled indulgently. "Don't worry, Professor. Nothing will be printed in black and white without solid research. I'm nothing if not fair." She turned to leave. "I'll let you know what I discover before any story goes to press. Deal?"

"Okay, thanks," James agreed quietly.

"And don't worry," Murphy threw back over her shoulder, "your Spring Fling still gets the front page no matter what. After all, you *do* have an 'in' at *The Star.*"

James was almost afraid to open his eyes that Saturday morning. The local news had predicted a day of heavy downpours and the entire event was outdoors, from the pig races to the kids' games. Hesitantly, he got out of bed, stuffed his feet groggily into an ancient pair of maroon slippers, in which the big toes on both of his feet had poked holes through the material, and eased back his bedroom curtains just enough to catch a glimpse outside.

"Eureka," he whispered in relief. Though overcast, the sky was already elbowing its way through the dense knot of gray clouds, in a show of strong blue ribboned by pale peach and salmon hues. Toward the east, a foggy patch of sunlight scored its marks across the shadowy trees and gently eased the darkness out of the woods. James exhaled happily. It was going to be a glorious day. He felt it in his bones.

Throwing on his favorite pair of jeans, which had become distinctly loose at the waist and baggy in the rear, James was pleased to note that he was pulling his brown leather belt a full two notches tighter than when he had first begun the Witness to Fitness program.

Even though it was barely seven in the morning, Jackson was already on his second cup of coffee and was engaged in a lively debate with the plumber over which brand of toilet was superior to all others. Their voices echoed around the cavities within the gutted kitchen and carried noisily up the stairs.

"You gonna stay and help us redo the pipes in here, Professor?" the young man named P.J. asked with a sly grin.

"Now you know he's got to raise money for the library today," Jackson answered, clearly seeking to continue the strain of friendly, argumentative banter. "It's men like you and me who can't get a single crossword clue right that've gotta get good and dirty." He eyed James seriously. "Still, it's never too late to show a young dog a trick or two. Maybe tomorrow you and I will have a little Carpentry 101." He chuckled. "Isn't that how they call them classes at college? 101 or 500 or 1000 whatever?"

"Yes, Pop. That's what they do." James filled his thermos from the coffee pot now set up in the downstairs bathroom. "I'd really like for you to teach me how to be a bit more handy. I know I'm not much good at it, but I'd like to learn all the same."

Jackson looked pleased. "Well, git on for now," he said hastily. "You've been sleeping all morning like Rapunzel. Those computers you want are gonna cost a few piles of nickels."

James almost corrected Jackson's choice of fairy tale heroine, but considering the overall feeling of harmony about the morning, he decided to let it go.

"That's Sleeping Beauty, old man," said P.J. as he put a dirty hand on his hip and threw Jackson a look of mock disdain. "Did you even go to *high school?*"

"Sure enough. And listen here, you little whippersnapper, that place has never seen a boy take so natural to shop class as when I was enrolled. Why, they had to come up with all new projects just to hold onto my attention."

P.J. nodded as if impressed. "So *you're* the one who came up with that tissue holder project. Thanks a lot."

Jackson grumbled something unintelligible and James left the two men alone to create an even bigger mess in the kitchen and to add to the growing tower of rubble in the backyard.

At the field where the Spring Fling was to be held, Scott and Francis were busily directing vendors as to where to set up their booths. Aside from two large food booths from the local businesses (Dolly's Diner and the Sweet Tooth), James had sought out two other vendors. These were Doggone It! Hot Dogs and Italian Sausages, from Culpeper, and The Way to San José, a Tex-Mex restaurant hailing from Blacksburg.

An area farmer had sold James a mountain of hay bales in order to create the pig's racetrack. There was no seating for spectators except for some extra hay bales set back from the racetrack boundaries, but James knew that no one would mind standing in order to view such an entertaining sight as five heats of pigs snorting and scrambling their way around a dusty circle while people wildly screamed out their names. James also felt confident that he lived in the kind of town where the few hay seats would be reserved for the elderly, disabled, or heavily pregnant women of the community. It was simply one of the many unspoken codes practiced by small towns all across the South. Another such code was to arrive at a fair in a state of near-starvation — breakfast skipped and stomachs churning — so that each and every type of food offered could be sampled before the day's end.

Megan Flowers was fully prepared for a ravenous crowd. James was amazed at the sheer number of sweets she had baked and at the amount she was apparently intent on making throughout the day.

"Like my deep fryer?" she asked James cheerily. "I'm going to fry Oreos and Twinkies and rice crispy bars. They were all the rage at the State Fair this year. We're also serving homemade raspberry lemonade. Some of Amelia's friends from school have volunteered to help us man the booth."

Amelia appeared next to her mother bearing a large tray piled high with layers of frosted sugar cookies divided by sheets of parchment paper.

"Look at these, Professor. Amelia came up with the design." Megan put a proud arm around her daughter's shoulders. "We call them our 'bestseller' cookies. Here, try one."

Megan placed one on a paper napkin. "It's almost too pretty to eat," James said. Each cookie was shaped like an open book. Vibrantly colored icing formed the edges of the book covers and thin, black lines of frosting created the appearance of stacked pages. On one of the open pages, a single word had been written. The cookie James held read *WISDOM* in script icing letters. The other open page was covered by wriggling stripes of chocolate, producing the effect of lines of text.

"We put words on all the cookies to remind folks of how much we cherish our library." Megan gestured at the cookie tray. James noticed other flattering terms such as *COMMUNITY, FRIENDSHIP, DISCOVERY,* and *LOVE.*

"Love?" he asked, raising his eyebrows.

"Hey, you've got self-help books, don't ya?" Amelia quipped. "Tell you all about loving yourself and others. Do I need to mention Dr. Phil?"

James bit into his cookie, chewed, and then smiled. "Amelia, if the clothes you design turn out half as original as these cookies, then you are going to take the fashion world and turn it right on its head."

Amelia flushed and moved away to unload more baked goods from her mother's van. James could see cardboard cartons mounded with chocolate brownies, butterscotch squares, éclairs and donuts on sticks, pretzels with dipping sauces, miniature Key lime tarts, bite-sized cheesecakes, and palm-sized pies such as pecan, chess, and Megan's mouth-watering caramel apple crumb streusel.

"You're going to make a killing," James commented, tearing his eyes away from the multitude of treasures within the van. "I'd better get out of here before I hijack that vehicle."

"Stop on by later and we'll fix you up a fine snack. On the house, of course. If things go well today, you might just have saved our business, Professor." Megan tied an apron around her narrow waist and began taping price lists to the front of one of the many folding tables set up to display her wares. A small tent provided shade and Amelia was beneath it, busily assembling the largest deep fryer James had ever seen. James was amused to hear both the women humming softly as they worked.

After leaving the Flowers women, he stopped at the other food booths in order to welcome the vendors and to purchase a large coffee from Dolly.

"You've got a winner with this event today, Professor," Dolly said, winking at him.

"Only 'cause you're here." James winked playfully in return.

Next, he helped Scott and Francis create an elaborate pen system using hay bales and chicken wire to contain the droves of pigs awaiting their chance to race. Both Jake and Lenny, the two farmers who had so thoroughly muddied up the library carpet, arrived shortly after eight in order to assist in erecting both the starting gates and the racecourse.

"It was awfully kind of you to help us out with this, gentlemen," James said in appreciation.

"Never mind that, sonny," Jake said, shifting a wad of bubble gum from one cheek to another. "We wanna make sure we know the turf so when that rat bastard Billy Ostler tries to pull some of his shenanigans, we'll be ripe and ready for him."

"Yessir," Lenny added, shifting his straw hat back and forth on his head as if scratching an itch. "It's gonna be a Shenandoah pig that wins this daggone race."

After about an hour of stacking hay bales, James pulled an irritating piece of straw from the inside of his sock and decided to leave the swine containment area in the more capable hands of the farmers and the Fitzgerald twins. He was not surprised by the brothers' adeptness at construction and engineering. After all, they had built the winning float for the town's Halloween parade and had claimed a handsome cash prize on the library's behalf. James watched them for a few minutes, his expression reflecting the affection he felt for the two younger men and then turned to check in with Mrs. Waxman and her troop of volunteers.

Mrs. Waxman was calling out orders in the same voice she once employed to settle down a classroom full of rowdy students. Middle-aged women fluttered to and fro, placing trash cans around the field, decorating the table where entrance tickets were to be sold, and arranging the judging area for the Ladies' Hat Contest. They jumped to obey their supervisor like fresh army recruits and James would not have been surprised to have seen Mrs. Waxman produce a whistle and command her troops to "fall in." Still, the bustling women seemed content as they fretted over who should be in charge of the cash box and whether the portable toilets would arrive before the attendees.

The few ride vendors had arrived the evening before, so the merry-go-round, Tilt-A-Whirl, spinning tea cups, magic train ride, and Ferris wheel were all in place and prepared for the children and adults who would hop onboard and squeal with delight or nausea, depending on how full their stomachs would be at the time. James was not a fan of rides, but he wouldn't mind one turn on the Ferris wheel, provided he had some company. He decided to ask Lucy to join him. He knew his supper club friends would all be at the Spring Fling and expected to run into Lucy at any moment.

The day sped by as James ran around the makeshift fairground checking in on vendors, ticket takers, and chatting with congenial townsfolk. At noon, he positioned himself at the racetrack in order to watch the five heats of pigs take two noisy turns around the circle. The crowd roared and laughed simultaneously, and James felt like a five-year-old boy as he giggled at the sight. There was something extremely comical about the frantic movement of those stumpy pink legs as they carried their rotund bodies in clouds of dust about the track.

He recognized Jake celebrating after his pig Rutabaga won the first heat. A young couple in overalls won the second heat with a pig named Pork Chops and Jake's friend Lenny was the victor of the third heat with Truffles. A young girl who James guessed to be about seven years old was congratulated for winning the fourth heat, and a man dressed in a pale blue suit and wearing a perfectly white cowboy hat with a turquoise stud in the center of the band won the final heat. James noticed Jake and Lenny sneering at their finely attired competitor and James could only assume that he was gazing upon the notorious figure of Billy Ostler.

When the final herd of pigs had been shuttled into the starting gates to await the onset of the championship race, two things became clear to all of the spectators. The first was that Billy Ostler's black pig named Stallion was twice the size of all the other swine and that Chester, the white pig with the black splotches on its flanks belonging to the little girl, was far smaller than its competitors.

As the announcers spoke the names of the pigs and their owners, the excitement of the crowd seemed to crescendo. When Chester's name was called, the townsfolk roared out their support, and the little girl, whose name was Becky Abram, beamed with pride. James noticed that her clothes were ill-fitted and faded and that she held onto the hands of two smaller children, most likely siblings, who were dressed just as shabbily. Behind Becky, a plump, weary-looking woman held onto an infant while a toddler tugged at her worn shirt seeking attention. Another small child was perched high on the shoulders of a lanky man who James assumed was the patriarch of the large clan. Like his wife, he wore patched jeans and a flannel shirt that appeared as though it had been slept in several nights in a row.

James looked back at Chester and thought about how much his family could use the prize money their pet had the opportunity to win. But Chester was so small, a veritable runt in a field of racing giants. Stallion looked like he would devour the little pig as soon as race alongside him. It must have been a fluke that Chester had won his qualifying heat. Everyone else seemed to be assessing Chester's chances with the same hopeless looks, but before anyone could ponder the dismal situation any further, a loud horn sounded and the gates snapped open. The race had begun!

James leaned forward in order to gaze downward as the pigs battled for an early lead. Stallion swung his massive head against Truffles's hip and the smaller pink pig stumbled and quickly lost her lead. From the corner of his eye, James saw Lenny shout out in anger as Billy Oslter grinned wickedly and cheered on his pig. Stallion decided to bully Pork Chops next and he literally pressed up against his rival until Pork Chops was forced to run smack into one of the hay bales. Squealing, he fell down with only one lap to go.

That's when Stallion made his fatal error. In the lead, Jake's pig Rutabaga grunted noisily along the course, dust flying from beneath his dirty hooves. Stallion was closing in on him rapidly, and with so few feet of track to go, it looked like the two pigs would end up in a draw, but at the last second, Stallion turned his head to the side, opened his hairy mouth, and tried to bite Rutabaga on the front leg. Tied up in this manner, they both ended up slowing down enough for Chester to shoot right on by. The congenial pig, who had contentedly run the entire two laps toward the rear of the pack and had therefore successfully avoided Stallion's bullying attentions, shot ahead and crossed the finish line a black snout ahead of his competitors.

The crowd went wild, throwing baseball caps into the air and onto the racetrack. James yelled as jubilantly as the rest and returned the merry embraces of the spectators around him. Taking the envelope containing the sizeable check for the first-place winner out of his pants pocket, James threaded his way over to Becky Abram and politely pushed his way through the assemblage gathered to congratulate Chester's family.

James shook hands with Becky's parents and then knelt in the dirt in order to present Becky directly with the check.

"As they say in *Charlotte's Web,* that's some pig you've got there, Becky."

Becky accepted the check, her face aglow with delight. "I begged Mama to let me enter Chester. I knew he was a pig with the heart of a lion. I had to use all my saved-up allowance to do it and Daddy was real mad when he found out, but I guess it's all right now, isn't it, Daddy?"

"Sure is, Pumpkin Pie. Your piggy bank just got a heck of a lot bigger." The man ruffled his daughter's hair. "She's a real big reader, sir. Saves all her nickels and dimes so she can buy books from the Goodwill store. Has got one in her hand all the time. Most of them are awful old though. Seems like we just don't got the time to bring her to town just to go to the library, so she can get the kind of books she hears about at school." He looked guilty. "There's always too much work to be done."

"Don't worry." James put a hand on Becky's shoulder. "You give me your address and I'll have the bookmobile swing by your place twice a month. That way you can check out new books all the time."

Becky threw her arms around James. "Oh, thank you, mister! This is the *best* day of my life!"

"And everyone in your family gets free lunch from Dolly's Diner today. *And* you can all pick out a cookie from the Sweet Tooth. Just tell the ladies working the booths that you won the pig races and Professor Henry is going to cover the cost."

The announcement earned him hugs from the entire group of children. By the time they were done, even Chester was brought over and shoved into James's startled arms. He then left them to their admirers and, smelling a bit like the barnyard, headed over to the food vendor area to fetch some lunch.

After loading up on two corn dogs, small fries, and some raspberry lemonade, James made his way to the judges' table in order to be prepared to deliver the check to the winner of the Ladies' Hat Contest. As the women paraded slowly in front of the judges, Mrs. Waxman made notes on a piece of paper and conferred importantly with her fellow judges.

More than fifty women had created hats with literary themes. James watched as each contestant passed the judging area and then returned to her place in back of a long line. He spotted Murphy right away, for her wide, flat hat sported a red wooden barn stuffed with livestock and the title, *Animal Farm.* Right behind her was the organist from James's church who had designed a *To Kill a Mockingbird* hat. This was a simple straw affair bearing a mockingbird who had been stabbed through the side using a toy knife. Other hats that caught his eye included an *Of Mice and Men* bowler on which the creator had sewn Ken dolls and plush mice and the *Lord of the Flies* crown that had dozens of rubber flies encrusted about its rim and flying skyward with the aid of nearly invisible wires.

When the judges announced the winners, James found himself in complete agreement with their choices. A teenage girl who had designed her own *A Tree Grows in Brooklyn* chapeau earned the second runner-up position. She had used Lego buildings to create a New York City skyline and made a beautiful tree out of papier-mâché and tissue paper. The first runner-up was Witness to Fitness's own Phoebe Liu. She had erected a boxing ring onto an old cowboy hat and instead of two human pugilists, had fashioned a pair of combative grapes out of plastic fruit. She added to her *Grapes of Wrath* theme by periodically ringing a small bell, as if a new round of fighting were about to erupt.

The grand prizewinner was Ms. Beasley, a mousy middle school science teacher. Her hat was based on *Cat on a Hot Tin Roof* and showed a two-dimensional feline walking across a piece of metal sheeting with buildings in the background. The minute windows of the town's buildings lit up and every now and then, a hiss of steam would escape from beneath the piece of tin and the flat cat would literally jump up in the air and land on its feet again. Children were especially entranced with Ms. Beasley's hat. They clustered around her immediately after James handed over the prize check. Ms. Beasley began to explain in excruciating detail how she used dry ice, battery components, and other scientific minutia until James found his attention wandering.

He gazed contentedly around the field, watching as families lined up at the food vendor booths or waited for their turn on one of the rides. He smiled as he walked by both children and adults trying their hardest to win plush toys in the games area. The sight of clusters of bright balloons, the scents of delicious food, and the sounds of bluegrass music being broadcast by the town's only local radio station combined to fill James with a sense of giddiness that he hadn't experienced for a long time. In fact, he hadn't felt this way for many months and the last time was right after he had kissed Lucy Hanover.

As James stood reflecting on that kiss, he effectively blocked the path of a large group of teenage boys wearing baggy jeans and T-shirts bearing a variety of different offensive expressions. Suddenly, the boys veered off toward the picnic tables, where a pod of teenage girls wearing heavy makeup and short skirts giggled and nibbled on bites of cotton candy. In the space the boys once occupied, James caught a glimpse of Lucy as she strolled toward the carnival rides. It was as if his thoughts of her had conjured her into solid form and he knew that her appearance was more than simple coincidence. It was a sign to seize the moment.

Dunking his cup of soda into the nearest trash can, James hustled through the crowds, all the while trying to keep his focus on the sunlit halo of Lucy's hair as she moved away from him. He caught up with her at the entrance to the Ferris wheel.

"Care to share a cab?" he asked breathlessly after taking her by the arm.

"I'd love to." Lucy gazed up at the multicolored wheel. "I'm totally into heights. How about you?"

James gulped. "No, not really, but I'd like to see how our blue hills look from up there." He pointed at the car that had just reached the highest elevation. As they watched, the ride controller began the long process of releasing people from their cars and loading on new riders.

"We're in violet — my favorite color," Lucy announced, sitting down. The car rocked unsteadily for a moment and then lurched violently when James stepped in. There was barely enough room for their two wide bodies and the flesh of their legs and arms was pressed tightly together.

Lucy laughed. "Guess we need to lose more weight."

"Aw, it's cozy. I like it," James replied and then fell silent until all of the riders had settled into cars and the wheel began to turn in its languid circle. As they rose above the field, a swollen sun was dipping toward the horizon and the sky was mottled with mango-hued clouds.

"It's so beautiful!" Lucy exclaimed as they reached the pinnacle.

James gazed at her and had just opened his mouth to speak when their car came to an abrupt halt. It swung wildly forward and James felt his stomach flip-flop as he looked down to see his feet swaying to and fro over the small heads of oblivious townsfolk below.

Lucy offered James a look of pity. "It's okay, James. This happens all the time on these things."

James cleared his throat and sat up straight. "Actually, I hope we *are* stuck up here and for a good long time."

"Really? Why?"

"Lucy." James took his hand and placed it gently on her soft cheek, turning her face toward his own. "I'm so sorry we were interrupted that day at Dolly's. I said I had important things to talk to you about and I allowed an insignificant, and unscheduled, meeting to get in the way of what I had to say to you."

"I understand," she answered tenderly, her blue eyes lit by the twinkling lights of the Ferris wheel. "But I'm still interested in what you wanted to tell me."

James exhaled nervously. "I'm never so happy as when I'm with you, Lucy. I know I turned cold after that one time we . . . ah . . ."

"Kissed?" Lucy offered helpfully.

"Yes! You see, I was so afraid you'd end up finding me dull like my ex-wife did and then I'd get hurt again." James felt that he was babbling and cringed, but couldn't bring himself to stop. "So I pulled back, but I still feel something very strong for you and I'd like to try to make it . . . to make *us* work if you were still willing."

Lucy's smile was filled with delight. "I'm still willing, James."

"But what about Carter?" James asked with concern. "I thought you were interested in him."

Lucy chuckled. "I was just pretending to have a crush on him to get a reaction out of you. I was trying to figure out what was going on in your head."

"A reaction, huh?" James faked a severe scowl. "How's *this* for a reaction?" And he pulled Lucy's lips onto his own.

The pair never noticed that the ride had started up again until their car reached the bottom and the controller began coughing loudly in order to attract their attention.

"Folks!" he finally shouted at them. "Let some other people see the sunset now. Come on! Out with you!"

James and Lucy separated themselves, their faces flushed in embarrassment. "Sorry," James said sheepishly and then grabbed onto Lucy's hand. "That's a pretty romantic setting you've got up there, though."

"I feel like celebrating," Lucy said as they drifted happily away from the ride. "What should we do?"

"Megan's probably got a fresh batch of fried Oreos waiting at her booth," James answered, only partially in jest.

Lucy raised herself up on her tiptoes and gave James a peck on the cheek. "Deep-fried cookies, huh? That sounds absolutely perfect."

# ELEVEN:
# CHICKEN FLORENTINE
# LASAGNA

Serving Size:
10 oz.

Witness to Fitness
Points

5

James took a rare personal day off from work the Monday following the Spring Fling. Though exhausted, he woke in a state of dreamy happiness as he replayed the look on Lucy's face Saturday night as it was lit by the winking, multi-colored lights of the Ferris wheel. Thinking about having her in his embrace gave him a feeling of invulnerability. As he stretched his arms wide and yawned, he had an overwhelming feeling that, suddenly, anything was possible. He could become the man he knew existed inside. His weight loss was progressing, he and his staff had organized a successful fundraiser for the library, and he had taken the first step toward having a good woman at his side to walk into the future with. Even his home was becoming transformed. When he heard the whining buzz of an electric drill coming from downstairs, James decided how he wanted to spend his unexpected holiday.

After showering, James phoned the Fitzgerald twins at home in order to alert them as to his absence and then suggested that they too should look over the schedule and rotate turns taking a personal day later on that week.

"No thanks, Professor." Francis rejected the idea cheerfully. "We love our job and get plenty of time off. Besides, we've got to figure out how to rearrange the fiction section in order to accommodate our new Technology Corner. College finals are coming up, and those new computers will be in high demand."

James was unsurprised that both of the twins refused to take a vacation day. They also shied away from the praise heaped upon them for all of their original ideas concerning the Spring Fling, just as they had done after winning the float contest in the fall.

"Without those pig races," Mrs. Waxman had gushed over them Saturday evening while fluffing the wild hair on the tops of their heads as if they were a pair of cute toddlers, "this might have been just another country fair. Then you went ahead and added the hat contest and this was transformed to a county-wide competition."

"If only you two were as clever about finding yourselves some girlfriends," Dolly had murmured while serving them all fried chicken, corn pudding, and green beans cooked with bacon.

"We're waiting for a set of twins who love Science Fiction, Dolly," Scott had replied evenly, his mouth stuffed with one of Clint's fluffy buttermilk biscuits. "We have to have our priorities."

"And it would be great if they liked video games," Francis had added.

"And *Star Trek*."

"And the Discovery Channel."

James laughed at how Dolly had shaken her head, perplexed as to how she could manage to find two young ladies in their early twenties who shared the passions held by the Fitzgerald brothers.

Thinking back on Dolly's comment, James decided that since he knew of no available female twins whatsoever, the least he could do for the brothers after leaving them in charge of the library was to order them a few pizzas for lunch. The Fitzgerald boys were always hungry and James knew that their salaries rarely allowed them to splurge on takeout. He was quite sure they would rather spend their hard-earned money on the latest technical gizmos highlighted in *Wired* magazine.

Dressed in a worn pair of sweatpants and an ancient but beloved William & Mary Athletic Department T-shirt, James arrived downstairs to find Jackson holding a cup of coffee as he surveyed the dust-covered room formally known as the kitchen. His toolbox was propped open on the floor and each metal item glinted in the morning sunlight. James didn't know the names of the majority of the gadgets within his father's red Craftsman box, but he knew he was seeing a set of tools that were lovingly cared for when he looked at his father's array of wrenches, pliers, screwdrivers, and a multitude of other mysterious implements.

Jackson eyed his son's attire with curiosity. "You havin' them casual work days now at the library?"

"No, Pop," James replied, stirring a liberal amount of fat-free half-and-half into his coffee. "I thought I'd take you up on your offer to learn to be a bit more handy. You're working on the floor today, right?"

Jackson took a deep gulp of coffee as if he suddenly needed something to do as he pontificated over his son's ability to successfully utilize a tool. Finally, he issued an amused nod and said, "Well then, let's start with a little demolition. There's nothin' like rippin' out some ole flooring to get your day goin' on the right boot." He paused and then patted his stomach. "You'd best swallow a real breakfast, though. Those bars you've been eatin' aren't workin' man's food." He pointed at the box of multi-grain breakfast bars sitting on the dining room table. "Those clusters of nuts and fiber are meant for bushy-tailed rodents and that's about all."

"I'll fry us some eggs," James offered. "Since the stove is about all we have left hooked up in this kitchen."

"With sausage and cheese?" Jackson

asked, a hungry gleam in his eye.

James hesitated, silently calculating the Witness to Fitness points such a breakfast would cost. "Sure, Pop." He shut off his mental calculator and went into the dining room to retrieve the frying pan from a haphazard pile of pots, pans, dishes, and cutlery.

Less than an hour later, James and Jackson were working side by side to remove the yellowed linoleum Jackson had laid down with meticulous care almost thirty years ago. He showed James how to cut into the vinyl using a razor knife and then to slowly and painstakingly scrape up the glue residue underneath using a razor scraper.

"You can't rush a job like this," Jackson warned as they got to work. "We're gonna need to take off all the glue and paper sittin' on top of the subfloorin' just as careful as wipin' a baby's bottom."

Jackson switched the radio on to his favorite country and western station and began to hum along with the latest tune by Toby Keith.

"That boy knows how to sing good American songs," Jackson grunted as he pulled off a large segment of flooring and launched it out the back door along with the rest of the kitchen debris.

James hated how the backyard looked like a work site. He had hoped to hold the next supper club meeting at his house by hosting an outdoor picnic. Now, without a working kitchen and a backyard area that could have doubled as a set for *Extreme Home Makeover,* he didn't see how he could invite his friends over at all.

"What's eatin' you, boy?" Jackson asked. "You're burrowin' into that subfloor like you're a dog diggin' for an old bone."

James explained his concerns, expecting Jackson to shrug off his problem without much care, but to his surprise, his father stood and reached for the phone book. "I was gonna order a dumpster anyway. I'll just make sure they come this week and get all this crap outta here. Then you can have your . . ." he swallowed as if choking on the words, ". . . supper group over."

"Thanks, Pop," James said gratefully. "Maybe you'd like to join us as well?"

Jackson began dialing a number. "I'm livin' and breathin' a bit more lively these days I know, but there's no way in hell I'm ready for a whole night full of jawin' and bad food."

James laughed. "Fair enough, but once we get this kitchen finished I *would* like you to have dinner with my special friend Lucy."

His father left a mumbled but officious message on someone's voicemail and then looked at James appraisingly. "So, you finally made a move. 'Bout damn time, too."

"You're right about that, Pop," James agreed, resuming the tedious scraping. "It was about damn time."

Over the course of the day, James and his father had completely removed the linoleum and had prepped the subfloor to be laid with tile. Both the new cabinetry and the pallets of tile were delivered that afternoon, and the mountains of construction materials in the backyard almost prevented the Henry men from exiting and entering their own house. However, Jackson promised James that both the dumpster and P.J. would be arriving the following day and that the kitchen would be complete by the end of the workweek.

Later, Jackson stood next to the oven as James heated up their dinners: a container of Chicken Florentine Lasagna (one of the Witness to Fitness entrées) for James and the leftovers of one of Dolly's succulent pot roasts for Jackson. James sprinkled a liberal amount of salt and pepper on his lasagna and began to eat, all the while trying to ignore the sight of the tender meat and plump potatoes that Jackson happily dunked into a pool of rich brown gravy.

"I'm tellin' you, boy. That's not man's food." Jackson took a greedy pull from his bottle of Budweiser. "You worked with your hands all day. You deserve a meal like I'm havin'. Go on, eat some of this," he commanded.

"I can't, Pop. Besides, this lasagna's not that bad. It just needs some more salt."

At that evening's Witness to Fitness meeting, James was already so sore from a day of squatting over the kitchen floor that he didn't think he could possibly survive a workout. Examining his callused hands while waiting for his turn on the scale, he began to worry about the frequent amount of cheat foods he had consumed during the past week. As he stood scowling at the thought of actually gaining weight instead of losing it, Lucy breezed into the cubicle area and greeted him with a radiant smile.

"Why the frown, Professor?" she asked him lightly.

James explained his fears and she nodded in understanding. "It's the food we're required to eat on this diet. It's getting old for all of us."

Several other people overheard Lucy's comment and began to complain to one

another about the entrées until an antago-
nistic buzz developed around the scales.

Phoebe listened to the griping of one of
the male clients as he was being weighed
and realized that she needed to address the
group's concerns. Asking for quiet, she
spoke gently to the disgruntled dieters.

"I talked to Ronnie last week about the
blandness of the food you've purchased. She
assured me that she really made an effort to
spice up this week's meals. Give them a
chance and then we'll see how you all feel
by next Monday. Does that sound fair?"

It was impossible not to respond to
Phoebe's warmth and so all of the dieters
immediately stopped grumbling and agreed
to give the food one more shot.

"So she's not here tonight?" James wondered, looking around.

"No, she says she's come down with a bad
cold," Phoebe responded and beckoned
James toward the scale. James thought he
caught a hint of disbelief in Phoebe's tone.

"Maybe it's allergies," James suggested.
"Not too many people get colds in this kind
of warm weather."

"Maybe." Phoebe looked unconvinced as
she shifted the levels on the scale. "You've
made more progress. Good work."

James discovered that he had lost two

pounds despite his lack of faithfulness to the food program. His feelings of invulnerability and good fortune surged.

"Lost two more pounds. Must be all the exercise," he whispered in Lucy's ear as she waited in line for her turn.

Giggling, she whispered back, "Yeah, especially on the Ferris wheel."

Embarrassed, James looked around to see if any other members of the Flab Five had overheard her comment. He realized that he wasn't quite prepared to flaunt his feelings for Lucy in front of his friends. After all, he and Lucy hadn't even been out on an official date yet, so James could hardly explain to their friends that they were now a couple. James waited for Lucy outside of the exercise room and then hastily asked her to accompany him to dinner and a movie that Friday night.

"Sounds great," Lucy answered while pushing her hair back into a headband in preparation for the upcoming workout. "What's playing?"

James shrugged. "Actually, I have no idea. I haven't been to the movies in so long that I've forgotten to even read the film section in the newspaper."

"I go all the time. Lindy and I saw a great period film two weeks ago. An Austin remake." She sighed. "There's something about those British men in breeches . . ."

"Well, you can choose the movie, but I'd prefer to avoid anything featuring dandies sporting breeches and ponytails tied with silk ribbons," James said gruffly. Then, noticing that Gillian and Lindy were approaching, he gathered up his bag and stepped into the exercise room. Turning, he whispered, "Just call me at work tomorrow and we'll plan everything."

Lucy looked perplexed. "Okay, but why are you whispering?"

Panicking at the sight of the other supper club women, James darted over to the water fountain as if Lucy hadn't spoken at all, his stomach fluttering with nerves as he watched in the wall-length mirror while she casually greeted Lindy and Gillian.

"How's it going?" a voice asked from behind James, causing him to jump.

He looked beyond his own reflection to see the friendly, handsome figure of Dylan as he waited to fill his water bottle from the fountain.

"Oh, I'm fine! Sorry to hold you up." James bent over to take a quick drink in order to make it seem as though he had actually been thirsty, but in his increased state of agitation he jammed the button in with too much force and water shot out in an arched stream directly into his face. James backed away and wiped at the moisture running off of his chin and onto his T-shirt with his forearm.

"It's got a finicky release button," Dylan said smiling. "Glad to see you're hydrating, though."

James nodded mutely and slunk over to his customary place in the back row.

Halfway through the exercise routine, as Dylan was leading the group in the first of a series of nasty lunges, James noticed a face appear in the mirror at the door separating the exercise room from the cubicle area out front. The face caught his attention because it belonged to a woman who was not enrolled in the Witness to Fitness program. The trim figure, clad in a neat powder blue pants suit, was easily half the size of any of the other exercisers' larger bodies and did not seem in accordance with the other heaving shapes moving about in the mirror's reflection. Murphy Alistair began making her way toward James, but he instantly stopped mid-lunge, swung around, grabbed her by the elbow, and led her out of the room.

"What are you doing here?" he asked in an anxious and hushed tone even though

Phoebe did not appear to be at her desk.

Murphy grinned wickedly. "I thought you'd be glad that I saved you from those lunges. They look like hell on the ass and thighs."

"They are, but I think that's the point." James dabbed at his face and tried to calm down. He was afraid that if Lucy spotted them together again she would leap to the wrong conclusion. He had already explained to her that Murphy was interviewing him on his weight loss experiences but Lucy firmly believed that Murphy had her cap set on James.

"There's a look she gives you, James," Lucy had said late on the night of the Spring Fling. "It's flirty and . . . well, predatory. Women recognize that kind of look much better than men do. Just don't be fooled, because I *am* the jealous type."

Now, Murphy was fixing James with a calculating gaze, her hazel eyes studying him as if trying to read his mind. "I wouldn't have showed up here if this wasn't urgent," she assured him. "I just wanted you to know that you were 100 percent right about those entrées. They are all store-bought." Squaring her narrow shoulders, Murphy took a deep breath and turned to leave, "But since I seem to be causing you distress merely by being in your presence, I'll tell you all about it tomorrow."

Not willing to take the chance that Murphy was only teasing him again, James danced in front of her and held out his hands in surrender. "No, no! Please don't. I'm sorry, it's just that none of us look too graceful bouncing around in there and it's kind of unsettling to have someone who's not . . . ah . . . in need of our class suddenly appear."

"Don't be ridiculous, James. Your group looks great. After all, you're the ones making things happen for yourselves. You're not sitting at home ordering products from infomercials because they promise to make you instantly thin without the need to diet or exercise." She moved into the doorway separating the two sections of the building and indicated the exercise group. "It's an inspiring sight, truly." She paused. "By the way, where is your fearless leader tonight?"

James reached out to pull Murphy away from the doorway but she was unaware of his motion and stepped farther inside in order to observe the workout. "Who? Ronnie?" James asked distractedly, his mind focused on one particular form in the mirror.

"Yes, Ronnie." Murphy cocked her head

and put an impatient hand on her hip.

James shrugged. "We were told she was home with a cold. Dylan teaches all of the exercise classes anyway. Ronnie just does the weigh-ins and the counseling sessions. I talk to Phoebe whenever I have any issues, so it's not like her absence is a big deal to me, except that it's noticeably quieter."

"Well, she may not be your counselor, but she collects your money, I'd bet," Murphy remarked sardonically, her eyes wandering over the group of sweaty dieters as they jumped in time to the music.

To his horror, James noticed Lucy catch his eye in the mirror. She raised a suspicious brow and then faltered while doing a leg lift. James hurriedly withdrew in the direction of the front door, forcing Murphy to follow. "So how were you able to confirm my theory about the food?" he asked.

"I have a chemist friend. I simply brought one of Ronnie's meals and the comparable store-bought meal to my friend's lab and she conducted an experiment after work. It was fascinating to observe." Murphy rifled through her bag and produced a notebook. "According to these findings, the only thing Ronnie did to doctor up the cheaper product was to add some grated Parmesan cheese and fresh parsley for garnish. And somehow, I don't think her expenses would total the $6.81 difference between the cost of the store-bought meal and the one she sold you for ten dollars."

"Especially since that's $6.81 times seven days of entrées!" James was furious.

Murphy nodded excitedly. "Exactly! That comes to a bit less than $48 per week, which really adds up over the course of the month. Even though Ronnie had to buy aluminum tins for all of the meals, they sell those in bulk for next to nothing at those discount warehouses."

James shook his head angrily. "That's where Lindy and I met her! She was probably stocking up in preparation to rip us all off!" Murphy shut her notebook with a triumphant flourish. "We need to compare the rest of the week's meals in order to firm up our research. Can I follow you home and get whatever you have left from last week's entrées? I know you mentioned having skipped some of the required dinners last week. The paper will reimburse you for the cost, of course."

James hesitated. If he left now, Lucy would be convinced that something was going on between him and Murphy beyond that of a simple newspaper interview. And since he had told no one that Murphy was investigating the nature of the Witness to Fitness meals, it would look exceedingly odd if he were to simply disappear in the middle of class.

"Can I meet you at my place after class is over instead?" he stammered. "I don't want to miss the rest. I need to be able to deduct these exercise points."

"Ah, such dedication," Murphy teased. "Fine, I'll see you at your place in about half an hour and don't worry, I already know where you live."

James was about to caution Murphy about both his father and the mess in the yard, but she slipped out the door and into the evening like a silent zephyr. James hastened back inside to rejoin the class only to find that they had all collected mats and were beginning their final stretches. Avoiding everyone's curious eyes, James grabbed a mat and began bending over at the middle.

Once class was finished and people were drinking greedily from water bottles or stuffing sweat-soaked towels into duffle bags, Bennett moved over to James's side and clapped him on the back. "That's one fine lookin' excuse to get yourself out of those Godforsaken lunges, my man."

"What?" James asked innocently.

"That cute reporter." Bennett stroked his

moustache and grinned. "She can ask me for *my* story any time, yessir."

"Actually," James lowered his voice, "she may have found out something pretty incriminating about Ronnie."

Bennett looked at him with interest. "Go on, now. You can't mess with a man by teasing him like that. What did our fine Ms. Alistair find out?"

"I'll tell everyone tomorrow, I promise." James shouldered his gym bag. "Murphy needs to do a bit more research and I've got to go meet her at my place right now."

"Lucky man!" Bennett grinned and was suddenly bumped from behind by a figure hustling toward the front door. "Hey! Where's the fire, woman?"

James sighed in resignation as Lucy, her shoulders set in angry determination, marched outside and got into her car without so much as a backward glance in James's direction.

"Must be that time of her cycle," Gillian sympathized as she watched Lucy's car peel out of the parking lot. "I always feel especially sensitive during my week, too. Ah, the ebbs and flows that make up the mystical tides of Womanhood."

"What *are* you talking about?" Bennett muttered in bewilderment and walked off to where his car was parked.

James waved to the others and headed for the Bronco with steps more weighted than normal. This time, he couldn't blame the exercise class for wearing him down. After all, he hadn't even participated in half of the routine.

# TWELVE:
## PRETZEL STICKS

Serving Size:
10 oz.

**Witness to Fitness
Points**

5

"We figured it all out, Professor," Francis said, leaning over the Information Desk while flourishing a piece of paper covered with his familiar chicken-scratch handwriting. "We can afford eight new computers —"

"As long as they come with only basic programs," Scott interrupted.

"Right." Francis nodded. "Internet capabilities and Microsoft Word and such, but no fancy graphics programs. So, if we buy everything during the Memorial Sale at Wired City we can afford to get eight computers, two laser printers, one color printer, and a scanner."

"Of course we'll have to charge our patrons a bit more per page for the color printouts than for the black and whites." Scott pointed at a red-and-white sale circular on which he had drawn a dozen black stars. "But since we don't have a color copier *yet,* I don't think they'll mind. Francis and I have already done all of the cost-versus-value comparisons on all of these machines using *Consumer Reports.* I think we'd be getting a darn good buy if we go to Wired City."

James looked over the circular while chomping down on a pretzel stick. "This is more than I thought we could afford. What happens to our old machines? Can we still use them?"

"Our current two might have to get nixed, Professor. They are pretty old and too slow, but we've got a buddy who might be able to add some RAM for a reasonable cost and bring them back up to speed."

"That would give us ten computers!" James exclaimed. "That's remarkable."

"True, but we'd have no money left over for the actual furniture to put them on," Scott said mournfully.

"If only we knew someone who could build stuff like that." Francis looked at the sales circular with a wistful expression. "We're pretty handy, but we couldn't make anything that looks as sleek as this stuff."

James pulled the circular a bit closer. "These prices seem even higher than the furniture in our library supply catalogs. Truthfully, we don't really need workstations with bookshelf space, we just need to make a big computer island."

"Like some huge dining room table?" Francis asked, trying to form a picture of what his boss was imagining.

"Exactly, but with holes in the middle for all of the wires and shelves underneath to keep the hard drives off the ground." James paused, chewing on a pretzel. "I may know just the person to construct this for us. Let's figure out some measurements and do a rough drawing. We've got enough money left in our quarterly budget to come up with the cost of labor and supplies for this kind of table. If I can get my friend to agree to build it, we'll be ready to open our Tech Corner in the beginning of June."

The three library employees went back to work. Scott resumed his station at the checkout desk where he assisted a young mother trailing three children, each of whom carried a stack of picture books almost as tall as themselves, while Francis directed a patron to the reference section. As James studied the circular, a slender and pleasantly perfumed hand covered up the photographs of computers, digital cameras, and plasma-screen televisions. James looked up to see Murphy Alistair grinning down at him.

"I just sampled some of that milk and honey hand cream down at the Food Lion," she stated, inhaling deeply. "Nice, huh?"

"Yes." James stashed his snack-sized bag of pretzels under the desk.

"That's not contraband, is it?" Murphy pointed at the desk's surface. "A jelly donut? A jumbo candy bar? A vial of cocaine?"

"No, just boring pretzels. Now, if I dipped them in cocaine, *then* they'd be contraband." James smiled and realized he was flirting with the attractive reporter. "Um . . . did you come to see me about the Witness to Fitness food?"

"Yep. I was hoping to catch you before you headed home. My friend the chemist worked all through her lunch hour and now we've got proof positive. Ronnie has been scamming all of her Witness to Fitness clients." Murphy tapped her notebook with a set of plum-colored nails. "I wanted you to know before the story hits the front page of *The Star* tomorrow morning. I'm expecting our local businesswoman to feel some serious heat by the end of the day."

"Starting with me!" James whispered forcefully. "Ronnie had better be handing out refund checks like water to marathon runners or she's going to feel more than heat. Someone will see this as a chance for legal action."

"You going to sue?" Murphy asked raptly.

"No, not me. I hate all of these civil suits that clog up our court systems. Someone else may go after her, though. I mean, isn't this an open-and-shut case of fraud?"

"That's what my headline says!"

James felt his cheeks growing flush with anger. "I *knew* she was too good to be true. I told everyone . . ." he trailed off, trying to get his emotions in check. "Look, thanks for looking into this, Murphy. I owe you one. I've got to run right now, though. I want to contact my friends about this."

James backed away from the desk.

"Sure thing, Professor. You can just take me out to dinner one night to show me your undying gratitude."

James absently nodded and then went into his office to call the other members of the Flab Five. "Meet me at the library right after work," he told them all. Even when he called Lucy, he refused to divulge any specific information other than to urge her to come into his office as soon as she arrived.

"Does this have something to do with that Murphy woman?" Lucy demanded tersely.

"Yes, but not in the way you think. Please Lucy, just trust me. Can you do that?" James waited on pins and needles for her answer. After all, he had asked her quite a loaded question without meaning to.

Lucy hesitated and then accepted that she would hear a full explanation when she arrived at the library. "I guess I can wait until then. See you after work."

"What's going on, James?" Lindy asked with concern when she arrived shortly after five o'clock. Bennett and Gillian hustled through his office door seconds later with the same question on their lips.

"Just give Lucy a chance to drive over here

and then I'll tell you all at once. Can you browse through some magazines or something in the meantime?"

Bennett shrugged. "All right, but you've got my curiosity as peaked as Megan Flowers's meringue kisses, so Lucy had better be breakin' some speeding laws."

"Oh settle down, Bennett," Gillian admonished. "Take a few moments to center yourself. I know *I've* been dying to get a look at the new *Llewellyn Herbal Almanac.* Maybe I should look up some relaxation herbs for you when I find it."

"No thanks," Bennett pulled a face. "I still remember the taste of that blue lotus tea you made me drink to cheer me up when Virginia Tech lost their bowl game."

Lucy arrived shortly after the other three had settled themselves into reading chairs and were flipping through magazines with all the false concentration of patients in a physician's waiting room. James shepherded his friends all inside his small office and closed the door.

"Sorry to make this seem so dramatic," he began, "but I have some shocking news and I wanted to tell you all before you read about it in tomorrow's newspaper."

"Is something wrong . . . with you, James?" Gillian leaned forward, her pencil-drawn brow creased in concern.

"No, no. It's just that we've all been cheated. Ronnie Levitt has been selling us store-bought frozen entrées since we joined Witness to Fitness." He paused. "Basically, she's made a nice pile off of us and would have continued to do so had Murphy Alistair not taken the meals to a chemist and had them analyzed."

Lindy laughed. "That's it? My God, James, I thought you had some terminal illness or had accepted a job in Alaska and would be moving before the week was out! So, we're out a few pennies, is that all?"

Lucy frowned. "Wait a minute. Just how many pennies are we talking about? None of us are exactly living high enough on the hog to just throw our money away — especially for someone else's profit." She looked at Lindy curiously. "Unless art teachers are suddenly being paid more these days?"

"Nope." Lindy scowled. "Same old measly salary as usual. But how much could Ronnie have tricked me out of? Is it really enough to get all steamed up over?"

James explained the total cost differences.

"Why, that bug-legged, pony-tailed cheat is gonna pay!" Bennett exclaimed. "I put off getting a new satellite dish in order to buy those meals and now you're telling me I could have gotten them at Food Lion for three bucks apiece?"

"Hold on, everyone!" Gillian raised her hands. "We are *all* getting very emotional right now. Let's just take a deep breath." She inflated her chest with air and then let it seep through her lips with a whistle. "We have to remember that we *have* lost weight on this program. Witness to Fitness has not been a complete sham."

"That's true," James said, imitating Gillian's calm tone. "But I'd attribute most of that to our exercise classes. We could have bought these meals ourselves and joined the YMCA for a fraction of what we've been paying Ronnie each week."

The rest of his friends grumbled in agreement.

"What do you think she'll do when the news hits?" Lucy looked at James for an answer. "You're the one who never really trusted her in the first place, so what does your gut instinct tell you her next move will be?"

"Guys, I wish that I had been wrong and that she was exactly what she seemed," James sighed. "Personally, I think Ronnie will deny the whole thing. Cut and run is the approach I see her taking."

"You mean she'll just close up shop?"

Lindy was astonished at the suggestion. "But she's got equipment, a whole investment there."

"What? A radio, two scales, and two cubicles?" Bennett spluttered. "She's leasing the space, so she could just load up her cute little car and start over in another town. Be gone before the ink is dry on *The Star.* Start her moneymaking scam all over again. You've got to realize that she's making this profit off of *all* her clients, not just us suckers."

Lucy sprang out of her chair. "She's not going anywhere with *my* money in her purse! I'm going to confront her right now, *before* the article comes out."

"What? Like, at her house?" Lindy's mouth fell open in surprise.

"Hey, I'm with you, sister." Bennett stood and squared his shoulders as if he were about to sack an unsuspecting quarterback. "Let's drag her down to the nearest ATM machine and get some of our hard-earned cash back."

James hadn't expected such a strong reaction from his friends, but a small part of him relished the idea of seeing Ronnie squirm in the face of their accusations. For once, that superficial smile might be wiped off of her smug face. Gillian was the only person who felt that they should give Ronnie a chance to do the right thing.

"Ronnie might very well refund our money tomorrow evening when we come in for class," she insisted quietly. "How can you all assume the worst of a fellow human being? She made a mistake. Let's give her a chance to correct it."

Gillian's pacifistic attitude gave the rest of them pause.

"You're right about giving her a chance, Gillian," Lindy said, smiling appreciatively at her friend. "However, I still think we should go over to Ronnie's house and talk to her. I think she should know how we all feel and I'd sleep a whole lot easier tonight knowing that she's going to do right by us tomorrow."

"All right then," Gillian stood as well, fluffing out the bottom hem of her black and chartreuse polka-dot blouse. "But we're *not* a lynch mob. We need to approach her with kindness and respect."

"You'd better be our spokesperson then, 'cause I'm not feelin' too kind toward that swindling praying mantis right now," Bennett growled.

"I'll drive," James offered as he locked up his office. "I know where she lives because I had to give her a ride home awhile back.

Plus, my truck can hold all of us."

"Yeah," Bennett made an hourglass figure in the air. "Witness to Fitness has slimmed us down, but not enough to squeeze all five of us into my old mail truck. Lead the way, James. I'm gonna shake the pom-poms right out of that cheerleader's hands."

James pulled into the Cozy Valley Town Homes and struggled to recall which unit belonged to Ronnie. Fortunately, her VW Bug was sitting outside her home. He parked his truck in the street and opened one of the back doors in order to let two of the ladies slide out.

"This place is so cute!" Lindy declared. "I love the replica gaslights and how everyone has flower boxes."

"Except Ronnie's daisies are fake," Lucy scoffed, pointing at the window box perched next to Ronnie's gray front door. "How appropriate."

"Now, friends," Gillian cautioned. "Let's get a feel for the tone we want to set here. Think gentle. Imagine yourselves approaching a scared animal. We need to speak softly and —"

"Carry a big stick," Bennett grunted, pretending to look around on the trim square of lawn for one.

James gazed up at the townhouse. "She may not even be home. Go ahead Gillian. You're our voice of reason."

With a take-charge set to her shoulders, Gillian tugged downward on her shirt and rang the doorbell. A tripping of chimes could be heard from within. They all waited. James pulled nervously at a jagged finger-nail. He disliked confrontation and wanted to get his money back and retreat to the safety of his home as soon as possible. He hated waiting for Ronnie to appear almost as much as he resented being swindled by her. Gillian pressed the doorbell again.

"Figures," Bennett huffed after a full minute had passed. "She's probably out on a leisurely and relaxing fifteen-mile run followed by a few thousand stomach crunches. Then she'll eat a wheat germ and alfalfa sandwich while watching exercise videos."

Gillian peered in the vertical rectangle of glass flanking the front door and said, "She's got to be in there. I see a candle burning on the table inside."

"Can you see anything else?" Lindy asked.

"No. I'll just knock once and then we'll have to assume she's . . . indisposed." Gillian raised her fist and began to pound heavily on the door. She uttered a startled "Oh!" as the door swung noiselessly inward.

"Guess it wasn't closed all the way," Lucy said in a hushed tone and James felt an inexplicable chill tickle the length of his spine.

"Ronnie!" Gillian called gaily. "Yoo hoo! It's some of your clients. We've come to have a dialogue with you." She paused. "Ronnie?"

James stepped onto the stoop and pulled at Gillian's sleeve. "Let's just go. She's obviously not going to come to the door."

Gillian sniffed. "Smells like eucalyptus. What a nice fragrance. Let me just tiptoe in and blow out that candle. If Ronnie's gone out, I don't want her to return to a house made of cinders just because she was careless."

"Why not?" Bennett asked crossly. "Would serve her right."

After casting a long look of reproach at Bennett, Gillian breezed inside while the others watched her progress from the open doorway.

"Uh oh," Gillian hissed back at them as she pointed at the table where the candle burned. "She must have company. There's an empty wine bottle here and two goblets." She gestured wildly toward the stairs. "Who knows what's happening on the second floor?"

"Get out of there!" James whispered urgently, but Gillian was too busy examining something else on the dining room table.

"What are you looking at, woman?" Bennett demanded, craning his neck.

"A plate of cheese." Gillian wore an expression of bewilderment. "It can't be fresh, though. Some of these slices of Gouda and Jarlsberg are hard as a rock. I think Ronnie may not be here after all."

"Or she's wasted and is passed out upstairs," Lucy suggested, the idea clearly pleasing to her. "Remember that she was out *sick* yesterday."

"I'm going to run up and check on her," Gillian announced. "There was a time, back in my wilder days, when I had a few wine coolers too many myself. I just want to make sure she doesn't need any help. I know some splendid natural cures for a hangover."

Before anyone could protest, Gillian began mounting the stairs. Pushed from behind by both Lucy and Lindy, James found himself inside the house, peering up at Gillian's form as she made her way to the top.

A door opened somewhere above their heads. "She's not in the bedroom!" Gillian called down. "But there are more candles aflame up here. They're all burned down pretty low, too." Another door was opened.

Suddenly, they heard a heavy thump.

"Gillian? You okay?" Lindy shouted.

There was no answer.

"Gillian?" Lucy yelled and then began running up the stairs. James, Lindy, and Bennett were right on her heels.

In the small, carpeted hallway, lit by a dim overhead light, they saw Gillian sitting on her bottom, her legs stretched out straight in front of her and her mouth hanging open as if it had come unhinged. Her eyes were glazed. Without turning to her friends or speaking a word, she lifted her right arm and pointed toward the open door across from her.

Following a hair's breadth behind Lucy, James entered into a bathroom. It took his eyes a moment to adjust to the darkness, as the only source of light emitted from half a dozen narrow white candles and they had burned so low that the wicks were smoking. Shadows bounced around the walls. James swept his eyes over the countertop, noting a bottle of Jack Daniels among the candles. It was about a quarter full. He saw a pile of towels stacked neatly by the sink, a toilet at the far end of the room, and a large whirl-pool tub to his right.

James sucked in his breath at the same

time Lucy released a faint cry. Ronnie was in the bathtub, her naked body entirely submerged with the exception of the tip of her nose and her knuckles and toes, which poked over the waterline like small archipelagos of flesh. Her brown hair floated out around her head like a Japanese fan and her open eyes stared up at them from beneath the stagnant water. Her arms hung weightless and her lips were slightly parted. The shapes of her small breasts were barely visible in the darkness and a series of deeper shadows kept her modestly covered from her abdomen to her knees. James couldn't help but notice the small tattoo of a multicolored lizard or salamander that had been carefully inked into the skin above Ronnie's immobile heart. The impression her lifeless body created was that of incredible relaxation, as if at any moment she would blink, or perhaps sit up and scream at them for invading her privacy.

James couldn't tear his gaze away from her sunken face. He could not shake the similarities between Ronnie's death pose and that of the drowned girl in Millais's haunting painting of Ophelia, only Ronnie was not surrounded by flowers but by tired candles and a bottle of nearly empty booze.

"We're too late!" Gillian wailed from the

hallway, breaking the silence. "She's drunk herself to death!"

It was then that James noticed the note taped in the middle of the bathroom mirror. It had been typed on a plain piece of white copier paper.

"What does that say?" Lindy murmured almost inaudibly, pointing at the note.

James leaned toward the paper and read its contents aloud.

To the Authorities,
I am responsible for the Polar Pagoda fire. I started it using whiskey and matches. I wanted Willy's business to fail and now I can't live with myself any longer. I am truly sorry.

After James fell silent, Lucy exhaled a long breath and then turned to the others. "We'd better back on out of here. We don't want to touch anything. Let's go, Gillian."

Bennett and James helped Gillian to her feet. She was trembling with shock. Lucy put an arm around Lindy and ushered her downstairs. The friends settled themselves numbly around Ronnie's kitchen table while Lucy called Sheriff Huckabee.

James examined the tableau before him. As Gillian had mentioned earlier, there was a bottle of wine, an inexpensive California Cabernet sold at most grocery stores, two goblets, a plate of cheese, and a breadbasket filled with an untouched loaf of what appeared to be the kind of miniature French Baguette only made locally by the Sweet Tooth. Lipstick marks ringed the rim of the goblet with a swallow of wine in its bowl while the second goblet, which seemed to be completely full, looked as if it had not even been picked up. James squinted in the light in order to see if fingerprints had marred the surface, but it looked fresh off the drying rack. In fact, there were even little watermarks that showed where Ronnie had missed a few spots in polishing the exterior of the delicate glass.

As Gillian, Lindy, and Bennett sat motionless and unspeaking, Lucy also began to inspect the area. She eyed the contents on the table as closely as James did, and then walked around the kitchen, her arms crossed, as she absorbed every little detail. As the sound of sirens invaded the still air, James met Lucy's eyes. There was a mixture of trepidation and excitement flickering within her blue irises, and James knew that she would have to handle all of the difficult questioning in regard to why the five of them were congregated in a dead woman's kitchen.

He nodded at Lucy as outside, the doors of the patrol cars opened and then slammed shut again. She stood a fraction taller and issued a slight smile for his benefit. "Don't worry," she said softly as she moved alongside James, "this will be a good test for me. If I pass, I'll know that I'm ready to get out from behind my desk." She gazed toward the front door. "Then *I'll* be the one responding to calls for help."

# THIRTEEN:
# KENTUCKY
# CHOCOLATE-CHIP PIE

Serving Size:
1 slice · 5 oz.

**Witness to Fitness
Points**

16

"I should have known you'd be here,"
Deputy Donovan snarled at Lucy as he
burst through the doorway, his gun drawn
and his body poised in an aggressive stance.
"You've always got to be in the thick of

things, don't ya?" He puffed up his cheeks in a childish attempt to impersonate a heavy person.

"Holster your gun, Keith. There are no assailants present," Lucy replied in a dismissive tone. "But you do look kind of cute when you puff your face out like that. I think I saw a similar mating technique on one of those Mutual of Omaha wildlife shows the other night. Yes . . . that's it!" she snapped her fingers together. "At first I thought it was the special on bullfrogs, but now I remember. It was a special on baboons," she lowered her voice, "and how they attracted females by drawing attention to their bright red asses!"

The freckles on Donovan's face merged into a crimson mass. Just as he was about to launch a full-fledged verbal assault on his co-worker, Sheriff Huckabee and Deputy Truett marched over the threshold.

"Evening, Lucy," the sheriff said as he glanced around the entranceway and into the front room of Ronnie's home. "You always seem to be callin' me away from a good meal. The missus made beef brisket tonight. It was as tender as a groom on his weddin' night." He frowned. "It'll never reheat as good. Never does. Now, you say we got a dead woman upstairs in the tub?"

"Yes, sir." Lucy immediately switched on a professional demeanor, completely ignoring Donovan as he rudely brushed by her and bounded up the stairs. "It looks like she had a good deal to drink and maybe drowned in the bath. There's a suicide note as well. None of us have touched a thing."

"Except for the cheese!" Gillian piped up from the other room. "I squished a piece or two to see if it was fresh."

Huckabee moved deeper into the front room and took in the foursome seated at Ronnie's table. "I can't for the life of me imagine what kind of party you've got going on here, Lucy. Why don't you tell me the whole story while we take a look-see at the scene?"

"It would be my pleasure, sir." Lucy began talking rapidly until her voice became muffled to the others waiting anxiously in the kitchen. After what seemed like an interminable amount of time, the two deputies returned from upstairs and began taking statements from them on an individual basis.

James was relieved that Glenn Truett was interviewing him. Truett seemed like a simple soul whose main purpose was to get his job done so that he could spend his time on other pursuits. Lucy had mentioned that he was an avid fisherman as well as an obsessive NASCAR fan. Truett jotted down a few disinterested notes based on the story James told, and then told him to swing by the station the next day in order to sign an official statement about the evening's events. Free to leave, James waited for Lucy and the others by his truck, but Lindy informed him that although Lucy was staying put, the rest of them were more than ready to go home.

"Here comes the coroner," Bennett noted as a small man carrying a toolbox in one hand and an old-fashioned, leather physician's bag in the other nodded politely in their direction.

"Well, you don't have to watch too many episodes of *CSI* to be able to make a ruling in this case," Lindy said as she issued the man a quick wave.

"Oh," Gillian moaned from the back seat. "I feel so *contaminated* from being in that house. I can't wait to put my feet up and sip some Lemon Myrtle leaf tea. You are all welcome to join me recover if you'd like."

"Thanks for the offer," James answered as they drove away from Ronnie's townhouse, now ablaze with light as a troop of uniformed figures moved about within. "But I think my recovery is only going to be helped

272

along by raiding my father's supply of Cutty Sark."

Lucy became so involved with work that James barely heard from her. She sent out a brief e-mail to the supper club members in order to inform them that drowning had indeed caused Ronnie's death, but that the coroner refused to label the cause of death as suicide. The astute man noticed that there were some suspicious bruises around Ronnie's ankles, implying that someone may have forced her head under the surface of the water by holding her forcefully by the feet until the oxygen in her lungs was replaced by tepid bath water.

"Her blood alcohol levels were through the roof," Lucy told James during a short phone call Thursday night. "She may have barely been conscious when she was drowned."

"It's a murder case, then?" James asked, both horrified and intrigued by the news.

"Oh yes." Lucy was in her element. "The whole townhouse had been wiped clean of prints. What's more is that bottle of Jack Daniels we saw in her bathroom had a familiar-looking residue inside."

"As in the bottle found at the Polar Pagoda fire?"

"Exactly! It's been sent to the lab for analysis, but I'd bet five bucks that the residue was left from crushed-up Valium tablets."

James felt his mind spinning. "But does that mean Ronnie actually *did* set that fire, like her note says, or did her killer start it? After all, I still don't believe she had any reason to put Willy out of business."

"I know." Lucy sighed into the receiver and then perked up again. "Another thing is, that note didn't *sound* like her. It was so flat, so . . ."

"Without personality?" James suggested.

"Yes! If Ronnie were to leave a suicide note, I could see it on cute stationery with a lot of exclamation marks, you know?" James heard a click and knew that Lucy was receiving an incoming call. "I'd better go, James. Can you fill in the others for me?"

James initiated the supper club phone tree by calling Lindy. Witness to Fitness was shut up tight on Wednesday with a sign taped to the front door that the business would be closed until further notice. James checked out a low-fat cookbook from the library and decided to create his own menus until Phoebe and Dylan were finished sorting out what would become of Ronnie's business. Murphy's headline in *The Star* about the

274

fraudulent meals was instantly forgotten after it was replaced the next day by the news of the death of the popular Witness to Fitness proprietor. Murphy had left James several messages to call her, but so far he had avoided talking to her directly about the case. He felt that if anyone should receive any limelight over the incident, it should be Lucy.

Lindy picked up on the first ring. James invited her to his house for their Sunday supper club meeting and then gave her an update on the investigation into Ronnie's death.

"Wow! Murder!" Lindy breathed excitedly. "Here I thought the case of the fire was all wrapped up with Ronnie's suicide. Now, we're just as confused about that as before. We've got two victims and no suspects. Looks like we make some mighty pitiful detectives." She paused. "I know this is totally off the subject, but what are you going to cook on Sunday since we don't seem to be full members of the Witness to Fitness program at the moment?"

James explained his plan and then asked Lindy to forward all of the information on to Gillian. Just as he was settling down in a recliner to finish the final chapter of the latest Michael Crichton novel, the phone rang and Bennett, sounding uncharacteristically unsettled, asked James to meet him at the Woodrow Wilson Tavern, the town's only bar.

"Now?" James frowned as he gazed longingly at his book and at his feet ensconced in his raggedy slippers.

"I need your advice, man."

"I'll be right there."

Bennett slid a mug filled with blonde beer in front of James as soon as he was seated on one of the Tavern's red leather-covered barstools.

"What are we drinking?" James asked, picking up the heavy mug and eyeing the generous head of foam appreciatively.

"Presidential Ale Light. Our faithful bartender Sammy bought it from a brewery in Staunton."

James caught the bartender's eye and raised his glass. "Here's to President Wilson."

"To Wilson." Sammy raised his own glass and took a sip. Froth dotted his gray mustache and he gave it a satisfied wipe with the hem of his apron. As always, Sammy wore a "Made in the U.S.A." baseball cap and his sideburns were as thick and unruly as a rock star's. Sammy fancied himself a dead ringer for the famous Southern Civil War hero General Joseph Johnston and styled his facial hair so that it mirrored some of the black and white photographs of Johnston decorating the walls of Wilson's Tavern. Sammy was a lover of Virginia history and he knew more about the Old Dominion than anyone James had ever met. The Tavern was located on a side road off the highway and was never short of groups of husbands avoiding wives, truckers seeking a respite from the long road, or friends coming together to relax over a cold beer.

Bennett cracked open one of the whole peanuts from the bowl in front of him and plucked the nut from its shell. "I've got a professional dilemma, James. As one of the supervisors at the post office, I am the man lucky enough to have to deal with all the customer complaints." He popped the peanut in his mouth and shrugged. "Usually, they're about nothin'. Mail got delivered to the wrong Mr. Jones, the protective wrapper on some guys nudie magazine is missin', one of our mail carriers looked sideways at some lady's prize pooch — that kind of thing."

As Bennett paused, James drank some of his beer. It was rich and honey-smooth on his tongue and for a few seconds as he swished it around inside his mouth, he was able to ignore the tension in Bennett's hands as his friend roughly cracked open another peanut shell.

"Anyway," Bennett continued, "I got a complaint on Monday that I normally wouldn't give a flyin' fiddle about, but since Gillian called me this evening and told me that Ronnie's death wasn't really a suicide . . ." Bennett shoved several peanuts into his mouth and stared at the counter with a pair of tormented brown eyes.

"You think this complaint might be tied to the murder, but you want to protect an employee?" James guessed.

Bennett nodded his head. "Pretty much, yeah. See, it's about Carter and how he's been hanging around Ronnie's place like a tomcat on the prowl. She is . . . or was, on his route, but the boy even switched his delivery times around so he could see her when she came home for lunch every day. I hear from the mailroom gossips that our fool man has even followed her around town, but that was off the clock and thereby none of my damned business."

"So who called in with the grievance?"

"That's the thing." Bennett tugged on his moustache. "Ronnie did. On Monday, right after lunch."

"Did you talk to her then?" James couldn't restrain himself and he gripped Bennett's shoulder with a firm hand. "That might be the last time anyone heard from her . . . alive."

"Don't I know it? But I didn't talk to her. She left a message on our voicemail and I hadn't even listened to it until yesterday. One of the sorters called in sick and I had to lend a hand. But look, there's no way Carter is some crazy killer. He just had it bad for that woman. If I tell the sheriff, the Lord only knows what's gonna happen to that boy."

James took a silent pull of beer as Bennett finished his mug in three swallows and signaled Sammy for a refill. "You're going to have to share that information, Bennett. I know you're worried about Carter. I feel the same way about the Fitzgerald twins, but if Carter's innocent, then it'll all come out just fine and he'll understand why you had to report Ronnie's call. It's better for the authorities to find out now, in an up-front manner, than if they discover Carter had been stalking a murder victim on their own."

"See?" Bennett looked hurt. "You're already throwin' harsh words around like 'stalk' and 'murder victim.' And that's just you! What chance does Carter stand against that red-headed pig Donovan?"

"I'm sorry. I didn't mean to imply anything." James cleared his throat and added hesitantly, "But you *do* have to wonder about why Carter didn't just go up and talk to Ronnie. Why not ask her out on a date like regular people do?"

Bennett spluttered in his beer. "I don't know how things were for you back in Williamsburg, but it's not exactly easy! I can't even remember the last time that I had the nerve to ask a pretty lady out on a date. Shoot, Ditka was probably still coaching the Bears. It's hard, man. Carter's just shy."

James nodded. "Then that's what the sheriff will discover as well. He's a good sheriff, Bennett. Have Carter come with you when you go to explain about Ronnie's voicemail. His cooperation will make a strong statement about his innocence."

For the first time since James had entered the Tavern, Bennett look marginally less worried. "Yeah, that's a good plan, my friend. I'll tell Carter all about the call first thing in the morning, then at lunchtime, we'll head on over to the Sheriff's Department and get this whole mess straightened out. Thanks, man." He managed a slight smile. "I knew you'd know what to do."

"Don't worry about it. Listen, you guys will probably be back delivering mail before your lunch break is over," James proclaimed, raising his newly filled glass against Bennett's in salute.

He was dead wrong.

"I'm not going to be able to make the movie, James," Lucy spoke into the phone in a crestfallen voice. James had just been preparing to leave the library that Friday afternoon when she called. "Bennett and Carter came in at noon today with some new information about Ronnie and I can't leave until I know what's going on."

"They're still at the station?" James asked incredulously.

"Just Carter. Bennett was told to leave. He looked awful." She paused, undoubtedly wondering why James seemed unsurprised by her news. "Do you know what this is about?"

James quickly recapped his conversation with Bennett at Wilson's Tavern. "I feel horrible, Lucy. I told Bennett that it would be a walk in the park as long as he and Carter were forthcoming about that voicemail message! Has Carter been officially arrested?" He heard his voice rising along with his stress level.

"No, not yet, but he's been questioned all afternoon. Donovan's having the time of his life. I can hear him shouting all the way down the hall."

James moaned.

"But maybe Carter *is* a reasonable suspect, James. The guy was obviously fixated on Ronnie. They say it doesn't take too much for a romantic obsession to turn into something darker. Maybe he didn't want to be rejected or he just didn't want anyone else to be with Ronnie."

"No one wants to be rejected, Lucy, but that doesn't mean they go around drugging and drowning the object of their desire, either!" He heard the shrillness in his voice and immediately calmed down. "Sorry, I didn't mean to yell. I just feel terrible for Bennett."

"I understand. I'm not saying Carter is guilty, either, but I do want to stick around to see what develops. I feel like I owe it to Bennett to keep an eye on Carter. Can we meet at Dolly's later for dinner?"

James thought back to his last meeting with Lucy at Dolly's. "Dinner, yes, but not at Dolly's. Let's go to that restaurant off the interstate instead. I forget the name. It has something to do with a farm."

"The Red Barn? The place with the buffet

filled with homemade Southern cooking? Mm, mm, you're on!" James heard men's voices in the background. "Oh, here they come with Carter. I'll catch you later," Lucy said hurriedly and slammed down the phone.

By the time they met at the Red Barn, dinner service was long over and only a few night owls were having cups of coffee as the waitresses wiped down the tables and dissembled the buffet. James and Lucy also ordered coffee and were given a piece of Kentucky chocolate-chip pie on the house.

"Y'all are here at the right time," their waitress said, plucking down two forks. "We bake fresh desserts every mornin' so we give away all the leftovers right about now. Thing is, we've been selling outta this here pie ever since the Derby. Can't believe there's any left. Guess folks are finally sick of it." She lowered her voice. "It's a damn fine pie, but I'm sure lookin' forward to gettin' back to our regular chocolate chess."

James and Lucy savored every bite of pie — each one a pleasant mixture of crunchy walnut pieces, soft semisweet morsels, and creamy chocolate. The crust was clearly homemade and had been baked a buttery, golden brown. It tasted more like a shortbread cookie than the customary piece of crinkled, bland dough.

"It's almost good enough to make me forget about today," Lucy said, licking some whipped cream from her fork tines.

James pushed his plate away a few inches, trying not to finish his entire piece. "So was Carter released?"

"Yes, finally. The coroner's report detailed that Ronnie's death occurred sometime between six and eleven p.m. on Monday night. Carter had a pretty firm alibi. He had dinner at Dolly's Diner and then went back to Clint's house while Dolly closed up. Carter and Clint have apparently become good friends. They both have this thing for *America's Most Wanted* and Court TV. The two of them split a six-pack and hung out until almost midnight. Carter provided a ton of details about the shows they watched as well as all the highlights of the Orioles-Red Sox game."

"There was a game last night?"

Lucy also pushed her plate away after dabbing at the last crumb with her index finger. "Apparently it was a makeup game for Sunday night's rain delay. Clint was switching to the game during commercials and Carter can practically give a play-by-play of the parts of it they watched. Huckabee was pretty convinced, though he had to give

Carter the don't-leave-town speech before letting him go."

"Thank goodness," James sighed in relief. "Maybe Bennett will speak to me again after all."

"You gave him good advice, James." She put her hand over his. "Your heart is always in the right place." Lucy smiled and then tried to hide her mouth as the smile merged into an enormous yawn. "I've got to go into work early tomorrow. The sheriff is going to let me go through some of the personal items they found at Ronnie's townhouse. It's a great chance for me to shine." She yawned again. "*If* I can find a decent clue about her killer."

"I'd better get you home," James said and paid their bill. He drove a groggy Lucy to her front door and kissed her chastely on the cheek. "Get some sleep. I'll see you Sunday."

The weekend flew by for James. On Saturday, he called over to Willy's house to ask if he would be willing to build him a computer table for the library.

"I'm right busy with Pet Palace projects, Professor," Willy answered. "But I'd be happy to build your library the finest computer table anyone had ever seen. After all, you and your friends welcomed me to this town straight off. Without Ms. Gillian, I'd be on the unemployment line by now."

"You're a true Renaissance man, Willy. You can run a business, keep the books, and you're a skilled carpenter. Gillian says you could assemble Noah's ark out of a pile of toothpicks *and* make it watertight."

Willy laughed. "She's too much!" He paused. "I am a grateful man, that's for sure, but I do miss dishin' out my custard. I love to see the faces on folks when they're eatin' my sweets and just lettin' all their cares drift away like feathers in the breeze. Not much company out here in this garage."

James felt tremendously guilty. It had been weeks since the fire and not once had he called to check on Willy. "How would you like to join our supper club for dinner tomorrow night?" he asked, confident that the others would approve.

"It'd be my pleasure." Willy sounded grateful to have been included. "Now, I'm going to head off to the library to take some measurements. You say you got some drawings for me, too?"

James told him that a rough sketch was behind the checkout counter and that Mrs. Waxman would give him any assistance he needed.

"See you Sunday," Willy said cheerfully and rang off.

After leafing through the pages of several cookbooks, James decided to make lemon chicken with lima beans for Sunday's dinner. He created an alphabetical grocery list and headed out to the Sweet Tooth in hopes of avoiding the early lunch crowd and scoring one of the prized parking spaces on Main Street.

James spent a few moments admiring Megan's new window display, which showed oversized butter cookies in the shapes of flowers, including pink and purple tulips, white and yellow daisies, and orange tiger lilies. Inside, the bakery was busy, especially for in between mealtimes. Megan and Amelia were both working and James recognized several of his fellow dieters from Witness to Fitness. Their purchases ranged from bran muffins, to more decadent hotcrossed buns, to downright sinful cannolis.

"Professor!" Megan greeted him warmly after handing a customer a loaded paper bag. "What can I do for you today?"

James selected a loaf of Italian bread for Sunday's dinner and bought a loaf of raisin bread for his father. As he examined the bread, he noticed the small French baguettes on display in a wire basket.

"Are you the only local baker who makes that kind of bread, Megan?"

"Sure am. Most stores sell the long loaves but that's too much bread for anyone's family unless they're all coming over for Sunday supper. Still, folks just buy more of the smaller ones from me even in that case. I think my crust is flakier than the grocery store bread."

"Did Ronnie Levitt buy one from you on Monday?" James asked in a low voice.

Megan frowned. "We're closed Mondays and Amelia worked the Sunday afternoon shift. You'll have to ask her." Megan's frown deepened into a look of concern. "Wait a minute. Does my bread have something to do with . . . with . . ."

"Oh no," James hastily assured her. "But if Ronnie bought it then whoever came to her house for a meal didn't. I just thought I'd find out. Chase down a lead, you know, as a favor to Lucy."

Megan nodded. The whole town knew about Lucy's longing to become a genuine deputy. After filling James's order, Megan whispered in her daughter's ear as Amelia carefully packed a cardboard box with frosted carrot cake muffins. Amelia mumbled something inaudible to her mother and then returned her attention to her customer.

"It was Ronnie," Megan said to James sotto voce. "She bought the bread at about three o'clock on Sunday. Sorry we couldn't help you more than that. After all, your Spring Fling combined with the whole scandal about those diet meals has brought *us* back to life." She put her hand to her mouth. "Oh, that came out wrong. I mean, I feel terrible about what happened to Ronnie and I wish I hadn't said anything negative about her. I'm just grateful to have customers passing through my doorway again."

"You didn't say anything bad about her personally, Megan. You were just worried about your business and your daughter's welfare. That's nothing to be ashamed of."

Megan nodded gratefully and handed James his bag. "I snuck a treat in there for you — one of our Raspberry Cheese Danishes. Have a nice day!"

On Sunday afternoon following church service and then a light lunch comprised of tuna salad, some crackers, and a juicy peach, James straightened up the backyard. He mowed the lawn and then planted tiki torches in the ground around the picnic table in order to create a more festive atmosphere. Jackson was decked out in his painting overalls, but instead of being holed up in his shed working on a bird still life, he was covering the kitchen walls with a warm, milky coffee-colored hue.

"I love this shade, Pop. What gave you the idea to paint the kitchen this color?"

Jackson jerked his thumb at an old *Southern Living* magazine. "Your mama had a page turned down in there. Told me it was her dream kitchen. I've tried to match everything to those pictures."

James picked up the dog-eared magazine and immediately found the page illustrating his mother's fantasy kitchen. Jackson had reproduced it almost exactly, right down to the stainless steel appliances, the terra-cotta tile flooring, and the vintage-style light fixtures. Now, he was completing the final touches by painting the room the precise color as the kitchen displayed in the glossy photographs. James stared at the magazine, trying hard to hold back tears. He hadn't realized how much his father had loved his mother, or how much he still missed her. Their new kitchen was a masterpiece, created in memory of a woman for whom one of life's great joys was cooking wonderful food for the two men she loved.

"Don't you have something to do with

your time?" Jackson growled, sensing the mood that had overtaken his son.

James laid the magazine back down, avoiding his father's sharp gaze. "I'm going to the garden center to get some pots of petunias. Be right back."

The lines at the garden center were long, however, and after James struggled to maneuver his loaded wheelbarrow around clusters of animated gardeners to the register, load up the truck, and return home, he barely had enough time to arrange the violet and fuchsia blooms around the Henrys' cracked cement patio before Lucy's Jeep appeared in the driveway.

"Boy," she began breathlessly, "have I been working like crazy! Sheriff Huckabee brought me two huge boxes filled with Ronnie's personal effects. There wasn't much that seemed personal about her life, though. No diplomas, letters, yearbooks, scrapbooks — just financial records and receipts and boring stuff like that. I *did* bring over two photographs, hoping that someone in our club might be able to identify the locations where they were taken." She paused, taking in the picnic table with the checkered cloth, the lit tiki torches, and the containers of vibrant flowers. "This is really nice, James."

"Hello!" Gillian waved the tail of a long,

gauzy, orange scarf in greeting as she and Lindy walked up the driveway. "We rang the front bell but no one answered . . . Oh, an outdoor dinner! How *wonderful.* We can dine under a tent of stars tonight."

Lindy peered up into the thick canopy of trees and smiled. "I don't know. We all eat so fast that it might not get dark enough to see any stars. Why, hello Willy!"

"Howdy all." Willy hugged the three women and handed James a bottle of sparkling cider. "You've got a mighty fine place here."

"Renovations still going on?" Bennett called out, appearing around the corner of the house. "That why we're roughing it tonight?"

James grinned. "Actually, the kitchen is so incredible that I was afraid to soil it making one of my humble meals. Make yourselves comfortable and I'll show you how it turned out after dinner." By that time he was hoping Jackson would be upstairs instead of holed up in the den, poised for flight like a caged hawk.

As James stepped inside to collect the pitcher of sun tea that he had let brew throughout the course of the day, he stuck his head into the den where his father was chewing on a bologna and cheese sandwich while watching the evening news. "You sure you won't come outside with us, Pop?"

Jackson eyed the doorway suspiciously. "I gotta keep current. Now, go on and shut that door and visit with your friends."

Gathering a wooden tray, the tea pitcher, and some drink glasses bearing faded designs of lemons and limes that the Henrys had used since James was a boy, he rejoined his friends as they poured over the two photographs Lucy had laid out on the picnic table.

"Is that Ronnie?" he asked in shock, pointing at the tall, strong-looking woman with glasses and a baseball hat. The thick bangs of her boyish haircut practically fell over the heavy frames of her round glasses. She wore a Red Cross vest over a dirty white T-shirt and a pair of loose-fitting walking shorts. She carried what appeared to be a Red Cross donation box and her face bore an expression of triumph. Her mouth had curved into a smile that displayed all of her teeth but became more threatening than appealing the longer James stared at it.

"I know it doesn't look like the Ronnie we knew," Lucy said. "She's not so bony here and she's got a different hairstyle, but it's her. The question is *where* is she?"

"That's easy." Bennett pointed at the

building in the background. "That's the Astrodome in Houston. Those blurred red, yellow, and orange seats in the background are in the upper section of the ballpark."

Lucy squinted at the photo. "Good to have a sports nut in the mix. Thanks, Bennett."

"And *I* can tell you where that second picture is taken." Lindy held her hand over her ample bosom. "My family would be sorely disappointed if I couldn't, considering I have about twenty cousins who live right there. See that art deco building off to the left? That's a hotel in South Beach. Some of my mother's family lives in an apartment across the street."

"Miami?" Lucy asked.

Gillian took hold of the photograph. "My, my. Ronnie is really young in this shot. She looks like an all-American girl."

James leaned over Gillian's shoulder and examined the image of Ronnie in her early to mid-twenties. She was lounging on a low wall next to a blooming bush of cherry-red hibiscus and seemed to be soaking up the sun like a tropical lizard. Her light brown hair was streaked with blonde and fell in soft waves almost to her waist. She wore spectacles with wire-thin silver frames, a blue sundress, a pair of white Keds, and very little makeup. Her eyes were replete with optimism and her lips curved into a modest smile.

"She looks like a completely different person in each of these shots," James observed.

"And totally different from the Ronnie we knew," Lindy added with surprise.

"May I?" Willy held out his hand from where he had been sitting quietly at the end of the picnic table.

"Of course, sorry." Lucy slid the photos in front of him. "I've just been dying to figure out where these were taken. I was hoping they'd shed some light on Ronnie's past, but no bells are going off in my head."

Willy examined the shot of young Ronnie and then pushed it aside. When he picked up the photo of her posing at the Astrodome he drew in a sharp breath.

"Well, I'll be damned," he muttered darkly.

"What is it, Willy?"

"I've seen this woman. On TV." Willy fell quiet.

James felt a prickle on the back of his neck. "That's what Pete said. That he thought he remembered Ronnie from TV."

"But in what context?" Lucy grabbed Willy's hand excitedly. "Does it have to do with this photo, Willy?"

"Hell yes it does." Willy exhaled heavily. "This picture was taken when all those poor folks that had gotten beaten up by Katrina were refugees in the Astrodome. Ronnie pretended to be collecting money on behalf of the Red Cross."

Gillian was horrified. "Pretended?"

Willy nodded sorrowfully. "So many folks showed their generosity of spirit durin' that awful time, but the snakes came out of the grass as well. Ronnie was one of the lowest of those snakes. She collected money for days from the volunteers that had come from all over our nation to help, from the fine people of Houston, and from any givin' soul who would drop a dollar in her box. Then she ran off with every dime."

"What a terrible creature!" Gillian exclaimed.

"Well, she was caught." Willy's eyes gleamed. "Not all of the scoundrels were, but she was. She got jail time for it, too. Her story was all over the news for nights on end. I think the media used her case to show other thieves and sneaks that people were now wise to their kind."

The group was silent for a few minutes and then Lucy sat down and cradled her head with her hands. "This doesn't help me narrow down a list of suspects. It's as long as a country mile. People would take a number like they were at the deli counter in Food Lion to get revenge on such a piece of scum. To take advantage of such a tragic situation . . ."

James felt himself unintentionally staring at Willy, along with the rest of his friends.

"Don't look at me!" Willy threw his hands into the air. "I haven't got a violent bone in my body. Besides, I didn't even recognize that wretched woman until I saw this here picture."

"We know you're no killer, Willy." A deflated Lucy reclaimed the two photos. "But Pete was able to identify her and someone else from her past did, too. But how am *I* going to figure out who?"

"It might help if you knew her real name," Willy suggested. " 'Cause when she got arrested she was no Veronica Levitt. I'm sorry I can't recall what she went by then."

"Hey, no problem. She's a bona fide criminal, so I know *exactly* who would remember her name," Bennett declared.

"Who?" They all asked in unison.

"Mr. Court TV," Bennett stated. "A.k.a. Carter Peabody."

# FOURTEEN:
# STRAWBERRY BANANA
# SMOOTHIE

| |
|---|
| **Serving Size:** 16 fl. oz. |
| **Witness to Fitness Points** |

Lucy was waiting for Carter outside the post office with the photograph of Ronnie in Houston clenched in her hand. Bennett had called his co-worker the night before to warn him that a member of the Sheriff's

298

Department wanted to speak to him before his shift started.

Carter was startlingly unfazed by his long afternoon of intense questioning the previous Friday and cheerfully told Lucy he had spent the weekend creating an outline for a screenplay he planned to write from the point of view of a postal worker turned bank robber. He told her he was actually grateful to have gained firsthand knowledge about the interviewing process and would love to be included in any investigation led by the Sheriff's Department.

Lucy refrained from telling Carter that he had a screw loose and showed him the photograph instead. He squinted at it for a few moments and then snapped his fingers and jabbed at the visage of Red Cross Ronnie.

"I remember hearing about her from one of the members of an online chat room from the America's Notorious Criminals website. I *knew* she was a woman with a criminal past." His face glowed. "I believe I have a genuine knack for tracking down felons. Anyway, her name when this photo was taken was Martha Hari. I think Ronnie picked it 'cause it sounded so much like Mata Hari, the famous spy."

Lucy's blue eyes narrowed. "What do you

mean 'picked it'?"

"Oh, come on!" Carter gaped. "It's gotta be an alias. No one's born with a name like that!"

"Well, we've got her prints and there'll be a criminal record under the name of Martha Hari." Lucy slid the photograph into her purse. "Maybe her true identity will show up on the NCIC database."

Carter almost began drooling. "You're going to do a search through the National Crime Information Center? Can I watch?"

"No!" Lucy barked and then immediately relented. After all, she would probably need to "borrow" one of the deputy's passwords just to access the database, so in some ways, she was no different from Carter. They were both amateurs looking to get a more legitimate taste of the law enforcement pie. "Listen Carter," she continued more gently. "I know exactly how you feel. *I'm* trying to solve this crime so that I can prove to myself and to my boss that I'm ready to take the written test and become a deputy." Her eyes grew glassy. "I might even be ready to take the physical this summer." Noticing the time, she shook off her reverie, pumped Carter's hand in gratitude, and then hurried off.

■ ■ ■ ■

Lucy replayed her conversation with Carter late Wednesday afternoon as she and James sat drinking smoothies. They were actually having their snack at one of the plastic tables set up outside of a large gas station, part of which served as a sandwich shop. While lacking curb appeal, the convenience store served the best grilled sandwiches and fruit smoothies within hundreds of miles.

"And what did you find out about Ronnie's past?" James asked, while taking a generous slurp of his strawberry banana smoothie. "Or should I call her Martha?"

Lucy stirred her orange crème smoothie and looked dejected. "Not much. She served less than a year out of a three-year sentence for her Katrina scam. Another case of overcrowding in our country's correctional facilities. She had also been brought up on charges of fraud in the state of Florida, when she was only eighteen, but her case was dismissed due to lack of evidence."

"Was her name Martha then?"

"No. Trudy Axelrod. That's actually her real name. Her birth certificate and social security number are both under that name.

301

I'm sure she has a whole slew of fake driver's licenses and other documents, but it looks like she was born in Coral Springs, Florida."

"What was the Florida fraud charge about?"

"Some kind of telemarketing fraud in relation to a phony investment. The legal terms were pretty confusing, as always, but Trudy claimed to be raising money to build a new senior center and casino south of Fort Lauderdale. The case fell apart because no one could link Ron . . . Trudy to the post office box where checks were sent or to the actual phone calls."

James angled his straw so that it could capture the last drop of red liquid in his cup. "She probably used a pay phone to make the calls. You know, there *is* research saying that the majority of the elderly are too polite to hang up on telemarketers. They are more susceptible to scams than the rest of the population." He laughed. "The experts should come do a study on my father! I don't think we've had a single repeat solicitation after Pop's gotten through with the poor fool who dared to try to sell him something."

Lucy offered up a weak smile. "Anyhow, at least the sheriff was impressed that I was able to discover more facts about our victim (all thanks to our Sunday night meeting), but as it stands, her killer has outsmarted our entire department."

"Why don't we go out and visit Mr. Wimple on Saturday?" James suggested, hoping to distract Lucy before she became too gloomy. "Someone donated the two latest David McCullough books in pristine condition and I thought, as a former history teacher, he'd enjoy reading them. At least it would take your mind off the case for a bit."

"That's a great idea, James. I'm sure he'd love to have the company and maybe he's remembered something else that would help tie Ronnie and Pete together. Have you called him yet?"

"No. Those McCullough books just came in this morning."

"Well, let me at least do that much. After we visit Fred at Wandering Springs, maybe we could go out for that movie I owe you."

"Sounds like a date," James replied, pleased that his idea had restored Lucy's good spirits.

It was difficult to ignore Lucy's nervous energy as she and James drove out to Harrisonburg. She rapped her fingernails on the passenger window, crossed and uncrossed her legs, and continuously changed the radio stations.

"You seem a bit edgy, Lucy. Have you got something on your mind?"

Lucy cast him an enigmatic grin. "Kind of. You'll find out soon enough what it is, but I just want to say how glad I am that you're with me today."

"Huh?" James was befuddled, but Lucy ignored his confusion and began to sing along with a popular song by country superstar Faith Hill. When she was finished crooning, Lucy asked James question upon question about his life in Williamsburg until he pulled his truck into the visitor's lot of Wandering Springs.

Fred Wimple was waiting for their arrival in the same chair on the sun porch where they had conversed with him during their previous visit. This time, he rose a bit shakily to his feet and greeted them eagerly. After thanking James profusely for the books, he turned to Lucy, his filmy eyes gleaming with the animation of intrigue.

"I investigated both of your requests," he announced as they took their seats in wicker chairs. "You were correct on both counts, young lady." He then brandished a cell phone. "Now, I borrowed this from one of my friends. I haven't had too much experience with one of these things, but I can call the right people if I need to. You just give me the signal and help will be on its way."

Lucy nodded. "That's an excellent idea, Fred, thank you. Shall we have some of that famous limeade while we're waiting?"

"Absolutely." Fred winked at his guests and raised a wrinkled hand into the air. As if by magic, a young woman appeared and took their order. "I'll bring y'all some Thin Mints, too." She smoothed down her stark white apron. "We had to buy so many Girl Scout cookies this year that we'll never get rid of them if we don't hand them out at every opportunity. Be right back."

"Would someone care to tell me what is going on?" James demanded quietly in what he believed was a tone of virtuous patience.

Lucy cast her eyes around the sun porch and lowered her voice so that the pair of elderly women who sat in matching rockers on the opposite end of the veranda would not be able to listen in. James doubted that they could hear anything above the sound of their own voices and the steady clicking of their knitting needles, but he leaned closer to Lucy so that she could keep her voice scarcely above a whisper.

"After you suggested coming to see our friend Fred, I started thinking about our last visit to Wandering Springs. At first, I was just longing for another glass of that delicious limeade." She paused as the drink she had fantasized about was placed before her on a linen napkin. Once a loaded plate of cookies had been deposited in the middle of the table and their server disappeared inside as silently as she had arrived, Lucy continued. "But then I began to suspect that the answers to all of our riddles lay within these walls, so to speak. With a little help from Fred here and your friend Murphy, I was able to confirm my suspicions."

"What suspicions? Can you *please* stop being so vague?" James begged and then crossly bit into a Thin Mint.

"Okay, okay! Sorry, I'm just having a good time now that I finally know the answers." Lucy helped herself to a cookie. "Do you remember the man Dylan was with when we were here before?"

"The one in the wheelchair who seemed to be suffering from Alzheimer's?" James asked by way of reply.

"Yes. That man is Dylan's father," Fred declared importantly.

James sat back in his chair, trying to figure out how that simple fact had any bearing on either of the two murders. "I don't get it. How does that secret being revealed connect to anything else?"

Lucy grabbed onto James's hand and squeezed. "Mr. Shane told us that Dylan was the best point guard in all of Miami. Remember? Who else spent time in Miami, James?"

"Ronnie. When she was in her twenties. So?" James absently rubbed Lucy's palm. "I still need more information."

"That's where Murphy helped me out." Lucy took a long swallow of limeade. "She researched any news stories related to the Shanes of Miami and discovered two terrible things. The first was that Mrs. Shane, Dylan's mama, died of uterine cancer. The second is that the person hired to nurse Mrs. Shane in their home, stayed on with the family after the mother's death. Somehow, this nurse managed to run off with the family savings and was never heard from again."

James felt the pieces of the puzzle come together. "Was the nurse's name Trudy Axelrod?"

"Actually, no. It was Stacy Weeks." Lucy shrugged. "And neither I nor Murphy could find out anything about this Stacy. It was as if she never existed as far as the databases containing Floridian records are concerned."

"But if we're assuming Ronnie or whoever she was back then was that nurse, Dylan would have only been a boy when he knew her. I'd say she was in her mid-twenties when that photo was taken."

Lucy popped half a cookie in her mouth. "That's true. Dylan would have been in high school. Still, I have more proof to tie him to the murders."

Fred cleared his throat and looked around. "That's where I came in. Miss Hanover phoned and filled me in on the latest murder. She then asked me about Mr. Shane. Once I had confirmed his identity, this astute young lady requested that I do something highly irregular. Basically, she required that I become a snoop."

Fred abruptly stopped speaking as another elderly gentleman wearing a white and green argyle sweater vest over a pink golf shirt settled himself into a nearby chair at one of the glass-topped tables. Within seconds, two rambunctious boys joined him and began to set up a portable Chinese checkers board. As the trio began to play, the noise of their chatter swept over the entire porch, allowing Fred to continue in a more audible tone.

"Miss Hanover asked me to discover whether sleeping aids were a part of Mr.

Shane's list of medications. In order to do this, I had to access the confidential records, an office at Wandering Springs that is carefully monitored and in which residents are not allowed." He grinned mischievously. "Suffice it to say. I was able to gain entry during the wee hours of the night and found out that Mr. Shane had indeed been prescribed Valium to relieve anxiety, though not recently. However, each of the times he *had* been issued the pills occurred on a Saturday and by request of a visiting family member."

"Saturday. The same day of the week when Dylan regularly volunteers." James shook his head in disbelief. "But he is such a kind and positive person. I can't see him plotting to poison two people, let alone drowning one of them *and* setting fire to Willy's building. That sounds like the work of someone who has become completely unhinged!" He released Lucy's hand and rubbed furiously at his temple. "Can a person really conduct an exercise class and then run out and kill someone minutes later?"

"We'll see what caused him to act like a madman when we confront him." Lucy pointed off in the distance to where a figure pushing a wheelchair could be seen heading toward the mansion. "His exercise class has been done now for almost an hour." Lucy's eyes grew misty. "I wanted to give him a few more moments with his daddy before his life changes forever. That old man may never see his son again."

James gaped at Lucy. "But we don't have any hard evidence, do we?"

"Nothing that will hold up in court without Dylan's confession, no. That's why we need to corner him and pretend to know the whole truth."

"I still insist that this is a foolhardy arrangement, Miss Hanover," Fred cautioned.

"I firmly believe that Dylan Shane acted out of a desire for vengeance," Lucy stated calmly. "I don't think he's going to get violent with us."

Fred lifted a pair of binoculars from the empty seat next to him. "I'm going to call the authorities if I see the slightest indication that your brazen plan has gone amiss."

"Thank you, Fred." Lucy planted a kiss on the man's lined brow and stood, resolutely dusting crumbs from her lap. "Coming, James?"

Mutely, James followed Lucy as she strolled up the gravel garden path. It seemed surreal to him to be in this tranquil setting, with monarch butterflies hovering above clusters of bachelor's buttons and slow, fat bumblebees lazily settling onto the feathery heads of golden yarrow, with the goal of accusing a man of murder. The gravel crunched pleasantly under their feet and the twitter of wrens and finches visiting the feeders and bathing in the shallow cement birdbaths filled the air with an orchestrated harmony that served to increase the dreamlike atmosphere. Turning back to the house, James saw Fred Wimple raise his binoculars and fix the lenses of his apparatus upon Lucy's quarry.

Something in her bearing must have alerted Dylan that she was not approaching him in order to simply offer a quick greeting and he slowed his pace until he and his father came to rest next to one of the wooden park benches bordering the path.

"Hello Dylan," Lucy began almost sadly.

"Hi there folks." Dylan attempted to adopt his customary light tone, but the cautious look in his eyes betrayed his wariness.

Lucy sat down at the opposite end of the bench and James stood behind her, trying to be as tall and erect as a soldier. "How's your daddy doing today, Dylan?"

Dylan's lips narrowed and then sprang back into a smile. "Who?"

Lucy turned to Mr. Shane who was gazing happily out across the sweeping lawn. "Good afternoon, Mr. Shane."

"He's not my father. I told you before, he just gets confused." Dylan put on a show of being offended. "It's not nice to mess with folks who have memory loss."

"When did his memory loss first occur?" Lucy asked gently.

"Randolph's?" Dylan issued a covert look of tenderness at the man in the wheelchair. "I believe he was quite young. Still in his forties. It was a case of early onset dementia. Pretty rare, but very debilitating. Folks who are stricken with his condition at that age deteriorate faster than older people do. They forget stuff at home, at work. They end up being laid off from work. Take Randolph. He couldn't even remember how to make simple meals for u—" He checked himself and then continued, "for his two kids."

"You were going to say 'us' weren't you? *You* are one of his two kids." Lucy spoke quickly, giving Dylan no chance to continue his denials. Softly, she said, "I can't even begin to imagine what that must have been like for you. It must have been really hard, Dylan. Especially with the passing of your mama and then some nurse called Stacy Weeks taking off with all of your family's money. After all, you *were* just a kid," she added softly. "That's a lot for any person to bear."

Dylan stared at his hands and said nothing. The minutes dragged slowly by. James shifted his weight and wiped the perspiration gathering at the nape of his neck with the back of his hand. He wished he had another limeade and that they had chosen to sit on one of the benches in the shade. Finally, Dylan sighed and his shoulders sagged heavily. "What do you want?" he asked, suddenly sounding deeply weary.

"I know Ronnie and Stacy are the same woman. How did she succeed in ruining your future, Dylan? How did she get away with that kind of . . . treachery?"

Still staring at the crisscrossing lines etched into his palms, Dylan began to speak. "My father's illness was already beginning to show itself even before my mom died. He was an electrician. You can't make the kind of mistakes he started to make doing that kind of work. He almost fried himself a few times and his co-workers more than once before he was finally fired. Stacy knew right away what was wrong with him. She said she saw the signs when she was first hired as a live-in nurse by my mom."

He touched his father's shoulder and slowly continued. "Stacy volunteered to stay and help after mom died. She said she felt like part of the family and would stay with us until she could arrange for the insurance to pay for a substitute — someone from her nursing school program who could live with us and watch out for Dad while my sister and I went to school."

"I'm assuming she never contacted the insurance company."

Dylan shook his head. "Nope. She was too busy plotting how to get the right legal documents signed by my clueless father so that she could get her hands on his retirement and our savings accounts. They were both kept at the same bank. She just showed up with power of attorney and all these other official papers, had the money wired to a different account, withdrew every cent, and BAM! She was gone." Dylan balled his hands together and James watched nervously as the fists trembled violently.

Lucy gave Dylan a moment to get both his voice and hands under control. "How old were you?"

"I was a senior in high school. Had a full ride to U of Miami come the next fall, but there would be no college for me. That was the end of school and basketball forever. I went straight to work. I've been a garbage collector, a shirt presser, a short-order cook, you name it. I kept moving around like I was the one on the run. I couldn't settle down for long in any place or at any job. Then I started managing a gym in a little town in Tennessee. That's when I saw Stacy again, by total coincidence."

"In Tennessee?" Lucy was surprised by this revelation.

"Yeah, except her name was Kelly Davies and she ran a business called A Leaner You. It was just like Witness to Fitness. Same food scam. She made a tidy profit for about six months and then split. I had only lived there a few weeks, but I was pretty sure Kelly and Stacy were the same person. I followed her — even as far as Quincy's Gap. I guess someone was getting wise to her scam in Tennessee and Stacy was planning to set up shop all over again here as Ronnie Levitt. Since I wasn't worried about her recognizing me, I applied for a job so I could get close to her."

"You mean, so you could get even with her," Lucy stated.

Dylan turned to her, his eyes blazing. "There was no getting *even*. She destroyed the lives of *three people*. Me, my father, and my kid sister. She took everything from us and right after we had just lost my mom to cancer!" He slammed the bench with his open hand. "We couldn't even mourn for her, my sister and me. We were too busy figuring out how to pay bills or make macaroni and cheese or keep my father from wandering around the neighborhood like some total lunatic!"

Seeing that Dylan was getting worked up, Lucy quickly asked, "Where's your sister now? Is she doing okay?"

Dylan exhaled a long breath through his mouth. "Julie's still in Florida. As soon as she turned eighteen she married an old rich guy. She's had four *older* husbands and never loved any of them, but she told me once that she never wanted to feel as insecure as she did after our mom died." He gestured toward the mansion. "She's the one who pays for this place." He sighed again. "From the outside, we seem like such lucky people. Good-looking and friendly. Julie's loaded, I'm popular with the ladies, but both of us are haunted. We can't get close to anybody because we trust nobody. We've just been drifting through life."

James and Lucy both let their eyes rest upon Mr. Shane. He had said nothing during the entire exchange but seemed to be extremely content following the haphazard flight of a pair of bumblebees. For a few moments, no one spoke.

"So you know all about my motives now," Dylan said as he also watched his father. "You here to arrest me?"

Lucy handed Dylan her cell phone. "I'm going to let you turn yourself in. It will go easier for you that way. Just press down on the 'send' key and your call will go right through to the Sheriff's Department."

Dylan accepted the phone and nodded grimly. "I want you to know that Pete's death was an accident. Ronnie *did* start that fire but it's my fault Pete couldn't get out of there alive. The spiked whiskey was meant for her and I had no idea she had given it to Pete until I read about the presence of drugs in his body in the local paper." He abstractedly rubbed the surface of the cell phone. "I'm glad this is all over," he said, smiling weakly at Lucy and James. "I searched for that slime of a woman for years and I have used up so much time and energy seeking revenge. Now that I've got it, I just want to sit still for a while and not feel anything." He leaned back against the bench and lifted his face to the sun. "Right now, I think I am older and more tired than most of the residents here."

"I'm sorry about your daddy," Lucy replied and took Mr. Shane's hand in her own. "It will be hard for him not to see you."

Dylan pressed a button on the phone. His eyes grew watery as he looked at his father. "He hasn't recognized me for weeks. He won't even know I'm gone. I guess I can count that as a small mercy."

"We'll check up on him and so will our friend, Mr. Wimple," James spoke for the first time, pointing at Fred, who lowered his binoculars and waved hesitantly.

"Thanks." Dylan glanced up at the sun porch and then turned his attention to the speaker on the phone. "Yes," he began, his gaze locked onto his father's serene face. "I'd like to make an appointment to see the sheriff." He paused. "Well, I think this *is* a priority. It's about the death of Ronnie Levitt. See, I'd like to make a confession."

# Fifteen:
# Sweet Lucy Light
# Frozen Custard

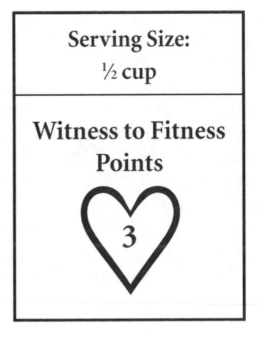

Serving Size:
½ cup

**Witness to Fitness**
**Points**

3

The first Friday evening in June was a bit on the hot and humid side, providing the residents of Quincy's Gap with a glimpse of the uncomfortable summer Mother Nature had in store for them. Willy had requested that the five supper club members, Carter Peabody, and Phoebe Liu attend a special "unveiling" ceremony and of course, they all agreed to come.

Lucy invited James to a casual dinner at her house prior to the evening's mysterious event. As the afternoon grew late, James showered, put on a bit too much aftershave, and drove to the closest florist where he deliberated over bouquets for a full twenty minutes.

"Why not just get red roses?" the saleswoman asked, growing frustrated with James's dillydallying.

"Too cliché." James looked around. "I want something vibrant, with lots of blues and purples." He smiled happily and mused aloud, "My Lucy has the most beautiful eyes. They're like cornflowers."

The saleswoman was unimpressed by his simile. "We don't carry cornflowers. After all, those kinds of flowers are like *weeds.* They grow in *fields* all over Virginia. We offer a more *sophisticated* selection of blooms."

Normally, James would have been put off by the woman's snobbery, but he was feeling too buoyant to allow her sourness to affect him. "Then I'll take a mixture of irises, statice, white lilies, and those cream-colored roses." He paused and cast his eyes around the shop once more. "With some greens and Queen Anne's lace mixed in. And I'd like it tied up with a lavender bow please."

Although the woman grudgingly gathered the stems, James was pleased to see the care with which she assembled the bouquet. After he paid, he whistled his way to the front door and then stuck his nose into the bouquet. The scent created by the lilies immediately made him sneeze. He sneezed three times consecutively while reaching for the door handle.

"I hope your *girlfriend* isn't allergic to lilies, too," the woman chided in farewell as he opened the door.

"Or to these Queen Anne's lace," he said, sniffling on the threshold, "which grow in *fields* all over Virginia." Pleased with his departing retort, James stepped out of the shop and recommenced his whistling.

When he arrived at Lucy's, James was relieved to see that her three dogs were safely penned in the backyard. Lucy threw open the front door before he had the chance to ring the doorbell and upon seeing the flowers, threw her arms around James so forcefully that he nearly fell backward down the porch steps.

Once they were both inside, Lucy filled

up half of the double kitchen sink, plopped the stem end of the bouquet into the water, and continued to show her appreciation to James. The pair engaged in passionate kisses until Bon Jovi, Lucy's largest male Shepherd, raked at the screen door leading from the kitchen to the back deck and whined. When he was ignored, his whine turned into frantic barking until Lucy finally broke away from James, laughing.

"I guess we'll have to close all the blinds whenever you come over," she nudged James playfully. "My dogs might think that you're attacking me instead of . . . well, what we were just doing."

"They're going to have to get used to me, because I plan to spend a lot of time here, if that's okay with you," James replied, tenderly stroking Lucy's hair.

"That's more than okay with me." Lucy gestured toward the kitchen table. "Um, shall we eat? We've got to be back in town by seven."

James looked at his watch and then pulled Lucy to him. "We've got a few more minutes yet. After all, I'm a very fast eater."

Outside the back door, Bon Jovi resumed his mournful howling.

Willy's unveiling ceremony was held in the

parking lot adjacent to the site where the Polar Pagoda once stood. By seven o'clock, all of the other businesses had closed and the only other living creatures in occupancy were the gnats swarming beneath the parking lot lights and a few hundred ravenous mosquitoes.

Willy greeted his guests warmly with hugs and handshakes all around, his face glowing with anticipation. Once everyone had arrived, he asked his friends to take a seat in one of the folding chairs Phoebe let him borrow from the Witness to Fitness storeroom. Apparently, Phoebe was one of Willy's regular customers and had been sneaking over to the Polar Pagoda during her lunch hour ever since Witness to Fitness opened.

Facing his seated audience, Willy held out his arms and began by thanking Phoebe for the use of the chairs. "Phoebe told me that she's movin' on to greener pastures. There's a Weight Watchers center over in New Market and she's gonna be one of the counselors there." Willy gestured for Phoebe to stand. "Tell 'em all about it, Phoebe."

Phoebe smiled shyly and smoothed down the front of her meticulously ironed white cotton blouse. "I am moving, but I am not abandoning my Witness to Fitness clients.

All of you will be given a free month's membership at Weight Watchers so that you can continue with the excellent work you've begun. I've also spoken with the Membership Director at the YMCA and he has agreed to let you try out their exercise classes for the same period of time." She held out a copy of *The Star Ledger*. "I've placed an ad in this weekend's paper to tell all of the Witness to Fitness clients this information, but I'd really appreciate it if you five could help spread the word about my leaving and the two offers. No one's weight loss success should be halted by . . . um . . . the unpleasant events centered around Witness to Fitness. You five alone have lost between fifteen and twenty-five pounds each. I hope you realize how incredible that is and I hope to see you at future meetings. Thank you."

Exhausted from providing such a long speech, Phoebe sank gratefully into her chair. Willy led the group in a round of applause for the taciturn and gentle nutritionist, and then opened the lid of a large cooler with a flourish. Reaching inside, he cupped his hands around a pint-sized Styrofoam cup and held it aloft before his friends.

"I'd like to help all of those folks who are fightin' the good fight to get in shape by givin' them a special treat to enjoy this summer. Y'all have had some mighty big stumblin' blocks with all the goings on around here, so I've created a new flavor of custard to keep your spirits up as the numbers on the scale keep goin' down."

"What's the flavor?" Bennett wanted to know.

"I am *so* glad you asked that question, my friend. It's a light-as-air, sweet cream vanilla with a hint of honey and a fairy dusting of cinnamon. I've named it Sweet Lucy Light in honor of the brave and intelligent lady that I am proud to number among my friends. Without you Lucy, things would still be right messy around this town and I would have never gotten a check outta those tight-fisted insurance folks. Now that I have, I can start rebuilding my dream and it's all thanks to you."

Willy handed out quarts of his new flavor of frozen custard to all. Lucy accepted hers with tears in her eyes. After one taste, James couldn't believe the custard was the sugar-free, low-fat mixture that Willy claimed it was.

"It's just too rich to be light!" he exclaimed to Willy.

"Oh, it tastes like it just fell out of heaven." Gillian congratulated the ice cream man on his invention. "And what a tribute to our Lucy!"

"Too bad that mutt Donovan took all the credit for solving the murders," Bennett said dourly after swallowing a bite of custard. "You did all the legwork *and* confronted a murderer all by yourself. You should be gettin' a medal."

"I'll stick with the ice cream name, thanks," Lucy replied graciously. "I felt pretty sure that Dylan was only after revenge. I know it sounds screwed up, but once he had accomplished that, he kind of lost his whole purpose in life. Besides, James was with me, so I had no reason to be scared."

Lindy caught the warm smiles exchanged between James and Lucy and put her hands on her hips. "Say, is there some hot romance going on with you two that we should be aware of?"

"Maybe," Lucy said enigmatically and winked at Lindy.

Carter was too impatient to learn about all the details of Dylan's arrest to allow for any other subject to intervene. Stepping in front of Lindy, he pointed his plastic spoon at Lucy. "Just how *did* the other deputy steal your thunder?"

Lucy shrugged. "Simple bad luck. I had

the Sheriff's Department's central number programmed into my cell phone, but the weekend dispatch operator on duty that Saturday patched Dylan through to Donovan instead of Huckabee. Dylan assumed he was talking to the sheriff so he just began to spill the beans about both deaths. Donovan told Dylan to stay where he was or he'd be in some seriously hot water. As Donovan was driving out to Wandering Springs, he called every reporter he knew so that they could be at the retirement center with their cameras loaded in order to get shots of him taking Dylan into custody."

"Where were you and James when this happened?" Lindy asked.

James put a hand on Lucy's shoulder. "We promised to look after Mr. Shane, so we wheeled him inside so he wouldn't witness his son's arrest. It's true that he doesn't even recognize Dylan these days, but we didn't want to take the chance."

"Of course, Donovan tore up the driveway with his siren going full tilt." Lucy rolled her eyes in disgust. "Dylan was just calmly sitting on the same bench where all of us were sitting when he made the call. There was no need for that kind of display by Keith. Those poor old people! Huckabee wouldn't have approved of frightening them half to death. So like I said, it was just a matter of bad luck."

"But that red-headed limelight hog is now the town hero!" Carter spluttered. "His picture's been in every paper from here to the Mississippi and he got free meals at Dolly's for a week! It's just not right."

Lucy laughed. "Well, that kind of food would be bad for my diet. Besides, I don't want the publicity. The sheriff knows what my contribution was and he is really starting to see me in a new light. *That's* what I really want — to break into the All Men's Club and fit in. I'm going to take the deputy exam this summer 'cause now *I* know that I've got what it takes."

Carter frowned. "There's still something that I don't get. How did Ronnie end up with the bottle of tainted Jack Daniels? The one with the drugs in it that knocked out Pete?"

"Even before Witness to Fitness officially opened, Dylan pretended to be interested in Ronnie romantically," Lucy explained. "He went to her house and snooped around one night while she was fixing them dinner. He saw a bottle of Jack Daniels in her wet bar and figured that he had found an easy way to kill her. He bought a bottle of the same whiskey in Waynesboro, where no one would remember him, steamed off the black label sealing the cap to the neck of the bottle, put the Valium inside, and glued the label back into place. The next time Dylan was at Ronnie's he switched bottles, removing hers and throwing it out. He expected Ronnie to drink the liquor and die quietly at home, with no one the wiser. Unfortunately, Ronnie brought that bottle to Pete. I guess she got him drunk enough on the drugged Jack Daniels to be able to pump him for info. I guess whatever whiskey was left over she poured on the T-shirts and started the fire."

"But I saw her at the Brunswick Stew Dinner. How did she have time to start the fire and get to the dinner?" Lindy asked.

"She was pretty late getting there," James said. "I know because I was one of the last people in line for food and she was right in front of me." He thought back to that evening. "I remember her making a point to speak with Mrs. Lowndes and Mrs. Emerson. She must have been making sure there would be witnesses who could attest to her presence at the fundraiser. Still, she would have had plenty of time to dump some liquor on the shirts, light them up, and drive to the fundraiser. She even mentioned the shirts to the other two ladies."

"Yeah!" Carter shouted. "Ronnie must have found out that Pete remembered her from the Red Cross scam so she got him loaded and then set fire to the building! Poor Pete. Then she just sits down and eats like nothing happened. What a sicko."

Lucy nodded. "That's about right, from what we can figure out using the evidence we have combined with Dylan's statement. Of course, Dylan felt horrible about Pete, but it didn't stop him from wanting his revenge. According to his statement, when he went back to Ronnie's for another date, he noticed a pack of Pall Mall cigarettes on the windowsill of her kitchen. He asked her about them and she said she only smoked when she drank. *The Star* had printed every tiny detail about the Polar Pagoda fire and Dylan remembered that the butts found at the scene of the fire were Pall Malls. He then knew that Ronnie had deliberately set fire to that building knowing Pete was passed out inside."

"Do you think that's why he held her under in the bath tub?" Lindy asked, both intrigued and horrified. "Because he was angry about Pete's unnecessary death?"

"I do," Lucy answered soberly. "I think it nauseated Dylan to get physical with Ronnie, so he wasn't able to plot her demise until they had had a few more dates. On that Monday she called in sick to work, Ronnie was at home and in perfect health preparing her place for a night of romance. That's why there were candles everywhere you looked."

Bennett chuckled. "Looked like a fire hazard if you ask me."

"Dylan had obviously led her to believe that they were going to sleep together. He got her good and drunk on wine, followed by the spiked Jack Daniels," Lucy continued. "According to his statement, Dylan suggested they take a bath together but he never ended up removing any clothes. As soon as he saw her chameleon tattoo he knew for certain that Ronnie was Stacy. He had seen the same tattoo when she wore a bikini while sunbathing in their backyard." Lucy smirked. "I guess that was the perfect tattoo for such a changeable person. Anyway, he felt taken over by vengeful anger and that was that. Ronnie was pretty far gone when he grabbed her ankles and held her under, but not totally."

Everyone reflected on the body in the bathtub.

James still had one question about the evidence. "If Ronnie was a smoker, why didn't anyone find cigarettes in her townhouse after her death?"

"Dylan took the cigarettes with him the night of the murder and smoked every single one of them on the way home to Harrisonburg to calm his nerves." Lucy dabbed at her lips with a paper napkin. "And Ronnie didn't have an ashtray. Dylan claimed she used regular drinking glasses to catch the ash and then just put them in the dishwasher. I think she was kind of a neat freak."

The group finished their ice cream and lapsed into silence, each pondering the shocking events that had taken a hold of their little town that spring.

Lucy stood and walked near the wreckage of Willy's former business. The bright yellow tape put out by the fire department had faded from a lemon to a buttery hue. Even the black lettering warning "Fire Line Do Not Cross," had turned to a dull shade of gray. She rubbed the tape pensively with her fingertips as her friends noted the solemn expression on her face. "Maybe you should be naming a custard flavor after Pete instead of me, Willy," Lucy said. "It seems like we're the only ones left to keep his memory alive. Us and dear old Fred Wimple."

Willy drew Lucy away from the tape.

"None of us will forget about Pete. I'll get a plaque made for him and hang it when I set up shop again. Let's turn our thoughts toward havin' long, lazy summer days with one another."

"Here, here! That's enough talk of murder!" Gillian declared. "Aren't we really here tonight to celebrate?"

"Yeah, Willy," Bennett nudged his friend. "What gives with the easel? You going to start painting and end up a millionaire like James's pop?"

"It's no painting, it's a sketch of my new ice cream parlor. The Town Planning Committee approved my proposal this afternoon." He lowered his voice and grinned crookedly. "Word had it that a Mrs. Savannah Lowndes was on vacation this week, so I rushed in my plan and it got passed by just one little vote." Willy chuckled with glee. "Y'all ready to see the design for the all-new Custard Cottage?"

"Yes!" his friends yelled in unison.

Willy whipped off the sheet to reveal a colored drawing of a violet Victorian cottage, complete with a white picket fence and loads of creamy gingerbread trim that seemed to drip down the building like warm icing. Giant-sized lollipops and gumdrops in a rainbow of colors dotted the roof and side walls of the building. A path made to look like pinwheel mints led to the double front doors. Four café tables with striped umbrellas were set outside, and the trash cans were shaped like enormous ice cream cones.

"I feel like Hansel," James said as he admired the sketch. "That place looks good enough to eat."

"I'm going to carry bulk candy as well as frozen custard and ice cream. That'll help me pay the bills during the winter." Willy looked at his friends. "Construction starts at the end of the month."

Lindy put an arm around Willy's back. "This is wonderful, Willy! We are all so glad that you're staying in Quincy's Gap."

Willy harrumphed. "Well, I'd better sell a hell of a lot of ice cream this summer, 'cause I gotta pay extra for the fancy new sprinkler system I'm having installed!"

"I say the Custard Cottage is enough excitement for the town of Quincy's Gap this summer," Lindy commented wryly. "Personally, I think we all need some peace and quiet for a change. *I'm* going to lose a few more pounds and then spend a week at the beach, turning my bronze skin a few shades darker."

"I'm going to study for that exam," Lucy

announced and Carter gazed at her with admiration. She smiled in his direction and then added, "Since you seem to know so much about crime, Carter, maybe you can help me study."

Carter looked very pleased as he nodded his agreement.

Bennett thumped manfully on his chest. "Carter isn't gonna have too much free time, Lucy. He and I are gonna start a post office bowling league. It's about time someone took on those boys from the DMV. They've won the league trophy five years in a row." Bennett flexed his arm. "Now that I'm gettin' some muscle tone back, I think I can whip a fourteen-pound ball down the lane."

"Looks like I'll have to hire someone to take Willy's place with Pet Palaces," Gillian sighed. "That might take the whole summer to do. Your kind of creative instinct and positive energy isn't easy to find, my dear friend. You don't have a twin, do you?"

Willy laughed. "Aw, shucks. Don't go makin' me blush. No, I've got a sister, but she's not too handy with tools. She can cook up a storm, though, when her nose isn't stuck in a book. Speakin' of books . . . what about you James?" Willy asked. "Got any immediate plans for the summer?"

James shrugged. "I haven't thought too far ahead, but I know what I'm doing tomorrow. I'm going to drive to that big mall in Charlottesville and go clothes shopping, something I usually hate doing." He tugged at the waist of his chinos and was able to hold several inches of extra fabric out in front of his stomach. "For the first time in ten years, I actually want to go buy a new pair of pants."

# ACKNOWLEDGMENTS

The author would like to thank the following people for their expertise: Holly Hudson; Deputy Chief Louis Aroneo of the Stirling Fire Company, Stirling, New Jersey; Jessica Faust of BookEnds; and the team at Midnight Ink. As always, thank you to Tim, Owen, and Sophie for bringing me joy and to the rest of my family for cheering me on.

# ABOUT THE AUTHOR

**J. B. Stanley** has a BA in English from Franklin & Marshall College, an MA in English Literature from West Chester University, and an MLIS from North Carolina Central University. She taught sixth grade language arts in Cary, North Carolina, for the majority of her eight-year teaching career. Raised an antique-lover by her grandparents and parents, Stanley also worked part-time in an auction gallery. An eBay junkie and food-lover, Stanley now lives in Richmond, Virginia, with her husband, two young children, and three cats. Visit her Web site at www.jbstanley.com.

The employees of Thorndike Press hope you have enjoyed this Large Print book. All our Thorndike and Wheeler Large Print titles are designed for easy reading, and all our books are made to last. Other Thorndike Press Large Print books are available at your library, through selected bookstores, or directly from us.

For information about titles, please call:
(800) 223-1244

or visit our Web site at:
www.gale.com/thorndike
www.gale.com/wheeler

To share your comments, please write:
Publisher
Thorndike Press
295 Kennedy Memorial Drive
Waterville, ME 04901